MATTHEW ANDERSON

Love in Doom and Secession

First edition

ISBN: 9798705034826

Cover art by Rachel Silver

This book was professionally typeset on Reedsy.
Find out more at reedsy.com

To lovers past present and future

Contents

Foreword

I began writing seriously in January of 2020. When I say seriously, I mean to distinguish between when I wrote intermittently as a child, some not so scary stories that arose out of my affliction for Goosebumps, Stephen King and the like, and when I decided to take up the vocation in a disciplined, dedicated fashion. In between lies a long period of little creativity. I forgot about my childhood affinity for reading and writing, doing so only in school or when it was otherwise required of me, enjoying it but never quite connecting the dots to realize I need to write like I need to breathe.

January brought the culmination of a few different catalysts. I returned to reading, prompted by a sudden realization that the content I constantly consumed on social media was a very poor replacement for the depth and satisfaction of books. That January was also the month I spent in Germany studying at a language school. I have found over the last few years that my experiences of *depáysement* always bring about fruitful periods of change and growth, and my time in Germany was particularly illuminating, despite its relative brevity. (It is perhaps not a coincidence that the title of the second half of the novel is inspired by a German phenomenon, though I am not one to confirm or deny, having only just recently noticed this parallel myself...)

But it would be neglectful and perhaps coy of me to speak of Germany as my muse without specifying that my most unforgettable experience on German soil was a boy. Our romance came totally by surprise: his Tinder had given me little indication that I would become so immediately enamored. I had had a string of disappointingly transient and superficial relationships at home, leading to a feeling of hopelessness; I had to bring myself up from a rock bottom of self-hatred to convince myself I was worthy of love, my own and that of others. With him it was magic, I finally loved myself enough to open up in a genuine way, to experience mutual infatuation at the speed of light.

Before I even returned across the pond, I began to write of him. I was processing this sudden glimmer of rejuvenating love in my life, feeling melancholy that it would end and yet hopeful that in the future I would find someone else, as I had finally convinced myself that I was interesting, worthy, and deserving of the fulfilling long-term relationship that I crave. And so I suppose my mind was on romance, specifically the particularities of relationships between gay men in this modern world. Having finished my piece about Mr. Germany, I wrote about other people who had entered my life under romantic pretenses, thinking one day I would make a compilation to describe my queer experience.

I had been experimenting with some other forms, including a return to the horror of my youth, when I came up with the idea to write a fictional account of Delaware becoming an independent country. But when I started to brainstorm, I found that there was so much I wanted to explore, so much I thought I could say; it grew very quickly out of the confines of the short story. Almost from the very beginning, it was clear to me that it would have to become a novel.

Only a few short months after I had taken up the pen once more, I was to write my first novel. My friends were excited, if not a bit puzzled or incredulous. And I had doubts that I would reach the end, too. I had never completed such an ambitious project, did not know how to begin. But step by step I found my way, through discipline and trial by error, and in the six months of quarantine that I used to write my first draft, it came together.

I have noticed some interesting reactions from people who ask me about the novel's plot. Some wonder if I am writing nonfiction, some sort of proposal to present to the Delaware government. Many others are puzzled by the idea that Delawarean secession could create a novel worth reading. It is certainly true that, if secession became a reality in the United States (a possibility I do not view as entirely improbable), Delaware would be the last to secede. Delaware is a mere geopolitical convenience. It is a non sequitur to speak of "Delawarean pride"; many Delawareans hold emotional ties to other places. If in some regions of the country it is a common personality trait to rave about your regional identity, like, for example, in the Pacific Northwest, we Delawareans define ourselves through the level of hatred we contain for our unfortunate place of residence.

But for my purposes, Delaware is the perfect candidate. In times of late capitalist decadence and white populist furor, I was asking myself: what are the extremes to which arbitrary ideology can be twisted? I thought it timely to provide a sort of circus mirror through which to view ideology as a concept; in other words, to portray the capriciousness of our current reality by satirizing it, stretching, distorting it. If it is absurd for Delaware to claim exceptionalism, what makes the idea of American exceptionalism any less absurd?

Forgive me if I cling to my home state, for it is the only place I feel comfortable claiming any sort of attachment to. My family is from the mountains of Eastern Kentucky, a place that I return to less and less and that feels increasingly more foreign. My family has no memory of our past before colonizing the American continent. I have tried to reconcile this sense of rootlessness by defining myself as a wanderer, learning new languages and trying to build myself anew through bits and pieces of places I come to know. But yet, in the six months I wrote this novel I was grappling with the fact that I would be leaving Delaware, which suddenly aroused a yearning in me for some sort of geographical belonging (not to disregard the cruelness inherent in such an endeavor on stolen land), so I wrote this novel as a love letter to my home, with its nonsense, its mundaneness, and its faults intact.

If this novel is a love letter to my home, the technical geographical space so defined as well as the more abstract concept, I return to my original aspirations by also writing a story of unapologetic queer love. I came into this novel wanting to fight back against typical ideas of queerness. I wanted to portray a realistic tale of two gay men, who fight with their own issues of self-hatred that lead to a fear and rejection of intimacy with the other, but who ultimately make the choice to fight their demons and commit themselves. I wanted to fight back against the idea that queer intimacy necessarily has to be transient and transactional, an idea with considerable influence in spaces both queer and not.

I don't think it's presumptuous to say that this modern era has brought new difficulties for everyone in the pursuit of healthy, fulfilling relationships. For Queer folk, we are caught in an interesting conundrum: though legal rights and recognition have increased over the past few decades (particularly for the more privileged white cis members of our community), we still find ourselves struggling with these decades of baggage interpersonally. But I wanted to portray a sort of rebellion, an idea that one does not have to simply resign oneself to what is most congruous with the norm: I hope that this novel can create a sort of dissonance within these ideological spaces and help inspire Queer folk to have the courage to insist on the intimacy they want and deserve, whatever that may be.

To each and every reader, I want to thank you from the bottom of my heart for taking the chance on my work, in a world in which it seems that the act of reading is increasingly threatened by quicker forms of entertainment. This is by no means a perfect work, but it is wholly mine, my first novel and my first great public disposal of my soul. Without a reader, a writer is merely a machinist, and so I am grateful to you, the reader, for engaging with my words and thereby turning them into a work of art, one to be digested, criticized, and hopefully, enjoyed.

Matthew Anderson
  March 27th, 2021
  Taiwan

Acknowledgements

I am indebted to two of my beta readers, Imane Echehbani and Victor Hanzen, who so graciously agreed to read an early and highly unpolished version of this manuscript. With the help of their extensive feedback, I was able to make improvements that otherwise would not have crossed my mind. Imane sent me corrections as well as a highly generous set of positive comments, which gave me the courage I needed to publish widely. Victor has been reading and engaging with my work since before I evan began this project, and so you may notice a character named in his honor. Obrigado, amigo.

In terms of the cover, I am so grateful for my friend Rachel Silver, who agreed to take on this project on a tight timeframe. It was so important to me to have a Delawarean artist give my work a visual aesthetic that matched the writing's local color, and I believe that together we have created a wonderful final work.

As for moral support, Krista Jarrell has been there for me through thick and thin, believing in me from the beginning. She listened to me bounce ideas, encouraged me when things became difficult, and even agreed to receive a proof copy to confirm all the formatting was in order. Since I could not have a copy sent to me here in Taiwan, I had to rely on a stateside friend to assist me, and I cannot thank her enough for accepting the trouble.

My sincerest thanks to all, those mentioned and those not, for helping contribute to my dream.

I

Secession

the fall of Rome

It was reported, through frantic text messages and haphazardly shared newspaper articles, that the Rehoboth beach tourist trade was in peril. Eager town criers and reticent foes of social media alike were inclined to recount that the tides at the beach, being higher and higher each year, had finally become too high to dismiss. This year, once summer came, towels could not simply be moved farther inward, as was once done with quiet obliviousness, because the tides, stubborn like unruly children, had pummeled the boardwalk, invaded souvenir shops, and made the seaside ice cream businesses unfeasible, threatening to turn Rehoboth Beach into an Atlantis-style civilization of folklore and ancient imagination.

And who would have thought that it should happen in the winter when the streets were quiet and abandoned, and there were no observers to remark, "It is gone, we have seen it, let us show our respects."

That no one had seen, as no one was present at the beach in January, made it harder to accept. It's a pity, for it was not for a lack of the balmy climes amenable to beach activities, but a deeply rooted belief in the rigidity of proper seasonality, and if the people had been willing to ignore that in January it "did not feel right" to lay on the sand and be harassed by the sun, perhaps someone could have seen the beach for the last time in its last hour. To this, the most morose responded, if they had watched the beach disappear, they would have had no reason not to be swept along with it into nothingness.

It seems that in the communal folklore regarding any tragedy, some details resurface again and again, gaining traction upon having touched a common nerve. In this case, it was the ice cream's sad state of inedibility that most touched the populace, the photographs of murky seawater having rendered both its taste palette and physical integrity beyond recognition. From mouth to mouth reports of the ice cream's acrid taste, lack of physical gumption, and loss of once lively color were shared mechanically, representing the greater idea that what was once simple and beautiful had been irrevocably corrupted, the social expectation in vogue being that the recipient of this piece of information, regardless of how many times they had heard it before, would lower their head in shame and grief.

The DuFrond company, spotting a prized opportunity to appease share-holders while improving public morale, offered to begin production of a magic polymer that would maintain ice cream's taste and texture when inundated with saltwater. The preliminary consumer surveys, however, revealed a lukewarm response on the part of the public, which caused the idea to be filed away and abandoned as unprofitable. *So much for making the world a better place*, pouted the corporation.

Some, of course, ignored the ice cream hysteria in favor of a mantra that betrayed their denial: "It's not that bad." It was all they could say to ignore the hordes of evidence that the sea had reclaimed the land, that treasured knick-knack shops and pizza establishments were brutalized by nature, proving existence was a privilege and not a right. Ignorance and denial were the only tools they had to distance themselves from facts, to preserve hope that maybe, upon summer's arrival, it would all seem like a bad dream, that everyone could return to virgin shores to frolic and make merry.

But over time, the people grew tired of validating the skeptic mania of others, and thus came to reply *it was bad, the beach is gone, now please stop, I'm still in mourning.*

* * *

It's a cruel January Sunday when Juneau Baker herself first hears the news. Though she had thought she had no extra room for gloom in the Sunday dreariness, life counters her with the reports of the beach's sudden disappearance act, and so she had to stop her day to accommodate for this new loss. Juneau, like any true Delawarean, is deeply troubled by this news, the obliteration of a childhood refuge, and so she poured her energy into the construction of a candlelight vigil.

The black she wears out of respect clashes acutely with the vivid colors of drunk reverie on display on the main boulevard of the university hamlet. Though she often feels isolated, and frankly reluctant to use the possessive pronoun for the institution where she just *happens* to study, she feels so more intensely on weekends. And even on a day like today, she is appalled by the fact that no one seems to notice or care that Delaware is losing itself, which she attributes to the fact that most of the people who eye her on the sidewalk while screaming in collegiate euphoria are not in fact from Delaware.

She enters the convenience store, looking to buy an assortment of candles with which to create an altar. But on the shelves sit only four candles, each claiming to be "deluxe", with a price Juneau finds ridiculous. And three of them beach-themed: *sea breeze, coastal linen, Mediterranean blue*, which seems to be in bad taste. Browsing the scant collection further, she decides on one birthday candle: number 8. She would have chosen her favorite number, 7, but they are all gone, so she highlights the beach's longevity with an infinite loop. Having paid, she rushes back home, fretting to hide and make believe she is somewhere else.

Once home, Juneau knocks on her roommate Victor's door to request that he participate. His eyes fuzzy from midday hibernation, Juneau asks him if he is dressed for a funeral. "I'm wearing black already, just need pants," he says, taking his time to shuffle through his drawer while ignoring the strangeness of her request. "What shall we mourn," she answers *the beach*, and thus he follows her to the backyard to go commiserate.

They stand around the flimsy black table on the porch (tossed along by former occupants for 30 bucks, they split it for 15 each) as Juneau explains her decorations. The bag, still sandy and reminiscent of her last trip to the beach, languishes next to the infinite candle.

"I've never been more grateful for stubborn sand," she says. Victor smiles softly.

Leaning against the naked umbrella pole is a piece of scratch paper with some words sketched in calligraphy pen: "Delaware has lost its diamond." Victor tries to convince Juneau that Delaware *is* the diamond, hence its name the Diamond State, and therefore has only lost a small part of itself. *Not the whole,* so his logic, *isn't that better,* but Juneau is in mood for such rhetorical twists. "Choose your phrasing as you see fit," Victor murmurs in apology.

She asks Victor for his lighter, knowing it would be in his pocket; he bestows upon the candle a flame. Victor asks if she has any words, she says, "all my words are on that paper." And so there they stand, free of speech and free of time, until Juneau suddenly blows out the candle, "c'est fini" she proclaims.

* * *

Wynona Baker is very, very proud of her daughter. She knows, of course, that all moms are proud of their children, or at least the ones that she cares to compare herself to, so her feelings are not unique. In fact, she believes that anyone who bears the pain and joy of motherhood *should* be proud, as children earn respect by virtue of birth.

Wynona Baker also knows a great deal about her. She knows that Juneau always gets As, that Juneau always says "thank you" to her professors when she leaves the room, that she has a force of will without parallel. Her only wonder, then, hearing from Juneau on the phone that all would be well and she would save Delaware yet, was where Juneau had inherited her resolution to act against life's injustices.

She knows also that, because her body refused her the privilege of more kin, her admiration is sharply focused on Juneau. *Yes,* she thinks, *I would have loved more children,* but that is not the reality, and it does no good to dwell on what she cannot change. If she celebrates every single one of Juneau's milestones, even when these are more like pebbles or grains of sand, it is only out of an imbalance between her boundless love and a shortage of willing recipients.

Yes, Juneau was her only gift to the world; oh, how she shone. Thinking of herself, however, Wynona feels decidedly average. An average woman, since men had failed her, left her to raise Juneau on her own. An average worker making precisely the amount of money required for her existence, with little leftover for "silly" expenditures (like new jeans, or a 401k). An average dreamer, for being content in the way that only the dreamless could be.

And maybe it is also average of Wynona to believe that everyone merits a few small pleasures. *How dull*, she thinks, *to live life so seriously*: however futile or facile, all beings deserve such gifts. In her pleasure, she is extraordinary not in her need for distraction, but her choice of medium. Television, for example, had lost her interest decades prior, and so the only programs she watches are documentaries and love stories she had preserved on videotape. Film, a medium she also has little interest in, had occasionally swayed her towards the theater, but her cinematic taste is also of a lost era, and so mostly she satisfies her desires for evidence of past grandeur through her video collection.

She does have one interest, however, that outshines all of the others in intensity and rarity.

It's so uncommon and so illogical that she hesitates to tell others about her affliction, even though doing so would be quite simple, supposing she had someone to tell: *I like coins.* Only *like* isn't an accurate word, really, because she adored it, could not live without it. "The time I give it," she would explain to herself, preparing for some imaginary interaction, *"like* just isn't the right word."

Like anyone who devotes grand quantities of time to a single pursuit, she has a personal niche. Wynona fixates on pennies, nickels, and dimes: the less they are worth, the more value she finds. This, she thinks, is the detail she would be least comfortable explaining: that a woman with so little money to spare would hoard coins that buy so *little.* Especially considering that her collection has its own costs, "the treasury" receiving its own place in her budget every month for its maintenance and expansion. No, it is not a hobby: it's a primal need, like breathing or eating, one she cannot do without, and no one can tell her she has no right to enjoy it.

Juneau asks her if she can pay her a visit that evening, to tell Wynona of her plans to save her home, their home, and Wynona confirms that nothing could make her happier.

* * *

Juneau arrives around 7:30, still mourning in her black.

Wynona is delighted, as much as she is left stunned by the beach's disappearance and the grim circumstances that had finally prompted Juneau to come visit. But she could forget all that, yes, so long as she could see her daughter. She offers Juneau something to eat, which she refuses, saying eating while mourning would be bad for her digestion. Wynona tries to convince her otherwise, to tell her that widows need food to have the energy to persevere, but Juneau cannot be convinced, and instead requests that Wynona tell her a story about the beach that is no more.

Struck by this request, Wynona thinks and thinks and thinks, and finally decides that if the loss of the beach is a sign of the inevitable, there is a story Juneau should hear. Juneau manages a crooked semi-smile when her mother says, "it's all about a quarter."

She rehashes the information Juneau had heard countless times: that some state coins are trickier to find than others, that proximity or distance from the state do not always determine which are commonplace and which are rare. Of course, she has a surplus of coins from Pennsylvania, New York, New Jersey, which she could never get rid of no matter how many times she offered to leave them to Juneau, but some coins make themselves appear in the strangest of places. Juneau had heard it before.

What Juneau does not know is what quarter she's referring to that had been so easy to find. She had never been told that the coin that started the collection was a quarter from Alaska, all despite the fact that she never been to Alaska, much less farther away from Middletown than New York City, where she once saw a play on Broadway as a girl. "And I found it here, in Delaware."

"Your father and I, the bastard" (Wynona never referred to Juneau's father, said to be "out in Las Vegas", without his suffix "the bastard"), "we went to the beach. It was summer, so we said we would go, even though I was sick to my stomach, had been for more than a week, and our relationship at that point was 90% theater."

"I had a feeling, you know…call it motherly intuition. So I got a pregnancy test and took it in the bathroom after we got there. It was one of those public bathrooms, the ones that always feel damp, you know the ones. I found out it was positive, but at the time I couldn't find it in me to tell your father… the bastard."

"We didn't stay too long. It was hot as hell. We stopped at a gas station, somewhere near Milford, and I went in to get some water because he neglected to bring any. So I paid with a five, which back then was a good deal more than the water itself, and I got back a bunch of dollars and coins, one of which was the state quarter of Alaska from 1967. I looked at the attendant and I said, have you ever *seen* a coin like that? I guess he probably had. He wasn't very amused. I got in the car, *he* was taking his time to fill up the tank, and as I waited I thought, *Alaska's gotta be beautiful this time of year.*"

And she says that right then and there, she knew she would have a daughter and call her Juneau. "I didn't need a doctor to tell me. I just knew." And in the passenger seat of that 1987 Volvo, fixated on the quarter's dull brilliance, she had said the word, tasted it, "Juneau," and thought, *how beautiful a name, how powerful a name, maybe it will give her wings to fly far, far away.*

Feeling heavy, Wynona rises from the table where Juneau sits listening calmly and disappears down the hallway, returning with a small jewelry box of smooth green velvet. She sits down, places it in her daughter's hands with a firm clasp, and says, "If you keep one coin of mine, let it be this one, that way you'll know where you come from and where you can go." Juneau holds it to her chest, her cheeks shiny with fresh tears, and hearing this story once she knows she will never forget.

the silence of calamity

Shortly after Delaware wrestled with the beach's death, another landmark turned moribund: the Kristina Mall, whose parking lots once overflowed like roofs impregnated by heavy snowfall, had also lost its pulse. If the Canalites had thought themselves immune before, they mourned dutifully now, knowing that to wrinkle their nose in supremacy would not protect against decline. The Delawareans once again rallied around public grief. If they sank into cultural blight, they would sink together, their low voices commiserating north and south.

People whispered about an "inadvertent redistribution of assets" within the New Jersey government. In this statement there was only a hint of the truth, that private bank account dollars had surreptitiously flown into the hands of the most prominent members of the "waste industry". But so soon, everyone had heard the full story already, so the phrase was used as shorthand to promote efficiency and civic ignorance in children. They universally condemned the governmental response. Some public officials feigned amazement, as the governor did in a press conference that ended much earlier and with more braggadocio than anticipated.

Others raised their white flags ceremonially on cue: "Caught me." Though the people felt some delight at the hand of New Jersey's misfortunes, few dared take too much pleasure, fearing the universe would pay them back with ruin. When they remembered that the absence of out-of-state revenue would almost certainly mean the mall's demise, they did not question the logic of their punishment.

Noble and sincere efforts were made to try to stop the capricious tides of demand. In a trouble press release, the governor shoved a hastily enacted policy of the "resettlement of goods," hoping that the displacement of inventory from the mall into the depths of the closets, garages, and backseats of his constituents could prevent the mall from closure.

Good intentions aside, there was no stopping the tides of demand, even if no one would forget the sacrifices they had made. Citizens patted themselves on the back with charity, wielding their wallets and stretching far beyond their purchasing powers. The rise in revenue was determined to be "embarrassingly below 0.1%," and so lacking the New Jersey super-shoppers (as well as those from Pennsylvania and Maryland and elsewhere who, sniffing retail decline, figured it would be best to support their own establishments anyways), the mall slipped into an inescapable red. Mall management released word to the press that the mall was dead just days after the beach had also passed away, avoiding any mention of the impotence of the Delaware consumer.

Some few cultural critics went to the papers to laud the elimination of the "Snooki diaspora" and all their bagel establishments from Delaware's borders, which had served exclusively New Jerseyans too obstinate to return to their state to fulfill their daily carbohydrate quota. The citizenry, however, was in denial, unable to fathom a world without greasy pretzels and bookstores to buy books they would not read. Many of them insisted on bringing up the topic in daily speech, as if their constant refrains could release an incantation that would bring the mall back to life. One by one, they all came to realize their fantasies could not save them; just as with the beach, those who had recently accepted this reality would plead with the clingers, *find your peace, please, it's been dead for weeks and we must move on.*

* * *

Juneau, for her part, is indifferent. She who had never claimed to have felt the presence of the Holy Spirit in a Forever 21, cannot understand those who claimed to have been "reborn" in the food court waiting to be admitted entrance to this or that chain restaurant. Although she has no room to be overjoyed, she's at least optimistic to hear that the mall will soon be bulldozed over to make room for "novel development." As the civic servant she envisions herself to be, she clings to this vacancy, fantasizing about its possible benefit to the community.

Emboldened by goodwill, she asks Victor what he figures it will be: "A playground? A school? A national park?"

"Perhaps a landfill," Victor responds, blasé.

Developers had also announced with great ostentation that the bare lot would be converted into a "Refugee Camp for the Treasures of Yesteryear." Victor investigated the bureaucratese to find that this "safe space" for "items difficult to rehouse" would be a junkyard for cumbersome trash, like decrepit cars and batteries with all the juice squeezed out. The announcement also raved of the land's potential for industrial use, emphasizing that any noxious fumes "would certainly rise only slightly above toxic levels."

Juneau does not hold a vigil.

* * *

Wynona heard it at work that day: *the Kristina Mall's kicking the bucket.* That night, she is polishing, her extensive collection of currencies, as she always does before bed: her pennies, her dimes, quarters from every state. Thinking of the giant coin fountain, she finds herself at a loss, wonders where on earth she will go to fish for coins.

No longer will she travel to the mall once a week, full of glee untainted by retail ambitions, hoping to excavate a rare treasure.

No longer will she cling to the idea that each day holds the possibility for greatness, the signature piece that could fulfill her indefinitely.

Though she understands on one level that her collection could never be complete and that, conversely, it would never complete her, another part of her does not know how she will continue to live or breathe confronted with such meaninglessness. *Perhaps it's time for bed*, she thinks.

As she tries to sleep, she weeps, led to despair by the growing realization that all could end, and for no good reason at all.

* * *

"I think it's an omen," Victor declares of what he calls the "waste disposal situation". Juneau thinks about the possibility that Victor is right, that such destruction would bode poorly for the future. "But an omen of what?"

"Well, that I could not say." Or, maybe he could. Maybe he's not truly incapable of completing his thought, just simply scared that words from the brain might inadvertently become the truth upon twirling through the air.

"Why so secret?"

Victor had never stopped to ask if his secrecy was destructive. But it makes sense to him. If, by being proven true, traveling words can portend evil, can't they also bring salvation by being proven false? He lives in an in-between, he recognizes that: that his speechlessness is a way to avoid the danger of altering reality. An omen of what, he cannot say; not for lack of lexical abilities, but because of his reluctance to be reckless with words.

"Victor?"

He embraces the cigarette's touch, taking a clean drag, nodding to let Juneau know she has his attention.

"Maybe there's room for hope."

Silence, wind.

batons de mort

Juneau is always eager to admit, to those not from Delaware, that Punkin Chunkin is an odd way to pass the time. Or at least that to those unfamiliar with the concept, it may certainly appear that way. It requires a lot of work and energy, for an admittedly anticlimactic payoff, and while there is certainly a sportsmanlike spirit that brightens the events, there are no losers and no winners. So what's the point?

Even in its home state, Punkin Chunkin had faded significantly in recent years. Young Delawareans, for example, had all but abandoned the practice, save a few Delaware geeks (Juneau their exemplar, uniquely comfortable around septuagenarians) who stubbornly maintained it.

Those who had left the state for university, who may have played once or twice in their childhood, dodged inquiries from curious parents by reporting that they could not find the wide expanses necessary in the urbes where they undertook their studies. They also noted that the *spirit* wasn't there, that there would have been no point in trying to keep it alive, which hinted at the truth of the matter; that they were actually relieved to be free of the collective madness, in their new metropolises where they could unbind themselves from this crazed sort of geographical belonging.

Those few stubborns Delawareans who still maintained the practice, usually the elderly or others who for some reason chose to live in another era, often came up against what they called "practical barriers". This, one can suppose, is a delicate way of referring to the year everything changed, the year it was said that civilizations clashed.

It was monumental, what happened on that fateful morning in 2001: some claim that it rocked the entire world. Others counterargue that it was no more than a justification for the way things were already going. Regardless, there are facts: on August 13th, 2001, a pumpkin flew out of range and landed directly on the windshield of a New Jersey tourist. Although there were no casualties, the 47-year-old man sued for damages to his emotional stability, and traffic was at a halt for hours as he and his family tried to come to terms with the catastrophe.

There erupted a foreign burst of outrage and indignance so resounding that Delaware legislators had no choice but to place harsh restrictions on the practice of the sport. They were already embarrassed by the practice, tired of how many out-of-state tourists would complain of the effervescent smell of putrid Halloween along the highway. Such complaints easily evolved into moral outrage, and when Delaware transportation authorities were bombarded with a deluge of calls demanding that such barbaric nonsense end, they chose to act fast.

The new laws stipulated stringent regulations that made it all but impossible for the Chunkers to practice their beloved sport. Where there was protest, those in a state of unrest were informed purse-lipped to thank their lucky stars that the practice was not banned outright. Among their restrictions, they mandated time, location, season, maximum angle of flight, minimum angle of flight, number of participants, proper attire and pumpkin variety. And when all the rules were compounded in full, in all of their various matrixes and combinations, chunking could only legally take place on the third Saturday in November, between the hours of 2:33AM and 3:27AM, in a plot at least five miles from any major roadway, with between 17 and 33 participants in bright yellow neon uniforms to promote their visibility, solely with pumpkins grown in New Jersey to fund reparations for the affected family. Needless to say, this affected the spirit of the sport, and people just shrugged their shoulders in their passive small state way to say, "I guess it's over."

Juneau found it very difficult at the time to accept that Punkin Chunkin could die. She was proud of her encyclopedic knowledge of Punkin Chunkin, drawing both from her extensive research in Delaware phenomena (including the direct memorization of not a few encyclopedia entries) and from her mother's own recollections. She envisioned it ever so romantically, that great equalizer: Wilmingtonians cheering with Southerners, Middletonians joining forces with Seafordites.

She was so convinced of its efficacy, in fact, that she felt it should have been a required unit in Delaware's physical education classrooms. As much as this perception was artificial and idealistic, Juneau knew the loss of Punkin Chunkin was a win for the beige curators of cultural suburbanization and McDonaldization of regional color.

One day, having returned home briefly to borrow some batteries, she is confronted with a heavy case of wistfulness while flipping through a photo album she had made of newspaper clippings related to the event. Though her mother is intimately familiar with everything from the process of catapult construction to the ins-and-outs of pumpkin selection, she had never spoken of actually launching one herself, so Juneau asks her if she had ever had the honor of launching a pumpkin.

"Oh no, not me, sweetie, I never had the gumption to be a launcher", her mother responds, drawing another cigarette from the pack.

"Daddy raised me to be a picker. Just about every weekend in the fall, he'd take me to the patch so he could show me which ones were good to chuck. They had to be hearty, but they also had to be real pretty, he always said, because they were going to be on the boobtube."

Juneau freezes in blue melancholy, pursued by an overwhelming nostalgia for a time she never knew. "Do you think we could bring it back?" Juneau asks, her words trying their best to combat the hopelessness of her thoughts.

Wynona sucks on her cigarette inquisitively. An exhale marks a period at the end of her sentence: "No, I think it's dead and gone."

* * *

These poor Delawareans, who every day were confronting the terrors of the world, began neutralizing their fears with new vocabulary. It became custom to refer to the most troubling concepts with particular nicknames, crafted by the market forces to put a positive spin on their fears so as not to immobilize the consumer with depression.

The short-lived wave of environmental advocacy after the beach's disappearance was particularly threatening to Delaware's corporate community. Protests in the largest municipalities urged the state government to act against mass extinction, for if the tides could swallow the beach, they could also swallow this whole small state in one miniature gulp. But this word, *mass extinction*, left such an acrimonious taste in the mouths of the DuFronds. Although it provided some revenue and profitability in the realm of Armageddon preparedness, it was decidedly "a bummer". They also found that, when not turning to the hoarding of supplies like radios and canned fruit, consumers are significantly less responsive when they are thinking of their imminent demise.

So the DuFronds launched a mass campaign, the extent of which had not been seen in the modern age. Public relations and marketing circles began to harken it to a "21st century Marshall Plan," though no one could ascertain if the term was in and of itself an intentionally designed logo. The campaign made use of technology that already existed: through the digital appendages that limited corporeality to the duration of the charge of one's earpods, electronic glasses, and undercarriage accessories, the DuFrond company's PR team blasted their messages, shouting into all devices they were capable of connecting to.

But they weren't actually so complicated: they most often simply consisted of the words "*GRAND DISPLACEMENT*", spoken by someone with a husky, reassuring voice scientifically proven to lull and make complacent. Market dudebros retorted with grins, "Thank God no body part must go without Bluetooth anymore." Such messages turned mass extinction into something sleek and sexy, packaging it into the new term *grand displacement*. Inevitably it came to be shortened, so as to be referred to as *GD*.

By this process of linguistic desensitization, the DuFronds managed to incorporate the phrase into every nook and cranny of public life, while also placing it so remotely from its original meaning that people no longer feared it, and indeed felt a newly invigorated desire to buy, buy, buy. Mass extinction was no longer what made you want to protest against government deregulation and fight the injustices of a neoliberal ecosystem. That was *old* news. Now, it had a cool, modern name, *grand displacement, GD* for short; it was a concept that your everyman could have a beer with, that the teens could parody endlessly, leading mothers wanting to be perceived as trendy to habitually look to the sky and say "No chance of a GD today!", and in the meantime everyone forgot what the danger really was.

* * *

Juneau feels so disheartened, thinking of the losses she has suffered in recent times: of the beach, of Punkin Chunkin, of other things she never became aware of and can only mourn vaguely. Armed with some years' worth of academic evidence that history is moving closer and closer to oblivion, Juneau wants to stand in its path, forcing the unwritten troths of the future to curve upwards towards heaven once more. But, as she furthers in her academic studies, she fears she will merely gain the vocabulary necessary to materialize the fact that pamphlets and radical car decals cannot save their souls.

She calls out to Victor: "Maybe we can reverse this course, the destruction of our beaches and our habitats and our livelihoods…maybe a bleak future is not an inevitability."

Victor likes to call his cigarettes *batons de mort*, meaning "sticks of death" in what he refers to as "frog tongue". Despite his typical lexical creativity, he is speechless in this moment, and so calls to his cigarette to ask its opinion: "*Baton de mort*, do you have a thought?" Victor shakes his head. "He says, *bah, c'est fini.*"

Juneau replies with Francophile curtness: "Ceci n'est pas une pipe."

Victor, whose *baton de mort* has just expired, extinguishes the weak flame that without reason clings to life, twisting it into the carpet and throwing its crumpled remains into the garbage bin. He proclaims then, "it is over," and they come to agree that the English translation sounds much more definitive.

to create hegemony

Juneau is fascinated by all sorts of words that she does not fully grasp. She is a fan of *mellifluous,* as much as she is enchanted by the word *saccharine,* words whose precise meanings ultimately evade her. Other words, having been fascinating to her at some point in the past, lose their luster. *Defenestration,* which had produced in her great wonder as a high school sophomore, became so mundanely pedestrian when she connected it with the French word *fenêtre,* which made its meaning much too transparent for her liking. Only some few prized words can manage to keep her attention for long.

On one Monday, sitting at attention in her international politics class, she becomes entranced by a new word: *hegemony.*

It had been brushed over, tossed into the air and abandoned so frivolously, as if it did not warrant an etymological discussion. *Hegemony.* It looms in her head, weighted with quiet monstrosity, she stares at it so long that she forgets which syllable to emphasize so as to bring the word back to life. But her pronunciation doubts cannot compare to her yet more specious understanding of the word's meaning: she can only intuit that it has something to do with the clash between something Big and Bad and another something small and unexpectant.

Ten minutes after the word's mention, the professor having already jumped from the Middle East across the Atlantic to Latin American *caudillos,* Juneau does not dare to stop the lecture for clarification, as much as her own thoughts have not moved on. It would be rude, and quite embarrassing, to admit that this lone word haunts her so.

So sets out on a mental voyage to see if she can collect some insight into this new phenomenon. She searches around in the annals of her brain, perhaps to dig up some historical consciousness that will shed some light, but she doubts she will succeed, as history is not her best subject. She cannot think of any examples, try as she does to make sense of the incriminating phrase "Western hegemony in the Middle East", tossed about as if she should recognize the concept without delay. On her circumnavigational journey in this frigid, inert classroom, she makes tenuous connections to her own personal life.

Juneau asks herself, what are things, big and bad like wolves hungry for meat, that control smaller things? Surely, she does not want to admit that Delaware could be in any way subject to such an arrangement, so vulnerable to outside forces. Surely, this can only happen between independent nation-states (altogether different from the US political subdivisions of states, and more akin to what one colloquially calls countries, she reminds herself).

But then, a lightbulb, yellow and sinister, erupts in her brain, the contents shattering with such force so as to temporarily cloud her eureka moment. Suddenly, as a Middletonian (a word that only she uses, and that had elicited many an eyeroll), she feels small, vulnerable in her Delawareanness. She thinks of acquaintances previously employed at the beach when the ice cream was still unharmed by salty tides, who complained about obnoxious New Jersey tourists leaving paltry tips and shouting expletives unnecessarily. She thinks of the wealthy Cherry Hill elite who study at the university, those who harbor a superiority complex towards their adopted state yet cannot bear an ounce of criticism of their beloved South Jersey. She thinks of the angry, ear-shattering discussions that occur between New Jersey residents over the sovereignty of the disputed territory of Central Jersey.

Suddenly, her blood begins to boil, excited but angered by this new discovery: that Delaware had been suffering New Jerseyan hegemony.

* * *

Nonsense.

It had been an ugly word. Long before the distance between Wynona and

Bill was a chasm, it had been his main complaint.

The potpourri throughout the house, all in their specific amounts to account for room size and other ambience factors, compulsion mandating their replacement every three months: it was nonsense. The programs Wynona enjoyed watching, so old and outdated: nonsense.

Wynona, for such a long time, had not the strength of will to point out Bill's own nonsensical idiosyncrasies. Was it not *nonsense* to be incapable of preparing own's one meal, to simultaneously condescend to and also be totally unfamiliar with the task of laundry-doing? Wynona had not been raised to stay quiet, and she did not appreciate that Bill wanted to disturb her fundamental nature, somehow believing he had ownership of her just because his irresponsibility made a human grow inside of her.

But at the end, quotidian nonsense accumulated to such a mass that brought a deeper, more sinister realization: that the nonsense in their lives consisted not only of Wynona's penchant for coin collection, or Bill's insistence on sneezing as loudly as possible. It became increasingly clear that the true nonsense lay in this insistence on staying together, in pretending that they could live happy lives, in bearing so much pain to avoid facing truth.

They had divorced just a few months after Juneau was born. Indeed, it seemed for a brief time, through the delirium of new life, through a lack of sleep, an abundance of caffeine, and a horde of strange hormones that perhaps they could salvage some of the initial spark of young passion that had so innocuously changed them both forever. But it was all a farce: when their lives stabilized and fell into routine, they realized that they truly could not resign themselves to coexistence. They had had their moments of feigned unity, of satirical domesticity, but that would be possible no longer.

It was October when he left, November when Wynona had made purge of his things, December when a legal proceeding made their separation official and legally binding; and yet already by February, they had resigned themselves to their future fate.

Wynona had believed for so long that she had rid herself of all of the remnants of his presence in her house. All that November had been spent groping into all the nooks and crannies of her petite one-story house. She had gone through the process with all of the methodicalness she could muster, feeling free to succumb to her deep impulses for order, those he had mocked in her for so long.

After a string of sleepless nights and frenzied weeks spent checking off lists, she reasonably believed that she could not have searched any further, and so she sent it all off in two separate jumbo trash bags: one to be delivered to him by mail, and one to be either donated or set ablaze. All the while she hoped Juneau would understand that mother's temporary inattentiveness would pay off in due time with the arrival of a new freedom; she pronounced such words aloud, hoping that if she could not convince Juneau, she could maybe convince herself.

The thought came to her mind, as well, that her ritual was also meant to cleanse Juneau of the same fate, to prevent Juneau from falling into the same nonsense that she had, but she could only pray that endless rounds of scrubbing and decluttering could prevent that wicked familial inheritance.

* * *

Juneau instructs Victor, finding him idle in his room as they both understand to be his custom, that it is time for him to get serious about the threat that lies just to the Northeast, lest they fall prey entirely to complete subordination.

Victor asks her politely to explain it once more without huffing and puffing, as it makes it hard for him to understand.

She recounts that New Jersey possesses an inordinate amount of power over Delaware, making Delaware dependent on their dollars at the university, at the beach, at the mall.

"Well, the beach is dead, and so is the mall."

"Yes, but that does not neutralize this threat! Until we free ourselves from the yoke of interstate aggression and hegemonic penetration, the people of Delaware will never find their liberation." Juneau's newest vocabulary ventures include words she has plucked from cursory, insufficient readovers of anti-imperialist texts.

"So, what are you saying?"

"I'm saying that it's time for Delaware to stand on its own!"

Victor raises an eyebrow: "Can a state like ours really stand on its own?"

"Well, sure! We can start from scratch! We can grow our own crops and become self-sufficient and create new systems that eliminate the exploitation of the worker and-" At this point, Victor finds it necessary to interrupt.

"No, no, no, I mean that sounds great, but I was referring to your expression. Can a state really *stand* on its own? I mean, as an imagined political entity, what legs does it have, figuratively or literally?"

"It's personification. You know, like if we described Delaware as a person and New Jersey as a person, we could say that New Jersey was a big scary man mercilessly mistreating the innocent cherub of Delaware. But who needs to get into such details? If the expression is provocative, it'll get Delaware sufficiently fired up to move it in the right direction."

And so Juneau goes on, explaining some of her more concrete ideas. Since Delaware is suffering from the loss of out-of-state revenue anyways, she argues, it would be the best time for a movement to sprout that would declare Delaware an independent nation-state, which would establish a paradise, "a shining utopia upon a hill".

Victor's fascinated, if not a bit dismayed; not by the topographical impossibility of Delaware being a utopia on a hill, but by what he perceives may have been a gross misunderstanding of the term "hegemony." Yet he himself feels he isn't totally sure he knows what it means, and he likes the idea of turning Delaware into a socialist paradise, so he tells Juneau he's on her side. Juneau replies that it would be best if they started working immediately on a manifesto to ground the movement and prescribe its speech patterns.

"Every great regime controls its vocabulary, you know."

She has several goals with these vocabulary changes: one of them being to orient the populace towards a more community-oriented way of thinking, another of them being to emphasize the geographical and cultural uniqueness of Delaware, and yet another being to suppress capitalist thinking.

In regard to her first goal, she would need a lot of help from Victor, being as unfamiliar as she is with terms like "subaltern" in the realm of anti-imperialist discourse. Juneau grabs a piece of paper and the first writing utensil she can find, a fuchsia-colored crayon; they sit at the kitchen table to begin their manifesto.

First, she writes down "subaltern", leaving definitions for later. Then, she feels that they should give a succinct name to the oppression coming from the Northeast. Her proposal is "Northeastern domination." Victor opines that this could be a little vague, depending on whether she wants to name New Jersey specifically or not, and Juneau appreciates the comment, because she thinks it's best to have as specific a target as possible.

Her next suggestion, coming to her slowly after a long pause of fiddling with the crayon to foster her creativity, is "Jersey yoke." Though Victor finds the term a bit obscure for her audience, it is catchy enough to captive their movement's spirit, and so he accepts it with an accepting "yes."

For their next task, they move to making Delaware nationalist sentiment lexically concrete.

"Every great nation has some friendly rivalry," Juneau informs. Then, she begins to speak in the impassioned way that makes her skip syllables and distort vowels, the way that signals to Victor that her rant will be long and hearty.

She starts to name pairs of cities: Lisbon and Porto, Moscow and St. Petersburg, Rio and São Paulo, Sydney and Melbourne. She continues with "Madrid and Barcelona," but Victor indicates that he gets the point. "These are the rivalries that nationhood is built on. This is the foundation of a healthy sense of belonging. Any sense of national oneness is a façade, so a healthy communal rivalry helps to dissolve that dissonance."

Victor knows what she means and admires her candor, but wonders if such a mission will not be laughably ineffective in Delaware, a place with a population below one million and no real large cities to speak of.

"Even Wilmington, the thing that would come closest to a city, is essentially just Philadelphia's sprawling wastebasket."

Juneau frowns with distaste upon knowing that he is right. She tries to put up a fight, claiming that Dover is urban enough to classify, or that perhaps one can lump strings of small towns in the South together to fight against Wilmington, but Victor pleads with her, *please, have some reason and have some respect,* and she realizes that their statemaking mission will have to proceed in a different manner.

So they transfer their efforts to where Delawareans had already made some headway: with the distinction between those who live above the canal and those who live below it, the portion unlucky enough to find itself below being referred to as Lower Slower, LSD for short.

"So, we have two parts already, but I want to provide specific endonyms for the people in both places. What could we call someone, for example, who lives above the canal?"

Victor suggests "Canalite," which sounds somewhat biblical, but they both agree that it's the most linguistically sound choice to represent the cosmopolitan, northernly sophisticated citizen they are trying to portray.

"And for those below?"

There is another pregnant pause, teeming with nascent nationalist pride, and then Victor says, "Perhaps they could be lowerites." Juneau's face contorts with a sourness that Victor hopes is involuntary, but after a minute, her facial expression morphs itself back into a polite consideration; she says she can think of nothing better, and that if necessary they will go back to it later, because she is fired up and ready to move on.

They've established words to describe the main rivalry, and ways for the rivalry to take form in the new nation: sports teams, musical ensembles, and other community organizations would compete along these boundaries, pitting north against south. That much is clear. But Juneau is thirsty for more.

She thinks that if Delaware is going to be a *real* nation, then there needs to be distinctions on a more basic level. How could Dover differentiate itself from Middletown? How would Seaford be different from Laurel, from Georgetown? It pains and aggravates her to admit that these places are united by many more similarities than differences, that any sort of differences would only have had a couple of hundred years to sprout and would never compare to the richness of cultural heritage in nations that had grown organically lacking the newness of conquest.

"You know, you can't force these things," Victor says, "too much difference could be a bad thing, anyways. I mean, look at Spain. They're a mess." That, Juneau has to cede, but it does not bring her much peace. He tells her, *why don't we move on to trying to suppress the capitalist ego*, she agrees that that would be the best course of action.

"First of all, the words 'productive' and 'useful' are out. Banned. Jail sentences for first-time offenders, guillotine for the rest."

Victor is taken aback by the cold-hearted dictator that emerges from Juneau when she talks of these linguistic preferences he didn't know existed.

Juneau writes the words on the page, then strikes them out and records the penalties for usage. She proceeds to speak.

"'A penny for your thoughts' is gone. 'From rags to riches' is of the past, because we won't have such a ridiculous amount of inequality. No one will *need* to use it, and they won't be able to, because it will be prohibited. 'Dime a dozen'? Gone too."

Having written down each letter, she then scratches the words out with such haste and such fury that Victor thinks she may really be able to enforce these rules through fear tactics alone.

But then it occurs to him that, even if they are somehow able to succeed in banding the whole state together in secessionism, that it will still be difficult to promote and enforce the usage of these words.

"Well, *we* don't have to be in power for these words to be used. We could distribute the list as a part of popularizing the movement."

"But who will see to it that these words are said often enough to catch on? You and I know well enough that we don't speak enough on a daily basis to be good promoters."

Juneau ponders, *good point*, but outwardly she is eager to find a way around it.

"Look, I'm not saying these will come in handy. But if these nationalist feelings are nascent like I think they are, then we may have a chance for those feelings to be expressed through these words. Comrade, these are the words the proles are in need of!"

Victor would say her vocabulary usage is flimsy and awkward, but he is scared to reveal himself as a dissident, and so he flashes a smile of unquestioning loyalty; Juneau begins to scribble onto the page with the assurance and hurry of ideological purity.

The Delawarean Manifesto

<u>Punkin Chunkin: A Sport Of And For The People</u>

In this grand stretch of sea-kissed coast, there used to be a tradition so noble, so touching, that it brought tears to all who bore witness. While visitors came from all corners of the universe to partake in our great performances, what mattered most in Punkin Chunkin was our own community. It brought Delawareans of all creeds together: the farmers of Sussex gathering with the merchants of New Castle and the bureaucrats of Dover to celebrate this centuries-old tradition.

Punkin Chunkin predates the arrival of Europeans on our great strip; it even predates Columbus' grand voyage. Since time immemorial, our Native American friends, our benevolent guides to whom we owe some of our great Delawareanness, have practiced this sport.

Originally, they would use their bare hands to toss the pumpkins into the air, and a tribal committee would determine, by virtue of the pumpkin's state of dismemberment, who was the strongest in all of the village. With the arrival of Europeans for our great sojourn here in the New World, the locals were eager to show us their ways. Humphrey B. DuFrond, said to be the first white man to land on these shores, was taught the intricacies of the sport by a member of the local Lenni Lenape tribe named Huato.

It is said that, though Humphrey was a man of sufficient means to have multiple translators on call, he insisted on going to his daily Punkin Chunkin practice unaccompanied, during which time his and Huato's joy and sportsmanship were more than enough to render verbal communications unnecessary. As their relationship grew fonder, Humphrey introduced his friend to the technology he had brought with him from across the pond: firearms, levers, simple pulley machines. The fusion of this ancestrally Delawarean tradition with new technology brought the sport into the modern era. Though the first Punkin Chunkin championship conducted with modern catapults was rumored to have brought on the premature death of a nearby village elder, who had been startled into an early grave, the people buried the man willingly when they were informed that it was a small price to pay for new technology.

For all of these very reasons, Punkin Chunkin is a Delawarean institution worth saving. It runs in our blood and epitomizes our greatness: we fling pumpkins, therefore we are exceptional. We defy the logic of gravity to create a sport that dazzles and amuses any and all who stumble upon it. It is therefore no surprise that the New Jerseyans should take issue with our practice.

They are threatened by this form of high civilization that so contrasts with their decadent roadways and carb-loaded breakfast sandwiches. They are deeply disturbed by our capacity for such technological prowess. Which makes it inevitable that they should want to destroy it: look around today, comrades, no Punkin Chunkin in sight, have you ever stopped to wonder *why?*

Let it not be forgotten that New Jersey tourists, who claimed to have been "irreparably mentally and emotionally damaged" by the slight embrace of a passing pumpkin, were the ones who infiltrated our government and put an end to the lawful practice of our great national pastime. They dismember us, the small pumpkin yeoman farmer of our great shores: just you go over to Trenton or Camden at Halloween time to watch how they reap our insides, fry us from within, and display us on the porches of their homes to display their bloodthirsty motives.

The image of the pumpkin resonates deeply with the eternal struggle of the Delaware people for agency, for a voice, for self-determination. It is time we say NO to New Jersey imperialism, NO to the cultural revisionism that aims to destroy the Delawarean national character, NO to foreign control of our great nation. We shall no longer allow ourselves to be carved for the pleasures of the foreign consumer: we, as the people of the Sovereign Nation of Delaware, demand a return to our national purity!

<u>Delaware Exceptionalism: A Beginner's Guide</u>

The Diamond State. The First State. We, as a people, have always been aware of our exceptionalism. We understand that our shores were handed down to us from great Druid powers with the specific intent that we honor their sacrifice with our purity. And yet, we are still shackled by a false sentiment of inferiority and small stature, so that we resign ourselves to the designation of "state": subcategory, division of the grand empire that oppresses us, the common people, and robs us of our greatness!

There is no question that our New Jersey conquerors have conceived a plot to destroy us. They feel threatened by the greatness of our beaches and the communal euphoria of our shopping centers, and so conspire to orchestrate our downfall. One only has to travel briefly on the so-called "turnpike" (an example of a superfluous switch in language usage meant to present a thin veneer of New Jersey exceptionalism) to see that their industrial blight has polluted our shores and warmed our air so as to cause our shores to rise. They have been perennially fearful of the cachet of our cultural institutions: of our Punkin Chunkin, of our horseshoe crabs, of our exceptionalism plain and simple, and so have come together to destroy us.

New Jersey is a settler colonial state of almost 9 million hegemonists; they are all liars. So how is New Jersey able to convince us of our ill suitability as a nation, while at the same time hiding their influence? It's easy – one must only look to Mount Hollywood to see how deeply the rhetoric of anti-Delawarean liberation pervades the media we consume. While our former rulers, in that empire to the North, West, and South, convinced us that films and television are produced in Hollywood, they neglect to mention how powerful New Jersey is in creating these narratives. And there is no question that New Jersey has an agenda to push. We must stand together, comrades, and demand independence.

<u>The Horseshoe Crab: A Radical Arthropod</u>

The Delaware Bay has the highest concentration of horseshoe crabs in North America. Because our colonizers lay illegitimate claims to the

Delawarean Bay, we have been pressured in the past to acknowledge that the precious arthropod creates its habitat on both sides of the bay. Yet another untruth that we have been forced to concede to appease the empire and its boisterous subjects.

The horseshoe crab has always been a symbol of Delawarean exceptionalism, and that will not change. Their struggles are our own: they worry about the encroachment of others on their habitat, fear the sullying of their aquatic hideaways. Just as the legendary animal must be turned on its side to allow it to ride into peace and liberty, we must turn each other over to wake our nation up to the great opportunity that we are missing.

You see, the Delaware nation is destined for greatness, and the most natural expression of that is true independence. Independence is the inevitable last step in our journey. Bound by the shackles of Northeastern hegemony, under the yoke of their consumerist decadence, we have no opportunity to rise to the great statures we are capable of.

We are all pumpkins; we are all horseshoe crabs. We, as Delawareans, believe that control of our natural environment is of the utmost importance for our sustainability as a nation. With the current congestion of our waterways with the gray smoke of Cherry Hill's looming factory stacks, with the harsh aroma of extra-strength hairspray, with the exhaust let off by their fleets of SUVs, it is a national security issue; Delaware has no room to preserve its own natural environment.

As a nation, we must demand the purity of our natural environment. We must institute, immediately, a breeding program for horseshoe crabs. As Delawareans, we will invest our resources into attracting and raising the libido of our treasured arthropods, and we will serve as their personal assistants to assure that their breeding process goes smoothly. As active participants in this national space, we will renounce the evils of the mad consumerism and flagrantly rampant capitalism from the North that subjugates us and impedes our ability to declare our own happiness.

<u>Glossary of Radical Vocabulary</u>

As a nation, we must unify our language to unify our thinking. As we create the utterances that will so define us as a national discourse community, we will erase the traces of the morally imprudent New Jersey-style capitalist ethos that forbids Delawarean nationalism to thrive. The system has always favored our DESTRUCTION, because they fear the logical final step of our journey; namely, the realization of the Delawarean Nation For The People By The People, in which we will no longer be the subjects of the robber barons of other, less pure shores.

Subaltern – designates and identifies the colonial populations who are socially, politically, and geographically excluded from the hierarchy of power of an imperial colony and from the metropolitan homeland of an empire.

As Delawareans, we have been placed in our subaltern position deliberately by the New Jersey Empire to convince us of our inferiority and to reap the fruits of our labor. The empire cannot allow us to maintain our ancestral Punkin Chunkin practices, cannot allow us to value our natural environment and the creatures that inhabit it, cannot allow us to value our retail paradises; for, in doing so, we would realize that our culture is actually superior to those of the ruling state, and we would rise. For this reason, New Jersey and its media empire ("Mount Hollywood") carefully craft a narrative around Delawarean inferiority, claiming that a place so small could never be powerful, and they forbid us the opportunity to exercise our cultural traditions, leaving Punkin Chunkin abandoned in the past. As an independent nation, we can fight against the subaltern designation that New Jersey has thrown upon us, this wretched Jersey yoke, and we can come to reclaim the glory of our ancestry.

Jersey yoke - the oppression and subjugation that Delawareans face as a result of the New Jersey empire's foul desire to integrate Delaware into their neoliberal, hyper-capitalist system of consumerist decadence. Also known as "bagel bondage."

Mission civilisatrice – The idea that New Jersey has a duty to uplift and enlighten the citizens of Delaware, as the superior race they deem themselves to be, thereby justifying their economic and cultural hegemony. Also referred to in New Jersey state-approved textbooks as "The Guido's Burden."

Any Delawarean who has paid attention to recent developments in the last few years can see that the outsiders have come to shove upon us bagel shops, lascivious 24-hour diners (where the waiters and waitresses accommodate *any* customer request for a quick nickel) and açai bowl franchises. To be acquainted with our hearty, Mid-Atlantic cuisine is to know that these new culinary patterns threaten the simple but proud tastes of our forebearers: crab, scrapple, pumpkin, the daily bread of civilized beings. In spite of the blatant encroachment into our cultural sphere, the phenomenon seems so disjointed that no one has been able to point a direct finger. For our own liberation, it is important for us to pronounce the true culprit of these horrors: the New Jerseyans.

As colonial settlers, New Jerseyans have long placed stressing on our great nation's institutions, and recent years have only accelerated their southward movement. Driven away by high taxes in the metropolitan homeland, they flock to their lowly colony to implant their way of life and drive ours out. The New Jerseyans have created a Delawarean economy that bows to their every whim. They infest our universities, crowd up our beaches, buy up our land. As the people undertake mass settler relocation efforts, to what they refer to as "South South Jersey", the communities change to adapt to their tastes. We did not ask for their carbohydrate-drenched breakfast foods, nor did we want their nefarious diners. We have allowed them to occupy our land, change our surroundings, and deny us our cultural expression for much too long. We have been convinced that we are an inferior people, and that New Jersey's colonial enterprises have been in our favor. That time is no more.

Though I am also burdened by these losses, we must see them as an opportunity to move forward: these losses, as much pain as they bring, also represent a great opportunity. How lucky we are, as a people, to receive this gift from the heavens. We cannot let the loss of our beach and our mall render us mopey and complacent. It is time for the people to RISE, to set our own demands, to put our own nation first. We will rid ourselves of the yoke of providing the New Jerseyans with cheap land and entertainment. We will no longer cater to their whims and consent to their market forces. It is time for the great nation of Delaware to focus on its own people.

There'll be no more talk of work. We will all contribute our labor to the same causes. We will produce our own food, provide for ourselves in a way that nourishes our environment and nourishes our souls. We will be independent: we will say NO to Guido capitalism and that Jersey yoke.

This is the opportunity for us to realize the final form of our greatness. We are being called: let us heed these ancestral pleas! As they see us succeed in ripping off the chains of tourist servitude, they will shower us with spiritual glee.

Imperialism – This is the (deeply biased) definition of the New Jersey Education Association: "The policy of a country that attempts to extend or conserve their domination over other people or territories. Imperialism is inherent to capitalism."It is my duty to show you, the Delawarean Folk, the ways New Jersey trains its subjects to dupe us time and time again.

New Jerseyans, in taking precious time to learn about such concepts, feel that they are cosmopolitan and benevolent. In fact, this pride in their education leads them to believe they are superior. And yet, they learn only that *countries* are the actors that create empires: not states. Oh yes, they can certainly look at *other* empires to criticize, just as they openly criticize the American one. Yet they have no frame of reference to understand their own imperialist actions: they are blinded by the enlightenment they believe themselves to have.

Comrade — A Delawarean; a compatriot; a fellow national citizen; a fellow believer in the moral and technological superiority of Punkin Chunkin, of our mollusk friends, of our natural environment, of this magical coastal strip.

Canalite - A non-pejorative term to refer to a resident from the northern section of Delaware located above the canal.

<u>The Construction of the Delawarean</u>

You might well be asking yourself at this point: how could New Jerseyans *do* such a thing? Why can't they bring themselves to build their own great universities to attend, or do their gym, tan, and laundry at their own beaches? From where does the idea come that they have not only the right, but the responsibility, to occupy our space and instruct us in their "civilized ways"?

Public education is the answer.

New Jerseyans cannot imagine themselves without the image of the poor, provincial, inept Delawarean. Their own self-image is constructed in opposition to the image their literature, media, and film has constructed of the Delawarean. It is an idea so deeply ingrained in the base national consciousness, that the citizens do not call it into question. This is precisely what makes this idea so dangerous – because no one acknowledges it, it is a self-evident truth and cannot be argued against.

Portrayals of Delawareans abound in the productions of Mount Hollywood. While some of these efforts are commercial, the industry produces most of these film nasties with the education system in mind. New Jerseyans are inculcated beginning from pre-school with the image of the provincial Delawarean and the benevolent New Jerseyan.

While I wish I could provide you with a comprehensive critical analysis of these works, I'm afraid that these propaganda films are protected forcefully by the imperial state from outside consumption. On school days when these types of representations are fed to the students, students must show proof of New Jersey residence, to prevent outsiders from getting access to their materials. In spite of these restrictions, I have in my exhaustive efforts managed to obtain a synopsis of one of such films from an elementary school textbook that illustrates my point. Please read with caution, for the following story is damaging to Delawarean national character.

<u>The Merchant of Cape May</u>

The merchant's smile was radiant under the early sun. He had counted his wares, counted them twice, and his voyage was about to begin. He thought: "How happy my customers will be to receive these tools, for such unbeatable prices!" His eyes were green with the thought of all the money he could earn, and all the people he could save with his miraculous inventions and gifts to industry.

He was told by others that to cross the bay was to play with death. "Beyond Cape May," they would say, "I do not stray." They would tell him that Delaware came from the French "De la Warr", meaning "of Hell": the people were unlearned in civilized enterprise, hostile to foreign involvement. They would recount that they performed savage rituals and communicated in a tongue unknown to the modern industrialist. These stories did not scare him. As much as it pained the merchant to leave his beautiful shores, surely incomparable to any other, he knew that his mission would help those on the other side of the New Jersey Bay. As he cast his sail upward to announce the beginning of his journey, he was happy to think that the divine would shower him with great wealth for his morality.

On the first part of his journey, he proceeded with calm, knowing he was of a superior race. It was only when he approached the halfway point of his trek that he noticed something was not right. Halfway across the New Jersey Bay, he could see two sides of the water: in the side he was still in, the water was calm, a royal blue. But across the halfway point, approaching the shores of Delaware, the water was tempestuous, of a bile-like green. As he entered this new stretch of ocean, he found it difficult to control his vessel. It was a constant struggle, him against the raucous winds, the stench of rotten gourds, the unwelcoming skies. He carried bravely on, despite these premonitions of doom.

The last leg of his journey was the slowest, and yet it put him at ease. He had been warned that the "other side" would be difficult to reach, and he had expected that the water in the last leagues of his journey would turn into thick sludge. He proceeded through the murky waters, entering into the oblivion of this swampy country. Docking, he was greeted by eyes all around.

Suddenly, his boat is attacked by savage forces in the shape of human beings: the Delawareans have not taken kindly to his arrival.

"These *men*, if they are truly human, are clearly incapable of self-government!"

The merchant fends them off with his superior weaponry, and steers his boat quickly in the other direction to escape, back towards the shining shores of Cape May.

those who worship gourds

Juneau adamantly refuses to redact their manifesto on the computer; she simply cannot trust that her work will not be infiltrated by the New Jerseyan state. Victor looks at her as if she is infirm but she does not waver in her decision to write out the entire work by hand. She shapes each letter of their dogma painstakingly in a cursive script carefully crafted to seem warm and welcoming but yet also revolutionary in its dance upon the page. Each scribble, each dotted i, she explains in the introduction, is "shaped with love", the love of home, the love of community, the love of radical change.

"I'm still not sure how we'll share it," Victor says pointedly, drawing attention to what he sees as a futile exercise.

"Haven't you ever used a copier?" Juneau asks, a question she instantly regrets, since of course she knows that he'll say "no, never," thereby rendering her question null.

"Well that's how it will be done," she declares, with a finality that censures all possible retorts. She announces that she will going to the library to make her copies; Victor assents.

Juneau has the option to drive to the library. It would be a five-minute drive, at the culmination of which she would have to find a parking spot and pay for her sloth. The walk is substantially longer, about twenty minutes, but she enjoys the fresh air, and besides chooses to walk even in the most torrential of downpours to avoid the dull horror of the automobile.

As she walks, she passes through rows of quiet residences, some filled with students, others occupied by real families, breeders and their kin somehow managing to live and breathe amidst a plethora of tumultuous jumps into adulthood.

She thinks it strange that she should see so few people on her Friday afternoon stroll to the library, given how remarkably unoppressive the day's weather had been, but then she figures that most of the students have other ambitions than to spend a glorious Friday surrounded by *books*.

She enters the library, a sort of personal heaven. More generally, it is a haven for *all* of those more comfortable observing alien social interactions than engaging in their own, for those who don't need many friends since in literature they find friends much more reliable than those who possess flesh. But it is nicer to think that this building had been built just for her pleasure and recluse, every hidden table and forgotten study corner, and so she allows herself this small fantasy.

She comes often to do her homework, though when she comes she cannot help herself but to spend twenty, thirty, forty minutes roaming through the tomes, and it was a rare day that she would not preface her studies by making her way up and down the alphabet, trying to decide which five books she would take home, an arbitrary number that she nevertheless considers very important to give books the attention they require.

But today, she is driven by a higher purpose, cannot be tempted out of her crusade by any sort of literary fascination. She has a mission. She picked a good time for it, too, since the printers are all open and ready for her use, and there would be no one to tap their foot and whisper with forced breath to tell her that her time was up. And so she gets to work scanning each page with care, after a time getting into a nice rhythm of key strokes, mouse clicks and page flips, is momentarily lost when she realizes the scanning process is complete. Then she remembers that these pages are not simply meant to rest in cyberspace, they are to be distributed and set free in the hands of revolutionaries, and so she begins to make copies.

She does not know quite how many copies it would be appropriate to make. 50? 100? 250? As a manifesto of many pages, she does not want to be remiss in considering the environment's needs, whose fate is already determined but does not deserve to be kicked while already down. So she thinks, why not 100, that most central and general of numbers, 100 should be fine. Then it comes time for her to wait. This, too, has its own rhythm, except it is much slower: click, click, wait five minutes, place it in her bag.

She watches as each copy came out with her words and her descriptions, Victor and her's ideas, warm and freshly pressed as she thinks her ideas deserve to be. She cannot help but be enamored by the romance of it all, of blessing her university comrades with revolutionary ideology: is there nothing more youthful, more universally ambitious than daring to believe that things are not immutable?

And yet it is also a painful image for her, watching the pages accumulate, thinking that once upon a time these pages may have been sheltering a wise old tree in the Amazon, whose rings could have wrapped around themselves indefinitely had it not been for human avarice. She becomes fixated on this image of this wise old tree, its top extending to the canopy of the vast forest, and she thinks she would have liked to hug it, to share her warmth with it, ignoring the rough reprimand of the bark. And she thinks, what if there were no more axes with which to chop, no more forests stripped of their oaky children, but the library is too silent to feel anything but slight dismay.

* * *

Juneau begins her journey to class with pride. Victor has overslept, a casualty Juneau is quite used to. It is a walk, in any case, that she feels she can only do on her own. She feels that there are only two real possibilities, both of them disheartening: that either she would find her manifesto flapping around campus like doves having only recently been permitted to use their wings, or the pamphlets would be engorging trash cans and recycling cans alike, for when the recycling cans can take no more, the students ignore their eco-alliances and take care of their business through other more nefarious methods.

Winter, or what had become winter, still grips her soul, making it difficult to hope. She had posited *before*, in times before difficulties piled together in such numerous heaps, that perhaps higher temperatures in January would be a good thing. Even though she is not the type of person to thrive in warmer temperatures, preferring instead the rare frosty times when she can bundle herself up and hide from the world, it's hope and positivity that leads her to believe that a balmy January could be good. She had ultimately forgotten to ponder that, even in a January that allowed for bare knees and shoulders, the days would still be short, and darkness would still hold dominance over its earthly kingdom. And so she feels, despite the pride that places vigor in her steps, that the brisk strips of the early dawn weigh down her soul.

The day prior, as she had stuck pamphlets in receptacles of all varieties, she had hoped that the element of surprise could induce curiosity. Might a curiously laid pamphlet, inexplicably showing up in the cafeteria line or in a store window, communicate to the reader that the messages contained were meant for them and them only? Or should she focus on those meticulous readers whose eyes were attentive to all of the correct places to obtain revolutionary reading material, like the library or the bookstore, would know that they, as the responsible, resourceful reader they knew themselves to be, were the intended audience, and so had an undeniable responsibility. In what she perceived as a compromise, Juneau had gone sticking her work in crevices and crannies that would seem preposterous, bathroom stalls, janitor's closets, and underground sewage systems being just a few of such locales she had chosen to attract a certain kind of alternative-leaning student.

As she comes closer and closer to the heart of campus, twitching with the anticipation of gauging the effectiveness of her efforts, it astonishes her to observe so many with a copy of the manifesto in their hands. She sees voraciously engaged readers run into electric poles, to then continue their reading with a hurry as if they cannot afford to lose a precious minute. She witnesses pairs of critics exchange quotes, ricocheting comments and critiques in revolver-like fashion. There are those who read it aloud, focusing on one groundbreaking inquiry or another, those who take "comrade" and burst into fits of example sentence creation. Juneau, jaw unhinged, wonders if she had ever seen her classmates so lively at eight in the morning.

Of course, for as many people as she sees precariously engaged with their reading, she sees just as many look on these readers with open scorn. She cannot help but notice that those with the nerve to curl their facial expressions radiate a sense of Megalopolis Riches, a feeling that implies they had been transported by car for too many hours on the turnpike just to go to university with some people who *read* for fun. Their rumpled faces express a disdain so sour that it can only mean they are covering their fear of the written word. *Fear implies guilt*, Juneau thinks, watching these people with family brand-name recognition give these readers the same look they typically gave her just for passing by their side.

The flurry of activity escalates as Juneau approaches closer to the center of campus, passing by the typical milestones: the library, the overpass, the preacher that comes every day to warn in his raspy alto of the dangers of lipstick and children's cartoons. Normally, Juneau does not pay Reverend Bridge, colloquially known as Reverend Smidge, much attention, but today, threatened as he may feel by the attention the students pay to a one particular pamphlet, his remarks flow across the air and attack her membranes.

"Burn all Ye in Hell those who worship gourds!" Juneau has to be impressed by his ability to incorporate this new manifesto material into his routine with such short notice. *Reading scares them all.*

"Pack your bags, children: you've got a sinner-class ticket to Hell!"

"So much talk of global warming, so little recognition of the heat you've produced through of all your fornication! Homosexuals and adulterers, all of you, you deserve the flames!"

And periodically, tiring of the imprecision of English, the Reverend would evoke his direct connection with the big guy in space through crashing combinations of guttural sounds and ancient-sounding vowels. He speaks some language, who knows if it is a different one each day or just one of a select few in a regular rotation, his tone moves up and down in predictable patterns; tiring of his ululations, his vocabulary perhaps being too limited in this adopted tongue to express his disgust accurately, he switches back to English.

Juneau, having stopped on the corner to listen to his tirades, wonders which sin of hers he will condemn. Seeing she is a virgin, he will have to come up with something creative out to punish her for her genitalia.

"God sees you wearing clothes of two fabrics, he sees you call others 'fools', his tears fill the seas and threaten the coasts!" Perhaps he is lucid enough to read her mind. Juneau, always being early, has a bit of time to spare, but has neither the time nor the desire to watch him all day. He's perceptive enough to see her presence, though she had tried to watch from as far away as possible; he prepares himself for spectacle.

"Watch as I turn water into wine!" *Sounds like a good business idea,* Juneau thinks. A couple of other students, seeing her fixated on him, stop as well to watch the farce.

He ceremoniously pulls out a bottle of water, announcing its brand name several times as if his quackery were corporate-bound, and dilates the contents into his mouth, his eyes wide with crazed confidence. His cheeks swell with the weight of the water, or the wine, whatever the liquid should be called at this point in the conversion process. He continues moving his head from side to side, mechanically as if classically trained as an animatronic performer. The liquid swishes from one cheek to the other. His cheeks, patiently waiting for the liquid to exit their auspices, remained inflated, but begin to erupt in a curious shade of purple.

He continues to shake his head back and forth, but his face begins to change color along with his cheeks. Juneau, along with the rest of the crowd captivated by the continuation of the performance, wonders if the body necessarily has to turn the color of red wine to reflect the chemical processes within. When the Reverend tumbles over and returns the contents of his stomach to the earth, the water shining clearly in streaks of his bile, Juneau comes back to reality and makes the more logical assumption that his body had gone chameleon in a state of panic brought on from a lack of breath.

After his bodily upheaval, he arises shakily, shouting "THE DEVIL, HE WATCHES YOU AS YOU WALK AWAY AND HE RUBS HIS GENITALS ON YOUR PILLOW", but the group of students had already moved on, having understood once more that they were watching nonsense.

Juneau moves on with her day, goes towards her classroom. As she walks, she fantasizes about a Delaware shaped by spiritual wellness. The public servant that she believes herself to be thinks of a great new wellness program she will one day implement to promote national cohesion. She imagines yoga teachers, inculcated with the Delawarean ideology and driven by a desire to serve the Delawarean people, renaming their poses in the honor of great Delawarean historical figures, adjusting their class instructions to incorporate the manifesto's lingo, co-opting the rites of Catholic exorcism to remove the last stubborn traces of consumerism from the Delawarean psyche.

As she advances on, paying little attention to her surroundings and allowing her memory to guide her steps, she collides with the front wall of the building that she had meant to enter through its door. She had miscalculated, gotten lost in thought. Perhaps it is contagious, the tendency to lose oneself in another world. Or maybe generational. Before she can trace the source of her mishap, she spots a poster coincidentally placed just where she had bumped her head. She peers at it to analyze what wisdom the world had placed in her path:

BUY IZEBURG WATER, LIVE FOREVER.

She shields her eyes, sighing, thinking of rain.

malleability

If there was ever a thing that brought Russell Brandt pleasure, it was his love for the radio.

He views his hobby as separate from those of other ham radio enthusiasts, from whom he always distinguishes himself clearly and with a dismissive laugh, provoking the chagrin of his wife who dislikes such outbursts. He is not, for example, a collector, as he only owns two, one for the house and one for the office; what he values most is his ability to spend speaking with strangers in faraway lands, though it could be said to be a poor substitute for the face-to-face conversations that Brandt definitively prefers.

In the 1980s, when Russell was attending the College of the State of Delaware, he decided for once and for all that the radio was the perfect form of entertainment, and on this he never budged. He lived through various technological fads and resisted them on all counts, with more disinclined fervor as his number of years increased and manifested on his face. He knew the television, of course, he was not so old not to experience its novelty.

If one stopped to ask Brandt what exactly was so superior about this form of entertainment, he would be hard-pressed to come up with any concrete answer. It was not simply a question of a preference for music over any visual form of art, that he knew for sure. He could enjoy the odd trip to the movies, or an occasional piece of theater. But on a day-to-day basis, and this only grew truer as he got older, he preferred to sit back and listen to a radio station, knowing that an announcer had chosen this sequence of music with intention. And with the impact of his opinion among a dwindling radio audience growing larger and larger, sometimes a thought crept in that the music had been chosen especially for him.

But that was never because he called in any requests. That was not his place. He was used to sitting back and listening to each piece of music carefully: sometimes classical, sometimes jazz, sometimes gospel when he was feeling most lost, and to enjoying the snippets of human voice in between that introduced and concluded the pieces. Truth be told he enjoyed these intermittent interruptions to similar (if not equal) degree as he did the music; they showed him that he was not alone in his pleasure, that he could perhaps control his exposure to the outside world and still remain a silent part of it.

And he saw it as his duty to cling to his preference, despite or perhaps because of the increasing obsolescence of the object of his obsession; in this antiquated mindset he retained a small part of the spirit of this university intellectual rebellion, even though in most areas of his life he had succumbed to the impotent monotony of mortgage and marriage.

He does not particularly like or dislike his position as the director of the Delaware Department of Motor Vehicles. In theory, it brings him pride to help his fellow citizens. As in most professions in which people assert a higher purpose, however, this feeling in much easier to appreciate in principle than in reality. Indeed, if he had ever gained the opportunity to see through to his vision of the world, in some dorm room managing to be simultaneously stale and full of wonder, his department would not exist, as cars would be a thing of the past, and people would make use of trains or bicycles or other, less monotonously melancholy forms of transportation.

But these ideas, leftover from a time when Russell was young and impressionable and believed the world would let itself be changed, are gone.

Still, he finds his own crumbs of hope from which to make pride. Russell, in attending regional and national transportation forums, boasts often that Delaware's Department of Motor Vehicles is one of the most efficient in the country. *Oh, paltry Delaware, it is only natural,* they would say, *you're not in the big leagues, see, you could not even conceive of the traffic we have here, our highways could very well earn a place as one of the wonders of this modern world.* He listens to them all, those that dismiss him, and pays them no mind.

Delaware is small and so are diamonds, that's how he always thinks, *what do you know about the riches that lie here.* It is his tendency to cling to ideas rather than things, as physical objects deteriorate just as quickly as time passes by, and so his pride in Delaware's efficient DMV he attaches himself to with as much quiet desperation as his radiophilia.

* * *

Brandt idles in his office, alternating between twiddling his thumbs and mindlessly perusing the office mail. Amidst the avalanche of junk advertisements and bureaucratic nonsense, a name on an envelope tips him off: *Baker.* Brandt finds himself in high school algebra, sitting next to a girl who made his heart perform acrobatics he did not vocalize. He had certainly thought of her several times over the years, perhaps upon inhaling a certain scent or seeing a division sign. The truth is, she would come to him quite randomly, as much as he would want to find a pattern, and he found himself happy to have the memory, remembrances of unrequited love that permeate his existence. In front of Baker sits not Wynona, the object of his desire, but Juneau.

He reads the proposal over with increasing interest, reading for detail, for hidden meaning: *Our goal is to free Delaware from the Jersey yoke.* Maybe Juneau's words, whoever she is, whether or not she has some relation to the Wynona Brandt wants to believe he still knows, are meant to provoke his political consciousness, but his thoughts wander into all sorts of unproductive dimensions. It occurs to him, as had occurred to him many times before in life but yet never with the same force, that each life is just as intricate and complicated as his, dare he think just as melancholy; he thinks of how people move on and grow from the memories they create, so much so that there is no way to say if the people we believe to remember still exist in the present.

As he connects the abstract strands of his mental wanderings to concrete yearnings, he wonders: what could have become of Wynona? There comes the thought that, if this is presumably her child, there must have been a father, and it shocks him slightly to discover a feeling of jealousy. The rational part of him knows he has no right, that even if they had had a physical relationship, he could never begrudge her to move on and live her own life. The feeling is ridiculous, as many feelings are, with respect to the human condition for the heart and the brain not to communicate.

* * *

It had been a Wednesday when Brandt received Juneau's letter, sent in a buff blue envelope the color of Delaware, and by the next day, he had arranged for a meeting, which would take place within some short few minutes. He is already impressed by the youthful determination present in her prose. *How good to believe in things*, he thinks; perhaps he can learn something from her. He cannot help but compare this image he creates in his head of this Juneau, an anachronistic warrior fighting against forces that could no longer be stopped, with the image he has of Wynona.

Although he censures himself for presuming to know what the depths of Wynona's soul contain, he begins nonetheless to be amazed by the ways children can drift from their parents. Wynona, to him, had always seemed like a wandering soul, smart enough to perceive life's offenses but too fleeting to do anything serious about them. To think that her daughter would be so political, so impassioned, frightens him, because it reminds him that he is conjecturing about a woman that he had only known for a brief time, when they were both just children. He thinks, once again: *maybe I am fooling myself, perhaps this Juneau Baker has no relation to my Wynona, the world has sprouted stranger things.*

Then he can contemplate no more, because the secretary arrives with a girl in tow: it must be Juneau. The girl he presumes to be her leaves no doubts: she marches in front of the secretary, who glares towards her with slight reproach, and announces to him with hand extended: *I am Juneau, this is me.* She is sure of who she is, sure of what she wants, two things Brandt can no longer claim for himself: he has to admire her strength.

"Hi, I'm Russell Brandt. Please, take a seat." He gives her a smile he knows

47

to be open and ambiguous.

She is seated. She scans the office, cataloguing the items in her mind. She wears a dusty denim jacket, paired with jeans of a tone that clash lavishly. Her glasses are thick, thick enough to appear to protrude away from her face and into Brandt's, penetrating his thoughts. Brandt starts to notice a certain something about her that reminds him of Wynona, strange as it may seem. It's not the way she dresses, and it's certainly not the confident way she strode into the door. It's something that he catches in a mere short glimpse, some sort of antiquity trapped in her eyes. He searches for this thing he cannot name.

Brandt begins: "I found your proposal intriguing."

"I've no interest in intrigue not backed by action."

"Intriguing enough to spur my action, surely."

"What's your five-year plan?"

He chuckles. "Quite daring. Really. Reading it, I feel that things could change."

This *something* about Juneau is shining. Yet that's all he can call it, despite it staring him right in the face: this *something* so palpable and nascent.

Brandt continues: "But I just have one question, something that bit at me all the while I looked at your proposal. It tore at me, really, and I do truly feel that I could not go any further in our discussion before gathering your input on this topic. So I ask you with the utmost seriousness: have you thought of the flag? I mean, the one we have now is so drab and dull, as you may have noticed. And that's done just fine, so long as we have been an interstate pit stop. But now we're aiming for higher, bigger things, no? No more buff blue, I would think. What do you have for me?"

"I haven't gotten that far. Frankly, it's not currently relevant."

"What's your *vision*, Juneau?"

Something in Juneau's expression denotes that she has noticed a nonpolitical bent to Brandt's inquiry. She pauses, sowing tension.

"I envision happiness, communal joy. I see happy neighbors, romping through fields of royal purple, spending their days creating, enjoying the creations of others. I envision a world in which all of us can be free to commit ourselves to beauty. I foresee coastal communes, where the people congregate together to sing and make merry by the mouth of the sea."

"How fanciful your imagination. Maybe you should be an artist."

"Or perhaps I should be a politician. Politics *needs* creatives: it needs people who are able to think outside of our traditional ontological boundaries."

"Is that so?"

"Well, sure. Just think of paradise. No one *works* in a paradise. People spend their days devoted to increasing the General Happiness Quotient. That's how our government will be structured. No one will be in want of food: we shall come together as a people to provide for ourselves. We will farm and reap our own benefits. We will be in touch with the supernatural, praise deities that we have forgotten, become one with our earth until no one can tell the difference between our bodies and our soil."

"It sounds fascinating."

Juneau frowns. "I guess you're not one for action."

"I think the idea is beautiful."

"That's it?"

"It's not all I feel, but it's all I know how to express."

Juneau thinks for a moment. Then she asks: "You are from Delaware, right?"

"Of course," he responds, with a hint of indignance.

"If we keep allowing New Jersey to hegemonize us, with their imperial Northeastern allies that litter our beaches, congest our highways and infest our universities, we will never make any progress." She corrects herself: "Litter*ed* our beaches…", emphasizing her use of the past tense suffix.

"Okay, I see what you mean. What exactly is it that you need from me, though? How do I fit into this puzzle?"

"I think what we need at this point is some sort of spectacle to show that we're serious. You read my proposal, and the vocabulary document I attached, right? We've got to create an ideology around this idea, get people on board. I've been doing a lot of grassroots efforts, but we're going to need some sort of…*happening* to get people's attention."

"And what would that be?"

"I think we should blow up the Delaware Memorial Bridge."

It is now clear why Juneau's interests lie in the transportation administration. "You want fatalities, or a clean swoop?"

"There's no need for blood to spill. No one uses the bridge these days. New Jerseyans came for either the beach or the mall. Now they have no reason to cross over; they maintain it solely as a symbol of our quality as their subaltern. And what self-respecting Delawarean *ever* crossed north if they didn't have to?"

"You, as the head of the transportation administration, have a great deal of power when it comes to these matters. You could block off the road, declare it unsafe..."

Brandt ponders. "But I suspect that's not *all* you want."

She smiles. "I suspect you're perceptive."

"No, Brandt, that is *not* all I want from you. The spectacle would ignite a wave of pro-Delawarean, anti-Guido fury. It's the catalyst we would need to declare our independence. Once we make our debut, we shall need a leader. Someone with a love for Delaware, someone who can play hardball with those Northeastern colonizers."

"And this new country will still be called Delaware?"

"You've got to focus! At a time of revolution, no less..."

"But shouldn't our regime have a name? I mean, is that not a logical step?"

"It's a logical step. I think it's just a bit more important to discuss the logistics of you seizing power before we get to that."

He nods in agreement, but Juneau can sense that he's not fully convinced.

"Look at it this way. It would be a *huge* blow to New Jersey. I mean, they wouldn't really notice the bridge at first. But maybe one day they might. And then it would be a huge middle finger in their faces! If they see it, I mean."

Brandt looks at her, admiring her moves. She knows where to appeal to him, right in his blue hen Delawarean heart. He, too, had been the victim of foreign scoffs at his home university, had been pushed off his own beaches by hordes of Sardinian sunbathers. She knows that pitting him against that malignant force to the Northeast would rile him up.

"Fine. I'm in." He wonders if Wynona knows of the plan.

Juneau does not look too surprised at having convinced him, but she does show pleasure. "We'll rule the skies!"

"We'll conquer the plains!"

"We'll build a paradise for the people!"

"Goodwill will flow through our veins!"

"Our ambitions shall have no end!"

"We will conquer the perils of modern humanity and be glorious in our vanity!"

Finally, Russell points to what that *something* of hers is: it is her ability to lead other people to believe that the human race has a fighting chance.

* * *

In the main conference room at the DuFrond headquarters, tense discussions are being had. Although Harry and his legal team are of a high stock and distinguished caliber, their sweat reeks with the scent of plebeian fears.

"Those damn reds!"

Juneau and Victor's communist manifesto had now exited the realm of the university and successfully circulated itself all the way up and down the Delawarean strip, provoking intense speculation, wild glee and a fair number of lexical questions related to the vocabulary, but nowhere had it produced as much panic as in the corporate headquarters of the DuFrond company.

"Government by and for the people," Harry had responded with mockery: "These ideas only work in theory, goddamnit!" And then he felt guilty for using the Lord's name in vain, for his God was a generous God who had proffered him and his family with all of his riches, taking from the greedy pockets of those unwilling to toil and boil. So naturally, it was in the realm of holy possibility for him to do all he could to prevent a common resurrection that could lead to dents in their profit margins. But it would not be easy.

Their suits are wrinkled from bodily excretions, palpable visions of financial calamity have them envisioning catastrophe. Truthfully, Harry is

51

embarrassed that the company had only just now begun to catch wind of the pamphlets, since it had been over a week since they had been widely distributed. He finds it most convenient to think of his family's company as having a variety of tentacles, reaching into various areas of life through an array of contacts in a myriad of industries. But they are tentacles of a benevolent octopus, of course, a mercantilist octopus that praises human ingenuity and does no harm to the odd human body in its midst, even as its goo becomes tainted by the sludge it inhales.

Facing this threat, Harry will tolerate no more delays.

"So, boys," Harry starts, "have any candidates for me?"

Landon shifts from one buttock to another. "Yes, sir, we believe we do."

Harry sees that Truman is about to continue where his partner had left off, to inform him of who the company could promote to take over the independent Delawarean state in case the situation gets to that point, but he cannot accept the seconds that lie in between:

"Well, if you believe you know, and you're both men of your word, then why can't someone TELL me who!" Harry stomps on the ground for emphasis upon reaching the phonological climax of his sentence (indicated here with capital letters). Harry is well known for his temper tantrums: he knows that, for some, discomfort leads them to the point of obedience, while for others it simply scares them into submission. Whichever way it works, he concerns himself not in the least; as long as his methods of control are functional, they are valid.

"We've vetted a c- candidate named Reverend Bridge," Truman states.

"Is that his *real* name?"

"That's the only name we were able to find."

Harry raises his eyebrows in a quizzical look of fury:

"You take me for a FOOL! You think we don't need to know who do business with?"

"Isn't this politics?"

"Same thing, you *imbecile*."

Landon takes over: "Well sir we could certainly do more digging, but I believe he's commonly known just as Reverend Bridge, so-"

"Enough of that you paltry manchild, just get him in my hands!"

"Well, sir, he's quite the evangelical, we believe that if we appeal to his religious sensibilities, we can get him on our side."

The two *sides* they are on are left unnamed, but they all know that they are focused on the unity between the common, uneducated man, and the corporation. The relationship is inherently unequal: most corporate types know this, they just do not find it a very interesting fact to consider and so do not think of it very often. But the corporation is also big and great enough to convince the layman otherwise: that, as the corporation destroys communities left and right, it shifts attention to polemics that create a common enemy, *the liberal elite*, in this way the masses become pacified and do not notice as the market comes to control all.

They can cry out against abortion, scream about the lack of prayer in school, decry sex education, blame liberal decadence on the country's falling status, all while ignoring the pressure the higher classes place upon their labor. As they continue their hysteria about the fall of Western civilization, their wages funnel up into the pockets of their overlords, except they do not call them as such but instead prefer "boss" or "sir," and there are enough appearances of mutual benefit to appease the Mountain Dew-loving factory workers.

"So you think he's *malleable* enough for us?"

"We do, sir. He's quite connected with the…*gutter* community, I believe that's the term they want us to use now…we're sure that he could translate our message into their words."

"Then set up a meeting with him. We can't lose any time."

Then Harry storms out of the room with self-important gusto, as if he has somewhere to be other than out of the building to have his chauffeur escort him home.

"If you see a panhandler, slam on the gas, I don't give a shit about red lights," he says, weary from so much knowledge of other peoples' problems.

* * *

Truman and Landon manage to secure Reverend Bridge's presence at the company headquarters the following Monday. They had worked that Thursday, Friday, and Saturday to synchronize all of the details of their meeting, of which a great part included making sure that the room they reserved would include all of the amenities that Harry required: cold water to drink, fresh water with sea creatures to observe, a cheese plate with an odd number of cheeses and an even number of crackers, a masseuse on-call for emergency shiatsu.

Reverend Bridge is overwhelmed at his being fussed over upon his arrival. Truman and Landon almost stumble over him as he walks into the building, asking him frantically about where his chauffeur had parked the car, then feeling great shame to know that he had driven himself and simply parked on the street. They look at each other, eyes wide with wrongdoing, as if in agreement not to tell Harry about their lack of prior planning. To their defense, they had been working nonstop with no coffee, no sleep, and no food, so they were feeling slightly heady, as if the world were just a hologram's reflection.

But then, the pair take a better look at the man they had been hired to catch, and they realize what they are truly dealing with: loose-fitting supermarket jeans, an old secondhand flannel, a discolored pair of value-brand sneakers. It is one thing to *read* and *analyze* the common folk, and quite another to experience their appearances and odors firsthand.

As they lead him up the stairs, Truman says: "There must be a lot of honor in what you do."

"A whole lot!"

The Reverend, thinking they are showing their deference to a member of the clergy, responds with pride: "There is!" He's not aware that they are assigning him honor to defray their own guilt at having pillaged the likes of him to reach the nirvana of expensive ties and gold toilets.

As they wait for the elevator, the Reverend offers to take the stairs, to which suggestion Truman and Landon laugh heartily and do not bother to respond with words.

"Some men use their own two feet," Truman says, his tone ambiguously crafted so as not to let on if he had mocked or not.

The elevator comes and dutifully drops them off on the fifth floor where Harry awaits them. They proceed to the door, knocking some message in morse code to warn any inhabitants of that space of their entry. What happens next is clearly, in Bridge's eye, not according to protocol: it occurs in such a flurry of flailing limbs and hurried voices that the Reverend cannot determine what exactly had gone awry.

Truman and Landon's eyes grow great and wide like two pairs of night saucers. Angry words are shouted within the room, then as the voice gets closer, the door opens, and the Reverend finds that Truman and Landon are sheltering a person between their huddled bodies, leading this person (likely Harry, but the Reverend has no way to be sure) to an office down the hallway, their legs wobbling to keep the hostage covered and out of sight at all times, from all angles. They disappear behind a separate door, then after a series of physical and verbal blows resounding across the walls, they come back out in the hallway, smiles wide, to lead the Reverend in:

"Harry will be with us in just a moment."

They sit. Truman and Landon occupy two seats at the far-left side of the conference table, and lead the Reverend to his seat on the other side. Truman and Landon, operating as one, fold their hands ceremonially on the table in front of them, smiling in intervals at each other and at the Reverend. The Reverend deduces that Harry enjoys being waited upon, and wonders if that has anything to do with the commotion of his entrance.

After a few strange minutes of silence, and a few unanswered attempts by the Reverend to engage his captors in conversation, Harry enters the room. Truman and Landon shuffle to get on their feet, while the Reverend stays seated.

Harry exclaims with calculated prowess: "Greetings, Reverend Bridge! Welcome to our headquarters! I assume you've been well taken care of by our team."

Bridge squeezes out half of a "yes, I have" before Harry begins to speak.

"Do you know why I have gathered you here today? No, you must not. I imagine it all seems quite confusing, no? For a group like us to take interest in someone like…like you."

Harry looks to the ceiling, hands behind his back with practiced reflection.

"But you are an important asset! We need you, Reverend, because we have big, lofty plans here at the DuFrond corporation. Say, do you know of the greatest rising economic threat of our time?"

The Reverend tries to think of an answer, hesitant as he is in matters of international importance. "China?"

"Wrong! That's *exactly* what they would have you think." Truman and Landon nod emphatically, up and down, to and fro.

"It is perhaps the greatest fake news campaign of all time. China has gone about strengthening its vocal cords, preparing itself for international media consumption. And the people have lapped it up! They sit prostrate, waiting for China to build their railways and give them their Chinese bread. It's *shameful*. But the truth, that is something most do not have access to. And here at the DuFrond corporation, we believe that truth should rest in the hands of the virtuous."

He picks up a book, tattered and worn not from heavy usage but from years of arboreal decay, and slides it across the table. It is a noble effort, but it does not reach the Reverend: in fact, in the position it lands, it's just too far for the Reverend to reach it from his seated position. Truman and Landon jump up to set the error right, vying for speed to see who can retrieve the book first and give it back to their superior.

"Give me another try," Harry states, muttering something about the finish of the table having been altered by either an overzealous or a careless janitor. He places the book in front of him, the webs of his fingers lightly gripping the cover, and slides it down once more. This time, the book lands even further from where the Reverend can reach.

The Reverend, in a display of compassion fit for someone infirm, stands up from his seat: "I got it." But Truman and Landon had already shot up out of their seats, butts spry as if controlled by springs, pushing their hands in his face and rejecting his proposal.

"That won't be necessary,"

"Give it another try,"

"Let him do what he needs to do."

At this point, Harry is starting to choke. The Reverend, peering at Harry all the way from the other side of the table, can still see that Harry's one eye had begun to twitch, and the same side of his body had begun to lightly writhe.

"Let's forget about what just happened, boys." Then Harry sits his book back into position and shoves it down to the other side, where his toss is finally successful.

As the Reverend hides his face with the cover, Harry continues, his voice level and calm as if the past had been erased: "Take a minute to flip through it, and let us know if you have any questions."

The Reverend is too confused to read, too distracted. He still cannot ascertain what this meeting is about, what they want from him. But he has to prove that he *can* read, even if he usually chooses not to read books that are not abridged Netflix versions of the Bible, so he ventures to a look.

He flips through the book: "Japan, the next conqueror." It predicts a huge rise in Japan's economic and cultural power. Although the book is clearly from an older age, likely the 70s or so, its arguments seem reasonable, and the Reverend has no other basis to argue that the facts are wrong, or misguided, or out of context.

"What do you see in these pages, Mr. DuFrond?"

Harry's face shows that he is not prepared to be questioned. His answer takes some time to go through his mind's censors.

"I just see words."

"You've got to look closer: you can find a *revolution!* The Land of the Rising Sun: it's rising further and will just continue to rise. Meanwhile, they've got no one paying attention to them: think of all of their lost souls! We've got to get on top of them before they *enslave* us, Reverend! Do you know how few Christians they have?"

The Reverend shakes his head. He does not know.

"We've got a big responsibility, here, Reverend. We've got to go and proselytize! We have to go there and teach them about Jesus Christ and how he died for our sins! How else will we meet our business partners in heaven?

And we've got to act fast, otherwise those damn stinky Frenchmen will get in there and beat us to the punch."

But the Reverend is not *that* unintelligent. He can perceive that there is something lurking, something deeper behind this façade they are creating for him.

"But what is it that you *really* want from me? To lead some missionary effort?"

"We've got a grander missionary effort for you. Oh yes, we believe you could be very powerful, indeed: a savior! You see, Reverend, this whole Japan business is but one of the many missions we believe you must help us with. Surely you've heard about this…separatist movement, no?"

When the Reverend does not respond, Harry clarifies: "The people that want Delaware to become its very own country, with its own rules and shit? Have you heard of it?"

"Yes."

"This movement could be quite dangerous. There are many directions that the people could choose. Some of them would be *devastating* to Christianity. Some of these people preach awful things – not to diminish your preaching, Reverend. They want Delaware to become a *communist paradise*. Do you know what communism is, Reverend?"

The Reverend cannot give a definition in words. "I know it when I see it."

"Communism is the lack of religion, the lack of moral value: the lack of souls! Communists burn altars. They sacrifice children and tie virgin Christian women to *trees*: they throw expensive leather shoes into big pits of fire! You wouldn't believe it!"

He really cannot. And yet he starts to see his own interest in what they wish for him: a new country under his exclusive dominion. Under the dominion of God, as well, of course. Though he is left with a feeling of suspicion, he feels himself growing more comfortable with the idea of power.

* * *

Juneau goes into the meeting with hope. The state legislature is packed to the brim with people anxious for independence. The voices of the people fill the walls; she can feel that the people are ready for action. Though when she notices that she has not been granted a seat in the front of the room, as had been promised her as the originator of the manifesto, she grows concerned.

She stands in front of the woman who appears to be the monitor of the town hall meeting, who pretends not to notice her for a few moments, supposedly in hopes that Juneau will just walk away. But she does not, so the woman raises her eyes slowly and with contempt.

"Can I help you?"

"I was under the understanding that I would be granted a seat in the front tonight."

"I can't help you, there's no seat free."

"You *could* help me, though. If you looked for a chair, for example."

"I don't make those types of decisions. You'd have to speak to someone else."

She repeats herself, enunciating like molasses and big, condescending eyes:

"*I cannot help you.* Do you understand?"

Juneau leaves disheartened, wondering whose movement this really is.

The meeting begins shortly after she sits back down. Victor had brought them both, driving down to Dover. But since Juneau had been delayed and Victor had not expected her to sit in the gallery, he had not saved her a seat; they must sit apart.

"Good evening, ladies and gentlemen," the woman announces. She wears a bulky purple blouse with gray slacks. She's the type of woman whose presence attracts attention, and so her approaching the podium and introducing herself is enough to settle the crowd.

"My name is Flora DuFrond, and I'll be monitoring tonight's discussion. Before we get started, I have to announce some ground rules. In the interest of the protection of Delawarean nationalism, we will be censuring comments that go against our mutual interest. We welcome all viewpoints, mind you, but those we cannot accept will not be allowed to continue." The audience does not protest.

"Tonight, we will be discussing Delawarean independence. At this time, we welcome comments and questions from the public to promote community debate." Juneau feels queasy.

A man in the front row raises his hand while standing up to speak. He removes his hat in front of the Delawarean flag placed in the front of the room, the American flag having been removed hurriedly at the last moment. He wears a camouflage jacket and hiking boots.

"Way I see it, we've gotta fight fire with fire," he says with confidence. "If those Yankees are gonna come down here and oppress us, we've gotta go up there and do the same. Tit for tat, like in the Bible." A man in a far-away row jumps up to scream "Hallelujah" uninvited. The man squints, but not too hard, and continues.

"We've gotta show them we're in for business. Maybe go up there, fire a missile or two. If we haven't started building up our national nuclear power inventory, we'd better get on that soon." The crowd erupts in applause for several minutes. Juneau is one of the only people left sitting when the applause finally dies down. Many people rise to clamor for the right to speak. The woman places two microphones in front of the two main aisles, apologizing for not having instituted the system previously, and lets the people line up.

A woman who appears to be in her thirties shows up at the microphone. She says she's from Wilmington. She begins:

"We have to opt out of capitalism and the market. Delaware for the people and by the people! It'll set us free-"

"Next!" The mediator had deemed her comment inappropriate. It's unclear what word she took issue with: "capitalism," "market", maybe "set," perhaps "and".

A portly middle-aged woman introduces herself as Shelby from Selbyville. She does not address the similarity between her name and the town she hails from, other than by declaring herself as the town spokesperson. She stands in front of the microphone for several minutes with her hands folded to the sky. People behind her, who want so badly to get to their own opinions, poke her gently and ask if she needs an aspirin or a laxative. She says she just needs Jesus, opening her eyes briefly. These interruptions seem to cause a disruption in her flow, which means she has to go through her secret rituals once more before speaking. She opens her eyes finally, whispering in a language no one knows, not even her, and speaks before the crowd:

"We have a mission here. Those damn Jersey runts think they've got some sort of Guido mission. They think they've got a burden, they do. Think we can't live without açai bowls and pork rolls, Taylor ham, whatever they say. How can we trust them when they can't even make their minds up on the name of a *sandwich*? They reckon that their best choice, their only choice, is to hold us in their hands, choke us, and tell us it was for our own good. Well I've got a mind to say that we Delawareans are tired of being choked. No one likes to be choked!"

The room is startlingly quiet.

"If they're carrying such a load, maybe we oughta help them out with our own mission. They tell us that we can't throw pumpkins at children, that we can't hang horseshoe crabs on our walls, that scrapple isn't a dessert. To me that is a sign of their *savagery*. Yes – they think we're the wicked ones. Well maybe they'll learn something about wickedness if we shoved our culture on them! How'd they like that? Bet they wouldn't be thrashin' about in their tight jeans then!"

She receives some enthusiastic calls of support. Juneau tries to piece together the argument she had left somewhere hidden in her speech. It becomes harder and harder as the woman starts to feel frustrated by the lack of response in the audience.

"You all can't tell me you *like* bending to their every will, letting them treat us like egg yolk! We're under their yolk. No more yolk!! We've got to put on our best slacks and paint their towns blue to show them just how merciless and purely Delawarean we are. We've gotta invade their schools and make Punkin Chunkin a required course for *all* grades. Do you hear what I'm saying? We've got to make like our horseshoe friends: show our feathers and prove our greatness!"

At that time, she is informed gently that her five minutes are up. She protests, saying she didn't know anything about any time limit, and the bulky security man tells her it's because she is special, they make it just for her. The flaps in her arm swing back as she pulls away from the officer's touch.

"You can't make me!"

But he does, alas, find the means to grab her and escort her to the parking lot, or the bus stop, or somewhere where her words are no longer heard.

A lanky young man does not notice immediately when it is his turn, and the commotion summoned by the woman's exit further distances him from this realization. When the purple woman called for silence and order, he was still thinking about licorice, and the many times he had eaten it expecting it to taste good against all prior experience. He gets a nudge and then a shove from behind, would have toppled over had he not held on to the microphone stand.

"Take it easy, man, geez" he says, dusting off the sleeves of his green bomber jacket and beginning to speak.

"Delaware's gonna need money, dude. Money makes the world go *round*. You know? It kinda works on a lot of ways, if you think about it. Shit's deep..."

"No swearing!" The purple woman commands.

"Oh fuck, that's my bad. Anyways like I was saying, Delaware should start thinking about its financial future. Right? It's never too late to start thinking about the future. Or too early. There's always a right time, and now is always it. So basically I think it would be best for Delaware to invest in bitcoin, and maybe do all of their operations entirely in bitcoin, I mean bitcoin is just going to get more popular because cash is just getting touched up and nasty all day so no one wants to-"

"I think that's enough, young man."

"Really? I mean I could go on for hours, man, ask my buddy Derek, like if you take the example, if you were to read a book upside down-"

"No more words from you tonight." He understands this command instinctively and begins walking out of the building before she had finished her sentence.

The purple woman gestures for the person up next on the opposite microphone to give their spiel. Here is a man who is ready for the occasion. He wears a tight black suit, perhaps one or two sizes too tight, causing his eyes to extend beyond his face. It's unclear if this is how his eyes always look, or if his nerves make them bug out like so, or if there is another factor at play. Though his suit is up to date, his shoes appear to be simultaneously mud extraction and semi-formal event shoes, so their black is tinged with the green and brown of some outdoor excursions he had at some time embarked upon. Victor thinks it is a comment on the duality of man.

The man makes great fuss of clearing his throat before speaking. He raises a Bible, flips through to a page he had creased heavily. He holds it directly above his head, as if taking advantage of a light source on the ground, and lets the crowd hold its breath as he finishes scanning the particular verse he had prepared to reference.

Finally, after much furrowing of eyebrows and much impassioned shutting of books, he declares:

"God is real."

The audience is not underwhelmed: in fact, the cries are so large as to crush the entire presentation for several minutes, despite the gavel that the purple woman pummels into the table. It finally stops when the man wraps his hand in a semicircle, calling for silence.

"God is real, and Delaware needs His help. The United States is sick, New Jersey is sick; Delaware is sick. There's no way around that. But we, as a chosen people, have been dealt some very serious wake-up calls. The beach, the mall: these are *warnings*, premonitions of the fate that will await us in that moggy place below our feet if we do not heed the warnings of our God."

"Delaware has a great opportunity to praise Him. We're at our wit's end, we're looking inward for ways to jumpstart our economy and save our people. We have forgotten that the He knows what we need. *He* is our insurance, *He* is our friend, our lover, our petsitter: we need no one else. So if I may speak frankly, biblically, we'll need a whole lot of Jesus in this new country."

The applause is deafening. It does not come from everyone, but those who are under the man's spell are unsatisfied with lapping up his words by themselves, so they go around forcing peoples' hands into the air, shouting ululations in peoples' faces until they go along, punching people in the face to induce the Holy Spirit.

Victor looks closer at the man being hoisted into the air by two of his eager supporters. Something about his voice had stricken him as familiar, though he could not identify it. Then he realizes that the man's clothing had deceived him and led him away from knowing the truth: that this man preaching to the crowd is the same one who lines up every day at the busiest campus intersection to inform "clamshuckers and queers" that they would spend eternity "roasting on the big red one's grill." Victor feels that any surprise he could muster would be useless and directed toward no useful end, so he discards the emotion, watching as the Reverend performs a baptism on a screaming woman using a confiscated pair of overalls and a few drops of pink lemonade.

yellow bits of snow

Juneau had convinced her bowling team to designate one of their weekly bowling outings as "Delaware Secession Night". It did not take much. Most of the members of the club, being stringent adherents of a *good vibes* ideology, were happy to cede Juneau this favor, so long as it did not alter the timbre of their marijuana-hazed bowling events.

"You're in, my dude," the president of the club had said to her, who had recently ascended to the role after the previous president was impeached for election fraud.

So Juneau had gotten to work doing the canvassing, doorbell ringing and poster posting necessary to promote her cause.

Victor told her, squinting with hazy eyes, that the event's title "Come Support Delaware's Independence From The Imperialist Giant of New Jersey and its Child-Eating Allies" could perhaps be improved upon; the font was too light to be legible, and Victor also thought the phrase a bit unwieldy.

"None of those words are superfluous, and I refuse to remove a single one." And so Juneau, newly determined to see her project through in the way she saw appropriate, got to work moving bowling balls, adjusting the size of happy-go-lucky humanoid pins, dragging her propaganda up and down, left and right until both her and Victor agreed that her message could be seen.

But even so, Juneau regretted to admit, the poster's effect on the public remained "complicated," so she quipped euphemistically. Many of the people who saw the flyer, in university dorm room hallways, in student center thoroughfares, or on trees up and down campus, simply ignored it. Those who noticed it did not take action, citing that they "weren't big bowling fans". Many of the posters were torn down, either by university administration or by especially disgruntled students, some of whom were malignant New Jerseyans set out to destroy the cause, others of whom simply had a personal vendetta against the bowling club for this or that personal injustice.

It occurred to Juneau that perhaps their message should be more widely distributed. Those who had the most influence on the process would be found in the heartlands of Delaware's suburbs, where there were no out-of-staters to complicate this local decision-making process. These were the *real* Delawareans, she had to admit even in contrast to herself; the workers whom academic pedantry had not gobbled up.

* * *

So she takes to the suburban streets of New Castle, placing a flyer in each mailbox she finds and starting up conversations with test subjects who happen to be mowing their lawn or pulling into their driveway at that unlucky moment.

Juneau spots an older woman returning to her home, directs herself towards this target.

"Do you like to bowl?"

"No. Well...*I* do, but my knees don't!"

"Well, we're holding a bowling event, open and free for *Delawarean* comrades, and we would love to see you there." The woman seems put off by the way Juneau winks and intimates at the sound of *Delawarean*, drawing it out with some sort of suspicious candor. Juneau addresses the issue head-on:

"Don't worry, ma'am. I have ulterior motives, but they're not sinister. I'm a secessionist."

"A podiatrist?"

"No, a secessionist."

"An ophthalmologist?"

"No, I'm not a doctor. Just a Delaware lover."

"Oh…well, thanks sweetie!" Then the woman, scrambling with the limited awkward speed she can muster, goes into her house and shuts the door. Juneau hears a sharp *click* as she fastens the lock.

Juneau wonders if her methods are effective, but then she is distracted by a sharp pain in the arch of her right foot, and all she can think of is when she will be able to see her podiatrist.

* * *

The climate at the College of the State of Delaware grows tenser as the movement gains more and more traction. In the majority of classrooms, in contrary to the customary etiquette that prevents students from moving their seats mid-semester, the students separate themselves into two groups: the Delawareans, who clump on one side of the room, and the out-of-staters (OOSs, an abbreviation used by the Delawareans, since their hatred is expressed so frequently as to warrant a shortening) on the other. Professors report an incessant amount of bickering between both sides, often on completely unreasonable grounds only tangentially related to course content.

The OOSs gripe that the Delawarean side of the room has better light, the Delawareans bemoan that the OOS side of the room is ventilated more properly, while each side both finds convoluted ways of affirming that yes, it *would* be typical for the other side to act like this or that, based on stereotypes that have developed rapidly. This is not to ignore the fact that some Delawareans do choose to identify with the out-of-state students, betraying the soil of their birth, or that some OOSs support the Delawarean cause, feeling that in their youth they may as well find some radical cause to support tacitly, no matter how ridiculous. On the other hand, or more literally, on the opposite side of the classroom, there are the Delawareans that have moved sides. Commonly called *traitors* by even the least radical of Delaware's sovereign supporters, they sometimes cite an upbringing in another state or relatives from another region as a motivation, but mostly just report that they don't want to be limited to Delaware in their job search.

Only one course on campus has managed to retain neutrality, somehow oblivious to the phenomenon. Their students maintain their original seats, the ones that some had ended up in as a matter of pure coincidence, the ones that some had chosen with very specific goals in mind. In this section of Sociology 101, the rhythms of classroom life had not been disturbed once by those first moments of awkward reconfiguration; students continue to laze around, eyes glazed over regardless of national credence, seemingly unaffected by the tense atmosphere that predominates in almost all other spaces on campus.

The professor for this course, ever so eager to ruminate on the sociological reasons for this lack of disturbance, cites a certain "lack of discipline" and "disinterest in any sort of mental engagement" as possible reasons for this phenomenon. This professor in particular laments that their group of students had not been able to articulate a single personal belief during the course of the semester, much less a strong political leaning. Other professors, upon hearing this remark, cite the common proverb "the grass is always greener," and then correct themselves, asserting that their grass is not really so green, since the students in their courses who affirm their loyalties do not waver in their academic mediocrity.

Professors whose classrooms are haunted by this issue (that is to say, all but one) complain most begrudgingly of the stifled dialogue in their classrooms. In using the words "American," they must be careful to make sure that they are referring strictly to *that* land that lies approximately ten miles (six kilometers in the new Delawarean system, a move made to signify belonging to the wider world) to the north or the east, lest a Delawarean raise their voice without a corresponding raising of their hand to force the professor to reconsider their remark and thereby validate the sovereignty of this weak baby state.

* * *

The weather forecasts had called for snow, hesitantly, for a few days.

Meteorologists imagined, a week before that fateful Friday, that their machines were overheated and confused. As the day approached, the forecasts did not budge; in fact, the event appeared more and more likely, and yet still no one dared to believe that snow could return after so many years away. When the news anchors had finally been cleared to announce it on television, they mentioned it hurriedly, sandwiched between stories that would produce less suspicion: the new record for western fires, bland numerical accounts of the dead and displaced in the last hurricane. People did not take it seriously until the very day it was said it would come, when come it did, and with ungentle gusto.

Since the early morning hours, even before the state's worm-catchers could catch a special glimpse of the sky, the snow fell in a massive deluge. The skies hammered down fistfuls of thick precipitation, unrelenting even as roadways and homes were draped in white. The skies were more than happy to return to pre-industrial ways, if for just a brief period of time; the people responded in kind.

Nature had imposed a holiday. Schoolchildren were relieved of their duties, workplaces shut down with only minor delay. Highways remained unplowed, but since the driveways were buried just as deeply, citizens all over agreed taciturnly to explore only where their two feet could bring them. It was a sort of celebration of a smaller world, a smaller time, an ode to the long-forgotten art form of the snowfall returning for a final encore.

Juneau bursts into Victor's room, rustling him out of his ten AM slumber. He awakens only with reluctance. She informs him that he would have missed class if classes had not been cancelled due to the snow.

"Interesting," he replies, his thoughts directed to the white wonderland he sees outside of his window. Victor wonders how long it had been since he had seen snow. Perhaps only when he was still a child, perhaps never; he can't tell if his memory is simply mixing with the TV specials he had watched in Christmas revery.

As he thinks, Juneau jumps into her room, scrambling back onto Victor's bed a few moments later. She's got no time to waste; she wills her aging computer to cooperate with her hyper-speed finger commands.

Juneau makes a sort of comment to Victor, eyes too occupied to engage her conversational partner in eye contact, Victor ignores it all to admire the snow.

"Don't you ever take a break?"

For five minutes Juneau continues to mash her keyboard incessantly, neck strained towards the screen; finally, she answers.

"I emailed all the people on my bowling team, all the people in my French class, and my Horsehoe Comrade email blast list and told them to gather at one on the main lawn. I can't squander this opportunity!"

"Such a blessing, and you're still a sheep of hyper-productivity."

"A blessing? Says whom?"

"It's *says who.*"

"No, it's not. You use *who* after a vowel and *whom* after a consonant. S is a *consonant*, Victor," as if that is the point of contention.

"That doesn't make any sense."

"You don't make any sense. You know, you would do better to follow the rules."

"Coming from the one who wants Delawareans to completely overthrow their current system of government?"

"Don't be so obtuse. You know you love violent rebellion." Victor disputes no further.

"What can you achieve with this gathering, anyways?"

"I want to establish a then and a *now.* Today, souls will be dedicated to the Delawarean mission with renewed vigor. This bounty from above is just a sign to work harder towards our glorious mission."

Victor smiles. "Save the rhetoric for them." Juneau wonders if she should laugh or be offended.

"But in the meantime, shouldn't we enjoy the snow?" Juneau's brain strains visibly to comprehend, looking in the most obscure folders of its memory filing.

"*Enjoy?*" Strange to her, but not in a frightening way: rather queer or peculiar, a foreign concept.

"Well, I'll *enjoy* it with everyone while we dismantle the New Jerseyan oppressor state."

"Come on, that's no fun."

"Well what would we *do* with snow?"

"You've seen movies. People create new beings by sculpting it into human forms. They go out pointing the yellow bits. They hold contests to see who can submerge their feet the longest without losing a limb. Where have you been?"

"Let us melt the snow and bathe in the waters."

"I forgot that one."

* * *

Victor goes on a rant, describing the physical and spiritual benefits of bathing in melted snow water. Juneau nods with polite interest, unaware that Victor fabricates all of his claims.

Juneau feels refreshed, ready to take on the world, perhaps even grateful to Victor for telling her to stop to sniff the roses. But these words will certainly not cross her lips. Having taken a few whiffs of these winter blooms, she gets the gist and returns to the lightning pace of her work.

Juneau dries herself off as she repeats for herself the goal of her meeting, recited carefully just out of short-term memory: "It is a snow day renaissance of our political consciousness." She would give a few remarks to begin: a speech of this omen of their great fortune, and how far they would go in honoring this bounty. They would free themselves of the Jersey yoke, taking control once more of their environment, of their economy, of their culture. She had come to realize that these speeches came easy to her, unlike most other situations where she had to communicate with other people, and she felt secure in her soothsayer abilities.

She adds that she also plans to submerge her followers in the snow for a few brief moments.

"I'll ask them if they'll commit to being a martyr for our cause. When they say yes, I'll plunge them down into the snow so that they can be cleansed by our blessing. And I'll keep plunging 'em down as long as there are still heads to dunk and eyes to gawk."

"What if they say no?"

"Why would they say that?"

"I don't know. It's probably not very comfortable to be shoved into a deep layer of snow."

"You think?"

"Maybe."

"If they say no, I will wait for them to say yes. It's no big deal. Everyone mispronounces words sometimes."

Something seems deeply religious about it all, submerging believers into a tub of water, and Victor wonders if the coercive aspect of it rendering it functionally obligatory makes it more or less suitable to a baptismal comparison.

"Sounds like a blast."

engorged with cream cheese

Juneau and Victor arrive thirty minutes early. Victor had protested, but Juneau insisted:

"We have to start the event with the right energy. It's our responsibility to get there and emanate goodwill."

"What if I just emanate depression?"

"Don't."

They take their positions on the campus quad. Juneau stares at the sky. The snow had not let up, not one bit. As the pellets blast her in the face, she takes a sort of pleasure in this cool feeling of exposure. It is a feeling she had thought would remain forgotten.

There they stand, right below the tree on the main lawn that Juneau had chosen specifically to attract the most foot traffic. There are plenty of students romping around in the snow, discovering it for the first time, piling on lighter jackets where their chunky winter coats had been long abandoned and packed into storage in another state, or maybe sold for the value of their fabric. Juneau marks the tree with a black sharpie: "REBIRTH HERE." She takes a picture and sends it out to her various blasts. In the background, he can make out some words of the religious tirades Reverend Bridge still gives during this most beautiful phase of the apocalypse: "FAGGOTS… SNOWFLAKES…DEVIL'S DESSERT"

Twenty minutes pass before their ceremonies grow beyond the two of them. A few of Juneau's bowling friends arrive, sporting remarkably inappropriate clothing for the weather and comic smiles.

"I saw you coming from like, two kilometers away." Victor gathers that this is Juneau's greeting.

"What?"

"Maybe one and a half."

"What?"

"Delaware's going metric, boys. You should study up. We've got to get the motherland's progeny to have a more international face." As she says this, she makes a mental note to review her own metric knowledge.

The bowling boys stand four in a row. The tallest boy takes a lengthy, generous hit from a dab pen poorly concealed in some pocket and passes it to the boy to his left. The second boy, visibly a follower in this hierarchy, makes some commotion. When his turn is up, he squats briefly onto the ground, then catapults himself in the air:

"Juneau, I'm just so *pumped!*"

"I'm excited, too," she lies.

"You know we should really talk about how we're gonna launch against the goddamn New Jerseyans and how we're gonna get our National Guard in order. Call me a Southerner but we've gotta assert our military power."

Juneau puts on her best PR face. "You know, I think it would be best for us to preach peace-"

"Peace doesn't win wars, or bring any national glory!" Juneau and Victor watch as the leader of the apes begins to jump and gyrate in masculine anticipation of conquest, observe with scientific interest as the betas quickly follow suit. Soon, Juneau's vision begins to be tainted by their hoots and hollers and "GLORY FOR OUR COMRADES". *Men do not bring peace*, she thinks. Juneau tells them to take another hit of the weed, hoping it will serve as a tranquilizer. It reduces the volume and frequency of their outbursts.

Juneau greets some people from her French class with a warm "Salut!" They plead with her to speak in English, reasoning that it would be most suitable for their nascent nation to conduct their business in that language. Juneau nods, seeing how the movement grows beyond her own visions.

It's one in the afternoon. Although the group is still not huge as supporters trickle in gradually, it is present enough to be seen and to attract others supportive of their cause as the event goes on. Juneau positions herself in the center of the misshapen circle and shapes herself erect to command attention.

"Welcome, comrades!" The new arrivals greet her with shouts and vague murmurs.

"Nature announces its opposition to New Jerseyan imperialism. Nature has aligned itself with our cause. To that, we shall all show our appreciation. Shout to the skies!" This is a command she means in earnest. The bowler boys begin to howl much before Juneau has finished her sentence, while others of a more subtle nationalist conviction bark only hesitantly at first. Juneau encourages them all to up their energy:

"The skies cannot hear you! Thank them for these auspices!" So their collective racket grows and grows, as do the pairs of eyes in their vicinity who look over with irritation, their romping through the snow having been interrupted. Their group grows slightly as random onlookers grow curious enough to attach themselves to this new organism.

"We must treasure the snow and the rain. Our earth is in peril, it cries out for our help. We have done nothing to heed its cries. We sit by, munching on processed foods, watching the world burn." The crowd's cries of agreement are more confident, and not just from the rowdy quartet.

"But we Delawareans, we will take a different path. For too long, we have been usurped by the great empire that surrounds us on three sides. We have allowed the United States, through its vassal state New Jersey, to trample on our independence and interfere in our path for greatness. I say no more!" They shout, NO MORE! The bowler boys shout much louder and for much longer. A couple of people from Juneau's French class withhold their annoyance, overlooking their enthusiastic comrade's social deficiencies.

"No longer will we look west, north, and south for our legitimacy. New Jersey, having placed us under their yoke, has propagated the idea of our inferiority, our incapacity for self-government. We will look inward and we will look to the sea, as we align ourselves with the benevolent forces of the universe!"

"We know what needs to be done. We, as the subaltern, need to FREE ourselves from this tyranny, create our own government that respects

Mother Nature and the humans that inhabit our lands. We will produce our own nourishment. We will provide for the material needs of all. We will FORBID corporations from inculcating us with the ideology of that evil empire to the Northeast. The people will rise, in cooperation with the terrain, to defeat our capitalist overlords!"

The crowd erupts. There were already itinerant eyes on them before, but now, there is a mass migration toward the tree that Juneau has chosen. This audience is a motley crew of the faithful, of the mildly curious, and even the inwardly hostile; but she has them, and as long as she has them, she can transmit her message.

In the midst of the explosive national furor, the entire student population in the area had spilled out from walkways, stairs of unoccupied buildings and other trees to hear Juneau's words. There is only one human unaccounted for, walking without hurry and without notice of the ruckus. She has on a jacket that covers her from the top of her head to her ankles, of a black fabric conspicuous enough to not arouse too much attention, but yet still smell visibly of upper-crust sensibilities. It is unclear where she could have procured such an item on such short notice. As she trots with a mini-pizza from the underground pop-up gourmet pizzeria, the one that denies entry to anyone without proof of New Jersey citizenship at the door, she speaks loudly and brusquely on the phone.

Juneau and the bowling alpha male are the only two to notice the girl as the rest of the crowd is wrapped up in newfound national excitement. Her appearance makes Juneau proud to be from the subaltern. As the boy stares, however, his eyes fixate on her with a hunter's precision and engagement. Juneau feels uneasy, worried about the tension that rises, and yet she feels powerless to change the course of future events.

She sees the boy descend to the ground to grab a chunk of snow. He urges his social subordinates to accompany him by his side to help him with whatever it is he has been destined to do. They work hurriedly, like bees under their honey queen, but Juneau cannot see what they are producing. Juneau's mind wanders, she envisions some sort of dubious conspiratorial project to create a mass weapon, *The Wilmington Project*, she hopes she is carrying herself away into fantasy.

The boy rises from his squat position confidently, a ball of snow in his hand, and some few moments afterward, hurls it directly towards the girl in black.

Having been attacked squarely in the back, the girl stops for a second before emitting a scream that emerges slowly but soon cascades into a full-blown irate symphony. The boy's henchmen follow with reinforcements that attack other parts of her body. Almost immediately, indignant blonde women loaded with identical knee-length jackets and cell phones ready to document legal transgressions come to march by her side.

There are suddenly two fronts, two legions of students, one facing the other. There is a sense of calm in the moments before what can only inevitably lead to a grander confrontation, full-blown warfare.

The foreign students, having savored some moments to regroup and learn how to form snowballs, return the blows. Snow in various shapes and forms flies back and forth across the battle line. Icicles find themselves impaled in a disturbing amount of hidden places. All the while, shouts are heard from both sides:

"DOWN WITH NEW JERSEY TYRANNY!"

"THE SUBALTERN RISES!"

"YOU MID-ATLANTIC SAVAGES DON'T DESERVE OUR HELP!"

"NEW JERSEYANS INVENTED THE AEROPLANE, PEANUT BUTTER, AND CUNEIFORM WRITING, YOU BARBARIANS"

In the midst of bombastic gunfire, Juneau has room to find it curious how the New Jerseyans themselves have begun to arm themselves with counter-rhetoric defending themselves against her own claims of hegemony and oppression. As arbitrary and fabricated as her ideology may once have seemed, it is clear to her now that she has unlocked at least some sort of truth, even if that truth had to be brought into reality through the force of a snowball.

The fighting continues, but not for long. Unmarked gray vans show up on the suddenly exquisitely plowed streets. Men in non-descript uniforms go about with specific, exacting criteria: *dump all Delawareans in the vans.*

Though some of the students wear pumpkin earrings or some other material ideological symbol to identify themselves, the men have to rely largely on guess work and profiling to identify the Delawareans.

They spare pretty girls in ankle-length expensive jackets. Those could only have been bought with major metropolitan area dollars. Those students who wear several jackets on top of each other to compensate for not owning a proper snow one are pinpointed immediately as Delawareans and dumped subsequently into the vans. They spare those who, when prompted to say the word "sorority," drag out the second O fiendishly as if it were a rogue A, and dump those whose Delawarean blandness does not permit them to pronounce it in this strange way.

It is not a perfect system, but they do not expect perfection, just fear, and that works well enough. Soon, Juneau herself is in a van, pressed up against a few boys from Milford. The vans go in motion only when they are so full that the doors refuse to stay closed.

* * *

Victor is standing in the basketball stadium with the several dozen students from his van, as well as students hoisted from other loads. He assumes Juneau is in there, as well, but he has lost her in the swell of madness. A jarringly loud voice repeats over the speakers:

"THIS UNIVERSITY'S EXCELLENCE OWES NOTHING TO ITS GEO-GRAPHIC LOCATION. WE ARE GREAT BECAUSE WE ATTRACT OUT-SIDERS. NEW JERSEYANS TOOK US TO THE MOON. IF WE WERE TWO MILES TO THE NORTH WE WOULD BE OUT OF DELAWARE. DELAWAREANS SMELL LIKE ROTTEN PUMPKINS."

The earbashing volume and matter-of-fact tone with which the mantras are repeated suggest that these are facts that he must internalize.

He and his new friends remain there for several more hours. Though the volume of the propaganda is excruciating, the hundreds packed into the stadium do their best to undermine the gathering by using it to talk strategy. They ignore the calls:

"THIS UNIVERSITY'S MISSION CATERS TO THOSE WHO ARE MENTALLY, EMOTIONALLY, AND MORALLY CAPABLE OF HIGHER INQUIRY, OF WHICH SURELY FEW DELAWAREANS ARE CAPABLE. DELAWAREANS ARE SCIENTIFICALLY PROVEN TO HAVE A LOWER IQ, ARE OBJECTIVELY MORE LIKELY TO BE ANNOYING. BOW DOWN TO YOUR BENEVOLENT OVERLORDS AND BE GRATEFUL FOR WHAT OUR PITY HAS BEQUEATED TO YOU, WEAKLINGS."

Many talk of how the Battle of the Balls (as the recent snowball battle had just been christened) had radicalized them, driven them to devote themselves to the cause. Victor smiles, pleased to see Juneau's vision having an impact, ruffling the feathers of those from above. Newly radicalized students idolize Juneau and promise that they will further the fight. The masses gather together to drown out the voices from above:

"THE LAMB RISES, IN ITS GREAT NUMBERS IT CAN DEFEAT THE WOLF THAT TORTURES IT AND TRIES TO RENDER IT COMPLA-CENT BY ENGORGING IT WITH CREAM CHEESE, CLAIMING THAT IT DOES NO WRONG."

god, glory, gold

Juneau had instructed Victor, the driver, and Julia, her fiercely nationalist Lower Slower friend from French class, to meet her at Victor's car at 5:50 pm. According to Juneau's collaborations with Brandt, the bridge would be destroyed at around 6:30 pm. Since Delaware City was 24 minutes away, they would need 7 minutes to park and 3 minutes to prepare themselves for the event, with at least 5 minutes left over for an inevitable error.

The bridge had been closed to traffic both originating from and into the imperial power to the Northeast on account of what Brandt had termed "construction," although he really meant its opposite, not deconstruction but destruction, since deconstruction, despite its formal similarity, is not a true antonym.

No one questions Juneau when she says, "it smells like Delaware". It is quite remarkable indeed that no one stops to ask her why. Barricaded in a car with its windows up, surely the stench of the cigarettes Victor insists on smoking in the driver's seat is too dominating to allow for any othr aroma. For Delaware to have its own symbolic nosefeel would generally be an absurd notion anyways because the Delaware Parliament had not yet voted on a national smell, given that it did not exist, as it was only just recently that people began to clamor for sovereignty, and also because even the most radical of stateless nations do not really claim to have their own unique smell. In spite of it all, Julia and Victor just choose to agree: "it sure does."

So it smells like Delaware, it smells like soot, it smells like amber tap water. Juneau asks her friends if they are excited for this grand event they are about to witness. Julia says she is nervous. "Southerners," Juneau exclaims with fresh minted national pride.

Victor takes a Continental Spirit cigarette, nearly limp, and crushes it into the cup holder of his 2004 Honda Civic, Juneau glances over from the passenger seat and requests that he avoid sullying her person. He then takes the pack, turns it upside down so as to pluck out a fresh stick of death, he calls it *baton de mort* because it makes Juneau sick; he catches one and puts it in his mouth. He nods to Juneau so as to say: "can you light me?" Juneau hesitates, so as to say, "stop bossing me around," but instead just finds the lighter, which had fallen to the floor beneath her, and gifts him light.

"What's your preferred brand?" Julia's question puts on airs of being innocuous, but her tone is less than such.

"I don't know, I like them all."

"No, you don't. You always get the Continental Spirit ones."

"No I don't."

"Yeah you do," Juneau confirms, showing her solidarity.

"Well, they don't have Delaware Souls, so I get Continental Spirit."

Julia frowns. "That's not what I mean. You always get that brand, and you always ask for the yellow box by name. It's like you're all about the aesthetic."

"What kind of aesthetic?"

"Nihilistic imperialist."

"If I were a nihilist, I couldn't be an imperialist."

"How do you figure that?"

"Think about it. The Spaniards had lofty goals. God, glory, gold. Nihilists are content to watch the world burn."

"So you are a nihilist?"

"No. I mean, maybe. Why do you care?"

"Because I'm not a nihilist."

Juneau hopes that parking the car will be less of an ordeal than arguing about cigarettes. But it is just as difficult, if only a different kind of difficult, physical instead of metaphysical. Not because there are mounds of spectators, but because the area surrounding the Delaware Memorial Bridge is so devoid of places from which one can gawk comfortably. There's a big landfill, a factory, and some other expanses of industrial wasteland, but nothing else in the immediate vicinity of the bridge. The design of the area is surprisingly hostile to these sorts of irredentist activities.

They know they have the option to watch the event on television, but that isn't the same, and Victor said he didn't trust cameras, to which Juneau had responded how can that be true, you love photography, to which Victor just smiled and condescended, "I don't trust *their* cameras."

So they are parked at the imposingly gargantuan factory. It is 6:23: Juneau overcalculated. Victor sucks on his cigarette with a tinge of melodrama. In the car, one can feel a sense of transcendence, as if they were on the bridge themselves preparing to become martyrs for the state.

Most of the other cars there are leaving, presumably uninterested or unaware of the history being made in front of them. Juneau thinks to herself, staring at the factory with its long slender tubes and labored breaths: *if I could survive the act of wafting the fumes emitted from those stacks*, wafting being a skill she mastered in 7th grade science, *would it taste like freedom or pain?* She thinks, *how beautiful it is that these fumes do not affect the radiant blueness of the sky, the dome that embraces this new diamond country*. The cars leaving are immune to such thoughts. They are hurried, their wheels impinged with the same necessity for immediacy as the drivers themselves, who are ready to hurl themselves onto the highway and rush into their suburban graves.

But a few cars remain, the same revolutionary flair gushing out of their own windows, and Juneau is proud to see they are not the only ones who want to witness this event with their own eyes.

"6:29," Victor says with a huff, as if the few seconds preceding the explosion, the 59 or 31 or 4 seconds in between, were unmanageable. Julia's eyes grow larger with each second, and as Juneau looks back to her to ask, *are you okay, do you need some water, this moment sure is monumental*, Juneau sees streaks of fire in her earthen eyes.

It is 6:30 on the dash radio. One second passes, and then another, and then three seconds of agony later, the image comes, the sound shortly after, but it just looks like a great big frightening mess of combustion, their senses do not perceive the milliseconds between these various eruptions. The bridge is in flames for some moments, their eyes looking to heaven, but then it is not, because the bridge ceases to exist. The silence is stunned.

Suddenly, as if the moment demanded more attention, a black bird passes astonishingly low, falling to the ground in a circuitous arc. Victor reckons that it was caught in the explosion and ended up with maimed wing, and that from there, it flew frantically trying to maintain itself afloat. Alas it was powerless to fight the work of gravity and so ended its life on the ground, far from where birds should fly.

"Exponential decay," Juneau notes.

"What can produce that does not also destroy?"

Juneau smiles. "You're smart for a Southerner."

* * *

In French class, Julia and Juneau sometimes have trouble paying attention. Julia diddles the time away sketching pictures of witches with cauldrons and shrunken heads. Juneau occupies her time with dreams. She wants so badly to participate in this language, rather than to continue studying it passively as if it were an artifact not to be touched. She envisions a move to Paris, prattling on all those days with her flatmates about EU politics, her tongue contorting the phonological manifestations of a cultural heritage not her own.

She wishes that class could be an extension of her longing for what she doesn't know and never could. As if class could be a theatrical production, an exercise in hiding ones' identity through a perfected French r, a training in performing French malaise. For as much as she identifies with the here and now, the Delaware in her, it would be another thing entirely for her to say that she did not feel every now and then that it would be nice to rip oneself out of one's roots entirely and adopt a new persona. Perhaps she would call herself Veronica, and live in the 8th arrondissement, and in this new place stop pretending that things could be made more than less unbearable.

Juneau is startled out of her fantasy as she overhears a classmate trying to explain her feeling about an upcoming sorority event *en français*:

" Je suis excitée ! "

Her professor, an American from Tallahassee, holds a 120-ounce NASCAR soda cup in her hand, showing she is firmly rooted in her New World sensibilities despite her Francophone academic pursuits. The student holds herself with an air of accomplishment, having spoken for the first time more than a heavily accented "si" or "non".

"In French," her professor begins cautiously after flashing an apple pie smile meant to encourage utterances no matter how horrid, "to say that you are *excitée* means that you are…". Turning red, she continues: "excited in a *sexual* manner."

The student bursts out laughing. She looks towards her sorority squad members, invoking their sisterhood to join her in her laughing spell to dissolve her discomfort. They guffaw for some long minutes. Juneau manages only a smile that barely upturns the right side of her mouth, leaving the left side limp and devoid of amusement.

"Well, how do you say you're excited, then, in French?" The girl is still barely composed.

"Well, you don't!"

The girl's embarrassment turns to dark confusion, visibly upset with the world. For a false friend to meet her on her path, that does not trouble her, as she does not see the language as words to be used in the first place. But for the phrase to not *exist*, so important to her very existence and her various monied plans for the future? That is simply unacceptable to her trust fund sensibilities.

"Why not? There must be a way."

"Well, the French just don't get as excited as we do. Unless it's sexually."

The professor begins to discuss the topic of today's class, but soon after, the girl begins to tear up. As the professor fingers a map demonstrating the geographic extent of French colonialism, the girl's tears turn into heavy sobs that ring throughout the classroom. Her bleating cries become hard to ignore, and after two minutes of this tension, the girl's friend escorts her out of the room with loud, sympathy-seeking gestures.

The professor continues her monologue, finally having switched to French for two minutes of classroom input, the words parsed out carefully to allow students to read her words in the air:

" Aujourd'hui, mes amis, on va apprendre sur le colonialisme français ! "

Around the room, a feeling of blank quasi-sentience prevails as the students push their brains to parse, word by word, this grueling foreign utterance:

Aujourd'hui means yesterday, *no wait it means* today, *okay so* today, *mes amis,* my…friends, *maybe?, I think,* today, my friends, *on,* one, *or is that un, why would she put it that way anyways that doesn't make any sense, on va apprendre,* one goes learn, today, my friends, one goes learn, *that sounds so stupid, okay now sur le colonialisme,* about the colonialism, *whatever the hell that is, le colonialisme français,* the colonialisme French, *or wait,* the French colonialism, *I think that's a type of artisanal handicraft they make over there in Europe, I heard about that when I was in Italy and was told the Italians weren't good at it, okay so* Today, my friends, one goes learn about the French colonialism.

By the time the other students get around to analyzing each individual word, Juneau has already long been moving beyond this sentence, thinking of patisseries and new existence as she is prone to do in these long stretches of mind-numbing class time.

Then the professor, an avid believer in the power of repetition, tells the class to repeat after her:

"Les Français ont coupé de nombreuses têtes pour nous amener là où nous en sommes aujourd'hui, soyons reconnaissants!!"

no mercy

At 12:00 AM, Sunday turns to Monday, "just a bit longer" turns into "I should really get to bed", and the gravity of Brandt's promise comes crashing down. It had been so easy, in his discussions with impassioned Juneau, for him to be swept up in her adolescent resolve.

"At 8 AM on the 24th, you will declare yourself the Prime Minister of the Nation of Delaware." Juneau specified how vitally important it was that the name of the head of state be changed. Governor was of a time of imperial subordination, and there would no longer be any higher forces to meddle in Delaware's affairs. President was much too reminiscent of that old empire Juneau wanted Delaware to rid itself of. Prime Minister was just right, implying broader international solidarity and hopefully making it easier for the world to accept Delaware's well-deserved place on the international stage, so was Juneau's logic. Brandt nodded placidly.

Brandt feels weak, as weak as he typically feels at such junctures when a day ceases to be, giving into the next. It's 12:02 AM, Brant gives in to restlessness, the stairway groans with his somnambulant weight as he descends to the kitchen for a glass of water. Fate can change in a day, as much as it can change in the blink of an eye, even when night's starry blanket still caresses its earthly kin. Tomorrow, highways will be built, forests defiled to make room for commuter lanes. Meetings will be convened and adjourned, press releases held to be forgotten in weeks or even days, reporters working earnestly will be silenced or sidelined in less dramatic ways.

Brandt fidgets for a glass in the cupboard with only the faint glow of the hidden moon to guide him. He walks with caution, trying to make himself undisturbing to the senses. He knows his wife will not awaken, sleeping deeply in the room she moved into alone years ago, but he cannot shake his sense of courtesy. After a ceremonial six months of customary co-habitation, she told him she was bothered by his snoring, which he accepted at first until he realized it was a thin falsehood.

Never go to bed angry. Or alone, but that point is moot. And he never did: he came to accept with grace the physical and emotional distance she had placed between them. He came around to the idea that their union had been doomed from the start, a utilitarian matching having little to do with romance. His loneliness being larger than this ego, he calculated with ease that any sort of silly, legal union would be better than being alone.

He walks into the bathroom, struck with a sudden urge to urinate. As he turns on the light, he looks into the mirror, stunned by the harsh glow. Normally a man with much to say and more to think, he has no words as he scrutinizes the wrinkles that disfigure his once youthful face, his once chiseled jaw. He can see that his face had been mistreated by time's hourglass and inner solitude. Then, a few short words appear in his brain, and stay with him until he crawls into bed, failing to find sleep:

Time doesn't change, it is we who are different.

* * *

Reverend Bridge awakens as he does every day at 6:00 AM, aided by the calls of his alarm clock. Sunday is God's day but Monday means the end of respite, the beginning of ordained efficiency.

He rises from his bed with a purposeful step and goes to perform his daily devotion. He self-identifies as a non-drinking man, which for him includes alcohol, caffeine, and anything with bubbles. All he needs is a healthy dose of the Holy Spirit to get him ready for his day, as coffee is a sin together with many other things.

He drops to his knees.

"Lord, I thank you."

"I thank you for showering me with your golden light, for washing me clean of this dirty sin."

"Your hands are what I need, Lord. For I am a filthy sinner, naughty swine like all of us living upon this rotten ball; I am dirty, I am FILTHY, I need Your cleansing light, send me Your love and I send you my devotion."

He reaches his hands crossed in prayer above his head, hoping to caress the hands of his beloved savior.

"This world…"

"This world, it is sick, Lord. There are many led astray, many who do not know You, Lord. If only they knew you like I do, as the Bible ordains! They are the Devil's children, conspiring to defile your name."

"But I, I know You, God, and I know that Your feelings for me are mutual. I can please You, Savior Sir, I know that to see these sinners, it pains You, and I can cleanse the earth of these impurities." His body tingles in an excruciating release.

"They must know You, You and all of Your delights, Your treasures, the sinews of Your taut body pinned on the cross!"

"Show me, dear Lord, how I may revere You!"

As he opens his eyes and shouts "Amen" to the birds and the trees and all other living beings in his proselytizing splash zone, his phone begins to ring.

* * *

Juneau does not allow Victor to drive them to the DMV in Delaware City. He is too slow a driver, much more concerned with his cigarettes than with his progress on the road. Today, Juneau commandeers Victor's beat-up car, because they have a mission and a destination and there is no time to be relying on Victor's blasé driving style. Victor, bothered by what he presumes to be Julia's pretension, tells Juneau as a condition of lending his vehicle that she would not be welcome to accompany them.

Victor climbs into the passenger side obediently, happy to hand over the reins. Juneau sits erect at the steering wheel, as she drives she changes lanes with fury and impunity. Brandt had agreed that Juneau would give him a call precisely at 7:34 AM (why 34 and not simply 30, neither of them knew, but it can be assumed that Juneau had a very good reason for her strange exactness), at which time he would confirm that at 8 AM, in front of a fleet of media, he would declare himself Prime Minister of the Nation of Delaware For The People and By The People, and then they would meet to think of a better name for the new state-nation.

"Can you give him one more call?"

Brandt ignores Juneau's call at 7:34, causing great alarm; her subsequent calls at 7:35, 7:37, and 7:40 are also left unanswered, which only serves to increase her panic. The ringing echoes in Juneau's brain as she curses the earth she drives upon, no one comes to the phone to ease her frustration.

"Still voicemail", Victor assumes.

Juneau takes a deep breath. She takes great care not to allow her stress to influence her driving, but in exacting such focus, her knuckles grow purple from gripping the steering wheel with too much strength.

* * *

8:07 AM. The cameras are mounted, the press is whispering among themselves: where is Brandt? Victor stands awkwardly, his loosely-fitting slacks adding to his perception that he is out of place. Juneau sweats bullets. They stand in the crowd, watching, growing old while young.

"Victor, do you know what a power vacuum is?"

"My mom used to have one of those."

A hurried reporter, shushing her cameraman while simultaneously beckoning him to follow with a stern hand, straightens her skirt and walks over to Juneau. Her heels clack tidily on the asphalt of the parking lot hastily turned into a press conference locale.

"I'm Candace Walters from WCOB News, you are Juneau?"

"Yes."

"I heard you've been instrumental in promoting Brandt's rise to power. Is this true?"

"I don't know if I should say yes."

"Well you wouldn't lie, would you? A girl like you who cares so much about the future of our state?"

"I don't know." Her words gush out like impatient pus.

"Is he coming this morning or not?"

"Uhh…"

"That's all we have time for." She gives a curt "cut" to the cameraman, who rushes over to follow her as she trots away.

* * *

It is 8:10 AM. Reverend Bridge repeats to himself the Lord's Prayer, asking for strength and support. He knows that this is the opportunity that the Lord has sent to him to prove his faith. Still no sign of Brandt. Reverend Bridge has already waited the ten minutes God advised him to stay patient. Now, all that is left is action.

Reverend Bridge approaches the podium, Candace Walters stands at the ready to proclaim a new state, Harry DuFrond stands in the crowd with a putrid grin…

punkins fly

Reverend Bridge's first action as Delaware's head of state, emblazoned upon helicopters commandeered from the National Guard: "Viva the Delawareans: let the punkins chunk!"

The helicopters float in conspicuous loops around the university, conveniently timed to coincide with a class break at 1:10. Delawarean students erupt in chaos, undulating and contorting with wild energy. Though for most of their generation Punkin Chunkin had been merely folklore, its cultural memory had still been floating around, just waiting for some plucky nationalist to harness its power; Juneau watches powerlessly as chaos erupts.

Clusters of New Jerseyans and Long Islanders band together, forming a coalition of rival factions to protect themselves from the nationalist fervor. Though their crooked faces of refined Northeasternness presume to admonish the primitive ways of this state-turned-nation, surgical noses turned upwards, their fear shows through their increasingly tribal proclivities.

Other foreign students make no attempt to disguise their fear. They take cover in their elite apartment complexes, shutting their blinds tightly so as to escape the views of mania that their vertically-privileged vantage points afford them. As the pumpkins begin to descend menacingly from the heavens, students inform their mothers of their altogether unprecedented status of persecution, sobbing and screaming intermittently whilst pleading that the family jet come to receive them at once lest the Delawarean airspace become unreachable.

Yet others, hiding behind dollar sunglasses, try to avoid the chaos as much as they can, seeming to notice little even when struck by a fleshy gourd; they simply continue waddling in the manner of those whose brains have been softened by drink, hoping to arrive at their ethics course in one piece.

Juneau fears what other kinds of jingoism Reverend Smidge, who is known for raiding the campus several times a year with a cohort of militant "Crusaders" donning rifles and hand grenades shaped as human fetuses, will perform to continue turning her dreams into nightmares.

* * *

With the weight of Delaware's future pressing down on her, Juneau makes the unusual decision to skip her classes and take a day for self-reflection and self-pity, and Victor follows her lead, never needing so much of a concrete reason to play hooky.

Victor, sensing Juneau's third cup of stale coffee is starting to wear off now that it's late afternoon, perceives that she is entering a darker, more introspective place, and hopes to ground her in reality through a conversation.

Victor asks, "what do you think he will call himself?"

"President, I guess. Maybe Reverend President."

"You think? I think he'll try to reinvent the wheel. If he's trying to build a nation, he's going to have to do some things differently to make us feel like a separate people, no?" But Victor notices from the hollow expression on Juneau's face that perhaps he has chosen the wrong conversation topic to attempt to free her from her own fears, and so begins another.

"If you could have a superpower, which would it be?"

"I think I would like to fly."

Victor responds, yes, that would be neat; if you could fly, where would you go?

"Everywhere, I guess. If I were to fly, I would want to cross continents. Fly across the Atlantic, maybe resting in the Azores to then arrive in the Old World. Or I could fly down towards Patagonia, see the snowy slopes of the south. But if you could fly, wouldn't you also get tired? Must be tiring to fly 8,000 miles. Or…"Juneau clacks on her keyboard: "12874 kilometers, I mean. And once you start flying, how do you know you'll ever go back from where you came?"

Victor nods with reverence. In pondering a response to his question that Juneau turns back to him, he thinks leisurely, lighting a cigarette all the while to boost his brainpower.

"I suppose I would go somewhere holy. Who knows where, perhaps Mecca or the Holy Mount or something like that. Those must be protected lands, the lands most pitied by the skies. When Kingdom comes, those'll probably be the last to go."

"Or maybe instead the gods would destroy those lands first, out of some sort of mercy, you know? To spare them from the end. It's like when people say it's better to burn out than fade away. Maybe the gods are of that opinion. So the last to go would be the most sinful places, those that flaunt their ungodliness most, to burn and scar without end in punishment for their wickedness."

Victor takes a long, speculative puff, the backlash of which erupts and leaves a pregnant pause. "I guess you mean Los Angeles."

Juneau laughs when she is sad; her small chuckle is bittersweet. As a former American she cannot help but retain a devilish obsession with the defiant landscapes of the West, where civilization erupts from desert as if to brag, *the continent has ended but we are rising*. In this lies their beauty and their wretchedness, she reasons, and though she does not wish for them to burn, the gods do not heed her opinion. They remain quiet as afternoon passes into evening and finally into night; they smoke like chimney stacks as they soak in the foretelling of doom.

* * *

Victor's Diary

The guy next to me in International Justice told me about when he hiked the Camino de Santiago some summer. He said he met some cute Australians, convinced them to get rid of their humorless German friend. According to him, the Japanese are the most methodical of the hikers. I asked him, how did you feel when it ended? Satisfied, he said, because he had paid for the damn plane ticket, or his father had, and now he could finally tell others he had *done* the Camino. He had a photo album prepared for when people asked to see the pictures.

All day I have thought of pilgrimages. I went to the library and checked out fourteen books on the camino, the librarian was nice but not yielding enough to let me go above my limit. She spotted my Spanish-English dictionary and wished me good luck. Must have been a slow day. Or perhaps she knew it was the beginning of an arduous journey, through these texts I can hardly decipher, so old, pictures in a faded black-and-white.

How can it be that well into the depths of night, I still cannot shake these visions.

I think, how beautiful it must have been, this ancient spiritual journey. I have sifted lustfully through these books, old enough to be written in a language destined for an audience of one's people and not all humans on earth. I wonder if I intrude, every word I look up is a little key, piece by piece I unlock a shred of lost wonder. Though at some point I know my research will not suffice, there'll be too much left to my imagination, I guess I've got to get there myself...

* * *

How curious it must have seemed when the New Jerseyans reported accounts of dismembered pumpkins appearing on their doorsteps, adorning their rooftops, and sullying recently teased hair. At first, it was believed that it was a Halloween prank, but this idea was quickly discarded when the citizens were reminded that Halloween was six months away. The suburbanites were as angry as they were confused, but since the culprit was not forthcoming, they had no place to direct their fury. Civilization thus broke down.

In merely describing the location of this incident, politics interfered. The New Jerseyans stayed faithful to their public school teachers and referred to the New Jersey Bay, whereas the Delawarean state media pointed to the Great Delawarean Sea, geographical accuracy being subordinate to national glory and the term's "mouthfeel". Regardless of the name, in affected communities along the southern coast of New Jersey, including Penns Grove, Pennsville and Cape May, pandemonium took hold. Angry women accused their neighbors publicly of having sabotaged their daughter's dance recital with a lurid tossing of produce, men with inconceivable anger roamed suburban streets asking to have a few words with the jackass who threw a pumpkin into their car motor, and in time entire neighborhoods were ravaged.

Public authorities, upon hearing of these accounts, knew that something must be done to identify the guilty parties at once, but a bitter turf war ensued over jurisdictions. The statewide public health agency believed it was in their right to investigate, claiming a common outbreak of hysteria was an infectious disease and therefore a public health matter, whereas the neighborhood watch group claimed self-governance and wished to deal with matters on their own. Ultimately public health won, scoffing at the idea that a lowly community agency should dare to challenge the ambitions of a statewide agency.

But the public health officials, hoping to open and close the case cleanly and with great haste, were dismayed to find that the facts were a lot more complicated than anyone previously thought. For one, gathering information through interviews with residents in the affected areas, they found that no one could ascertain specifically where the pumpkins had come from: those who had seen could only say that they were "dropped out of thin air" from a high angle. After interviewing everyone who could be reached and was not totally incoherent from hysteria, they had absolutely no clues as to the origins of these mysterious attacks.

Stumped, the public health agency assigned a few of its researchers to commit themselves fully to the pumpkin cause, under strict instructions to investigate any strange pumpkin occurrence no matter how seemingly small. Meanwhile, the affected communities were placed under martial law to stop the looting and chaos.

After a few weeks, they had found absolutely nothing relevant to the incident. For the three researchers on the case, the word "pumpkin" was quickly turning into a hateful mess of letters with no meaning.

Then, on one fateful day, head researcher Dr. Marsha Pagliaccio-Cartwright, heavily doped on caffeine, recalled the existence of the world outside of New Jersey's borders, and called for an expansion of their radius of research to include news media outside of the state. When Pennsylvania and New York returned no results, Dr. Pagliaccio-Cartwright reluctantly decided to cover all of her bases and check on Delaware. At first, her research was stunted by the language barrier: she could not understand what the newspaper meant by "punkin," and did not even think to connect it to the idea of a "pumpkin". But then, proceeding with her research, Dr. Pagliaccio-Cartwright was astounded to find that all throughout the state, in each of the however many counties they had, there had been manifestations of xenophobic pumpkin violence, some of which were located in neighboring communities on the coast just a stone's throw from the affected New Jersey townships. "But not a stone's throw," Dr. Pagliaccio-Cartwright announced with pain: "a *pumpkin's* throw." The office gasped and weeped as they listened to her read a newspaper excerpt aloud:

"In brilliant displays of Delaware nationhood, Punkins were released up and down the state, over the canal on to Maryland, and into the wretched towns of that oppressor state New Jersey."

It was the evidence they had been searching for, hidden across a small bay and over a bridge. She resolved to march right on over there to find a governor or a senator or whomever would receive her verbal lashings to arrange reparations for these heinous crimes. Two colleagues agreed to come for backup, agreeing that Delaware was too backwards and dangerous to visit alone. But as they travelled on the turnpike, constantly veering into the left lane to pass those on the right not yielding for the immediacy of their needs, they were astounded once again to near the bridge and find that where the bridge had once stood, an empty space dominated, impassable without wings.

Dr. Pagliaccio-Cartwright had been relying upon her colleague Sandra, a devoted Catholic, for directions and also as a cultural guide, as Sandra had once been to Delaware for a church-organized mission trip. When Sandra shrugged her shoulders, Dr. Pagliaccio-Cartwright didn't know where to turn.

While miles previously they had been forced to press themselves against other vehicles to navigate with speed, now their van was the only traveller in either lane, in the rush of the commuter afternoon no less.

It occurred to Dr. Pagliaccio-Cartwright that this escalation of the violence amidst the rising movement for Delawarean secessionism (a phrase she could not help but laugh at) may have had some relation to the destruction of the bridge. Sandra asks:

"What do we do?"

"What responsibility could we have here? We know who did it already. We'll just stick everybody on the Delawareans, and we'll wash our hands of this."

* * *

The report that was released for public scrutiny paid little attention to the events in Delaware that had led to the destruction. Instead, they focused on describing the damages in great detail and pointing their fingers: houses in shambles, cars undriveable, daughters unshowoffable due to the unfortunate orange state of their dance recital gowns. Though it made a passing reference to "secessionist ideologies" in Delaware, it did not focus on the matter, and as its residents were pacified, so the matter went to rest.

shut them out

When news of Delaware's "secessionist ideologies" reached the CIA, the intelligence officers were stunned. They did double takes, making sure that the New Jersey report wasn't referring to Chechnya or Catalonia, but Delaware, right in the middle of the country's greatest megalopolis. The lack of detail led them to speculate wildly: to think, that something so dangerous as "secessionist ideologies," not just one but multiple ways the people wished to separate themselves from the state, was festering in the humbum North-South can't-make-up-its-mind state of Delaware, was frankly cute. Some of them attributed it to growing pains: "sometimes, you have to let them whine it out." Just like a petulant child. The idea that Delaware could be the least infantile of any state, being so speedy in signing the Constitution that it was christened the First State, was unbeknownst to them.

It was 4:05 PM when the news came to the attention of the Domestic Terror division. Action was not thought to be immediately necessary. They spent some minutes dwelling on the folksy cuteness of the small state in rebellion. Another collection of potato-chip late-afternoon drowsy minutes were spent wondering if Delaware contained more than the highway between DC and New York. Leisurely, one colleague recounted tales of his romps at Rehoboth Beach and his future plans to bathe in its DuFrond chemical water, ignorant to the fact that Rehoboth was no more.

By the time they decided to return to some sort of work-related task, it was 4:37 PM, and they were all eager to leave directly at 5 to anticipate the traffic. So one of them suggested: "shall we send the governor a strongly-worded letter?" Though there were arguments over the best medium, no one had any objections to the idea itself, or rather couldn't think of anything better, so it was decided they would send a note along with a carrot cake for the Governor to remind him of his allegiance to the Union. Stanley informed: "let me handle the cake, I've got a guy", Mike drafted the note.

"Dear Governor Bridge,

This is Mike from the CIA. We hear that you folks in Delawear are having some interesting times. It was not very nice of you all to attack New Jersey with pumpkins. If I were being more technical, I could call it terrorism, or maybe assault. But I'm having a good day, and you seem like a nice dude, so I'll let it slide this time. (You're welcome.) I get it pal: no one likes New Jersey. But how would *you* like it if you got pumpkin in your hair? It's called the golden rule, and it's what we go by here in these United States of America: treat others how you would like to be treated.

Which I guess brings me to my next point. It has come to our attention here that there are some 'secessionist ideologies' brewing in your state. Now I may not read so well, or with any pleasure, but I know what communism is when I see it. And it would be a real shame if we had to come in there with tanks and guns and remind you what country you belong to. Right? It'd be a real lose-lose for the both of us, man. Lotta hassle. So, on behalf of the United States Government, I would ask you to kindly control the separatism happening in your state (still can't believing this is addressed to Dalaware and not Guam or some shit) and let your citizens know who they belong to. That's all.

Enjoy the carrot cake. My buddy has a guy."

The employee in charge of finding Bridge's address and sending it to the bakery, a task designated to him in the last minutes of the fourth hour, was not feeling especially assiduous. He decided it would be easiest to just send it to the state capital building, where someone would inevitably find "the goods" and deliver them. He didn't know what Delaware's capital was, but had heard of a city called Wilmington. He figured that Delaware was super small, probably about a half-mile wide and a half-mile long, so it would end up in the Governor's hands some way or another. He sent the address as "Reverend Bridge, Wilmington, Delaware," leaving out the pedantic formalities of address and zip code. "They'll figure it out", he said, having confirmed to the bakery that yes, those were all the specifics needed, just be sure to include the note. And with that, he turned off his computer, said "Adiós", and walked down to the parking lot.

* * *

"What a disgrace!" Bridge shrieks. He has not read the note but is appalled to find that they had the gall to send him a *carrot* cake; and one that had gone rotten quite some time before! Such is his distaste for carrots and for cake that he is immediately predisposed to respond to the note in a sour, sour way.

Upon reading the intelligence officer's words (rendered in a font that Bridge frankly finds garish and childlike, particularly with the national disgrace of a misspelling), he is even more enraged. "How dare they!" His hands are clenching, desperately in need of a stress ball or perhaps a vase to shatter, while his eyes grow large and small and large again, his jaw opens and closes with pure rage, and his ears collect goblets of steam. "An a- attack on my k- KINGDOM!" He needs something to throw – how could he not! He grabs a paperweight on his desk and slams it into the wall near him, only dimly satisfied by its faint clunk. Then he calls for his interns, who certainly have already heard the commotion and are waiting by the door as is unofficial protocol, and shouts: "CLOSE THE BORDERS!"

* * *

Mayors of towns up and down the state (even in the written word, one cannot escape the vertical nature of the Delawarean consciousness) held meetings to educate the populace on the significance of the new border closures. While these began with lofty goals, and some of them ended with such, many others descended to filling in the gaps of the public school system's failings. The people were lectured on the boundaries between states, nations, and nation-states, and given metaphor-laden recaps of the political events that had led

100

to the present moment. Specifically, many of these meetings spent a lot of time on Juneau's coinage: "Come Support Delaware's Independence From The Imperialist Giant of the United States of America." There was a lot of confusion over the term imperialism, the boundaries between pronouns like "us" and "them" that were before so crystal clear, and what "independence" would be defined as in practice. Below the canal, it had to be specified that these meetings were *not* preparations for war against New Jersey, and that citizens should leave their firearms at home, in case discussions got ugly.

For all of their various failures to understand, the Delawareans were by no means unenthusiastic. For many of them, this suggestion seemed to have awakened something in them, touched a cultural or economic nerve that they were anxious to do something about. If they could latch on to a vague, but flashy and dramatic, goal that could liberate them from their tedium and sadness, they were ready to believe in anything. Because, in the end, if Delaware had been a more interesting state with more activities for the doing, one could imagine that one would not need to amuse oneself with irredentist movements.

* * *

The university, of course, had served as the epicenter of the outbreak of nationalist furor. The bowling club had tripled in size and shifted in purpose in record speed, boasting a growing amount of capital from excited Delawareans who wanted to build this new civil society. The citizens, if they had been aware that secession would be achieved through a coup rather than a sort of democratic process, may not have been so keen. But these details were lost on the population at large, particularly since Juneau herself did not truly understand how she planned to institute Brandt into power, just as she failed to understand the true connotations of the word "hegemony." In this way, she was truly a leader of the people.

The social atmosphere at CSD had only continued to grow tenser. The divide between in-state students and OSSs (a term increasingly preceded by "those damn") was widening and manifesting itself in increasingly ludicrous

101

ways.

Traitor Delawareans, who saw the secessionist proposal as preposterous and extravagant, had assimilated with OSS groups as successfully as they could. The OSSs who saw grace and dignity in the humbleness of the subaltern's desires had taken on this identity, and were growing ever more feverish in their attempts to aestheticize the Delawarean ideals that had just recently been invented.

Other Northeasterners were rather neutral and apathetic to the matter, remaining in OSS groups purely out of convenience. They carried out their normal routines, swallowing themselves unconscious Wednesday through Monday and phoning home during their rare hours of lucidity to convince their parents *yes, anthropology is great, any money you send my way goes straight to my books.* Being so privy to not attend class in the first place, and certainly not sober, they failed to perceive any classroom tension, and so it resulted that they were some of the least affected by such events. And the elaborate parties they hosted usually catered to the more monied, those who did not see numbers but only possibility, of which the only Delawareans that could ascend to this level were indoctrinated in their Northeastern language, customs, and political beliefs.

Their main political concerns lay not in issues of national identity but in the preservation of their prized fraternal institutions. They ignored other sorts of political activity, being too strenuous for their 80-proof brains, except when the university wagged a benign finger at a sorority or fraternity, in which case a flood of Jasons and Ashleys and Chads would storm the administration buildings in spectacle to protest this heinous infringement on their civil rights. To them, Delaware's political existence did not matter to them or interest them in the slightest, because Delaware was just a shitty place they could manipulate and prance about upon with abandon, a place where no one lived and no one grew old that consisted only of the three mile radius that contained the campus and all of the liquor stores in the most vast of its stretches.

* * *

The College of the State of Delaware, reacting to new border measures, worked with frenzy to assure all "stakeholders" that their interests would be protected. To reassure out of state students, the president of the university announced in a lengthy email, hidden between impressively long paragraphs dense with non-information, that out-of-state tuition payers would have safe spots at the university. "We take great care to secure our assets," the president wrote, "and to make sure that we attract and retain the kind of human capital that only can be found outside of these state borders."

They say, and by they one refers to physicists, that every action has a reaction. In this situation, this quote has little relevance or meaning, but it has the semblance of describing the Delawarean nationalist reaction to such news in an astute way. The outcry from the Delawareans reached all corners of campus, and even extended to the college's secondary campus facilities across the nation. Protestors demanded that the president retract his statement about the intellectual inferiority of Delawareans and make a renewed promise to benefit the citizens of Delaware, which they also demanded be named a country and not a state. So, bending to this pressure, the president released an email twice as long and half as full with actual information, the only sentence with even a tinge of concrete meaning being "we would like to emphasize that we are committed to serving the citizens of the great nation of Delaware."

But then some out-of-state students, whose "blood ran blue and gold" as no blood-bred Delawarean would ever claim, were worried that the Delawareans had gotten a leg up on them, though the statement was largely decorative, and demanded retribution from the president. He later responded, "I don't know how to fix this anymore, I always say the wrong thing, please just don't forget in all of the chaos to pay your tuition because I need a vacation."

One struggles to imagine how the out-of-state students could have been pleased with this statement, but at a certain point the controversy died down, and everyone tacitly agreed to put the issue on the backburner, as humans are eventually wont to do even in the strangest of circumstances. The notion that non-Delawareans could possibly be stuck in airtight Delawarean borders had also, like many other things that had at first sounded too ridiculous to be true, become reality, and so New Jerseyans and Long Islanders and Pennsylvanians organized grand campaigns, on a level of political engagement unseen and unheard of before at CSD, to arrange for their home states to repatriate them in the event that the border situation got tricky.

"Dear state government, I know I have abandoned you in your time of need, but now that I am faced with this current situation, I hope you will remember the good times we had together, before I jumped ship, and come to rescue me in times of difficulty. Like, if you could come with a helicopter or a jet or some other kind of rescue vehicle to help me escape. For that I would be so grateful that I would promise to never leave your side, to support your economy by working in your state and providing you with a labor force in your golden hour by giving birth to many strong children." Or something very similar to such.

work makes free

FLORIDA IN SHAMBLES; DELAWAREAN PENINSULA BLESSED BY TOUCH OF GOD

It has been reported in the last year to the Delaware State News Agency that in the United States, that unwieldy country to the north, west, and south of our blessed realm, some longstanding demographic trends have been reversing.

Up until the last couple of years, the so-called Sunbelt, a region described as "God's chosen land of low taxes, guns as fat as people and bone-chilling AC" was the go-to choice for families in search of overflow garages and diet-soda cultural offerings with the fun watered out (for the sake of their vulnerable children). In fact, up until the last couple of years, states along that Sunbelt had been growing at an average rate of 7% per year, in stark contrast to the left-behind northern hamlets, particularly in New England, whose antique highways and quaint village roads are ill-suited to the great SUVs and monoculture particular to their so-called American Dream.

Recent environmental changes, however, including the Wave and Grand Displacement, have disrupted traditional season patterns greatly, causing residents to rechristen the seasons of the Sunbelt as "skin-deforming summer," "shed your life summer", and "Hell." In addition, higher rates of industrial activity have added to the unpleasantness of higher temperatures and humidity, causing locals to wonder if their sweat is caused by the weather or by the higher concentration of carbon dioxide particles in the air.

While higher temperatures are a major push factor, some residents, particularly in the ravaged remains of what used to be the state of Florida, have had no option but to move to higher lands. On the Floridian Peninsula, more than 30% of the land has been reclaimed by the sea, with the city of Miami already having passed into the yellow space of history books. The flight of coastal and Southern Floridians to the Panhandle has been no small reason for tension between these two culturally distinct peoples. A host of fascinating anthropological field studies have confirmed the disruption in the ecosystems of these communities by the arrival of key lime pie and Cuban sandwiches.

Due to all of these factors, migration patterns have turned increasingly northern and increasingly inward, giving geographers reason to designate the Great Plains and the Midwest as new growth areas. "In particular, we see great futures for Minot, North Dakota, Pierre, South Dakota, and Des Moines, Iowa. These cities are just bland enough to be attractive to America's greatest geographical opportunists, those wary of too much local spice, looking for locales with enough industry to give fathers the financial resources to impregnate their wives and create more sugar cereal-loving tiny consumers." The American geographer in question, [redacted], described Minot as "the next Kalamazoo" with great enthusiasm.

If you ask Canadian authorities, however, they will tell you that the northern drive does not stop at the 49th parallel: in recent years, the Canadian Border Patrol has tightened border measures to prevent American nationals from crossing the border illegally in search of more modest climes. "We never had a problem before," reported an unnamed Canadian Border Patrol officer. "I can't remember a time before when *anyone* even knew where the line was. When I got hired, the job was a lot simpler, eh."

He emphasized that Canada has begun construction of a large fence along the length of the border, in addition to increasing the number of officers on patrol and installing checkpoints where officers ask the potential crosser to pronounce "Toronto" to discern native Canadians from the southern imposters. When asked where Americans are sent, he referred to "some sort of underground latrine and storage area" that houses border crossers.

Conditions are reported to be sub-human, but not quite as sub-human as in the capture stations along the Rio Grande. "We don't have the gall for that kind of treatment, eh," the officer stated, blushing upon his horse.

Meanwhile, in this great nation of Delaware, our ideological purity has allowed Him to bestow upon us mercy and fair weather. According to the lead meteorologist of the Delaware Division of Weather and Divine Activity, the "Delawarean peninsula effect" produces a cooling such that the Delawarean climate has been invulnerable to greater climate trends in topologically similar areas beyond our borders. "The Delawarean spirit has blessed and cleansed our region, dispelling mutant, satanic forces of Heat and Drought, and curving hurricanes so as to forsake our holy lands."

In the most reputable of Delawarean meteorological circles, Rehoboth Beach's disappearance act is described as a "clever fluke." While The Reverend blesses our lands as best as He can, He cannot prevent that Lower Red One from penetrating our territory with his blight. Residents are advised to keep a safe distance from coastal locales, as the "suspicious activity" around the beach is one of the foremost examples of Satan's temptations, a great test for those who question the sanctity of Delawarean land.

"We have no higher temperatures, we have no hurricanes, we have no forest fires," Our Reverend Bridge has assured us. "Any time you witness suspicious activity that appears to be or represents some sort of holographic representation of a fire, high temperatures, or drought, please call the Delaware Division of Weather and Divine Activity to report high Satan activity in the area. If we are all active in reporting his falsehoods and tricks, we will be able to see more clearly God's blessings, the real world that he has in store for us, that sometimes appear to be challenged by the Lower Red One's curses."

Bridge has subsequently announced, as well, a divine message of territorial expansion. In his latest press release, He announced plans sent from Above to create artificial land masses in the Delawarean Purity Bay in an act of land reclamation. "This way, we can provide for our ever-growing population, so that American refugees and our kin sent from Above will have vast areas for expansion. Long live the Delawarean race!" In addition, he mentioned his visions for expanding the Delawarean Ethos to the greater Delawarean peninsula and beyond.

In a final statement, Bridge mocked the Americans' indifference to their land, in their abhorrent willingness to pack up and move on a whim attracted by "the Lower Red One's temptations of three-car garages and lawn space." "We Delawareans are committed as the pastors of this Holy Land that He hath bequeathed to us. In so doing, we will also be extending our arms to the wretched citizens of the imperialist giant to the north, who surely yearn for the purity and spiritual strength of our land. In the name of God, let us expand and spread our beauty!"

So far, Delaware has welcomed 14,978 refugees through newly-enacted asylum policies.*

*American citizens left in Delaware at time of gap included in total

* * *

Reverend Bridge claimed thereafter in a multitude of public speeches what he presented to be his policy goals. The term he used was his "campaign promises", seemingly unaware of the incongruence between this wording and his lack of a democratic ascendence to power.

Juneau and Victor tuned in to every televised speech, lifting their cable television out of obsolescence with pious regularity. In his first one, Bridge made an appeal for national unity. He referred to the "separate but equal beauties" of Northern and Southern Delaware, urging "both Canalite and LSD comrades" to come together as one. They had no joy in witnessing the inadvertently successful proliferation of their vocabulary.

In Bridge's second speech, he waxed poetic about the need for a return to morality. Hearing the similarity of this language to a moral consensus of the late twentieth-century in that country whose history still pervaded the common consciousness despite a new national credence, both Juneau's and Victor's guts shifted and rattled within them unsettled-like. Bridge referred to Delaware as a gift from God, a piece of continent destined to break away from the flames of sin coursing in those lands to the north, west, and south. And with eerie regularity, Bridge repeated a new mantra: "ethics of work."

Victor would have been happy to believe that this would be a noble campaign to remove the chains of subjugation from the worker under the employer, but he thought it much too cowardly to believe what was most comforting to believe in the face of an ugly truth.

Bridge subsequently cozied up with employers, stating that the concept of the minimum wage was tyranny in and of itself, and he announced his immediate revocation of "that great continental mistake". He then declared his intention to "free the common folk from the tyranny of the 40-hour workweek" and "protect the right to personal pet project fulfillment" by allowing employers to set higher minimum requirements for weekly work hours: 50 hours, 60 hours, 70 hours. There was no end: he announced in his following sadistic utterances the "elimination of Sunday Sloth," referring to a more general concept that would require workers to report all seven days of the week. Bridge pointed to a graph that by some illicit force of statistical fraud was able to depict an exponential relationship between an increase in work hours and "spiritual karma", beaming that he would do more for the worker than anybody else had under American rule: "One can only imagine to what level we will rise when our productivity is untethered by the periods of sloth and inertia that characterize 'weekends' and 'nights off.'"

Naturally, during the course of these orations, he always made clear references to Delaware's national struggle, setting clear boundaries between Delaware and "our former oppressors" . He criticized the "idolatrous Americans" and foresaw that the "Delawarean-Protestant work ethic" would lead them to glory, avoiding the pitfalls of Delaware's unfortunate previous attachment to the American nation.

Various groups of middle to low-class Delawareans, despite his attack on the notions of "leisure" and "slumber", received him with open arms. After their recent terrors, the people were ready to be called to strength, regardless of the horrors their labor would cause their joints and their gray matter, for they were serving the noblest cause there was, of course, and the people were bored, having long forgotten what it was like to have personal hobbies.

The upper class, including the upper echelons of the middle class, were undoubtedly receptive. As high-level administrators or managers, they could make their own hours and increasingly draw up their own salaries, adding zeroes as they saw fit, and so the new labor regulations did not apply to them. Furthermore, through the advent of new worker-beating technologies promoted by the DuFrond firm, their time in the office became largely ceremonial, so that in the meager minutes they spent at their companies each week they could attend to dinner reservations and the purchasing of foreign wine, which still was not taken to mean wine from California.

This is not to say that there were no signs of pushback or organized revolt. Among the most vulnerable in Delaware's population, particularly those that already worked multiple jobs to keep themselves afloat, it was impossible for them to add more hours to the day without forgoing sleep they needed at least occasionally to maintain bodily cohesion, so they were adamant that their standard of life had decreased sharply during Bridge's taking of power. But they were much too exhausted to protest these changes with any adamance, and so as the weeks went on those that were not forcibly removed from shelter perished from sheer exhaustion.

In the rare minutes of idle time that the people had, mostly chunks of five minutes or so during the workweek scheduled as "worker appreciation" to replace meals and sleep, Delawareans erupted with national pride. They shouted about some new production statistic that they had exceeded, they made Bridge's name rise, they burned the previous US flags and hung Delawarean flags in the embers.

It was on one of his ceremonial visits that the Reverend Bridge saw this take place. Upon setting his eye on the flag, he declared that the "colonial flag" would no longer do, that it would behoove them to find a new design that would be "deserving of our greatness." And the shouts of crazed rapture grew louder, people and machines screaming in equal frequency and intensity, the workers in their increasingly hallucinatory state of exhaustion growing ever closer to God.

* * *

By now, Juneau notes that it is tiresome and laborious to walk around campus, because of the continual reminders of Bridge's rule. The Christian community the Reverend Bridge had previously worked with so closely at the university celebrates constantly. Juneau thinks, for people that so admire Bridge's ethics of work, they are quite prone to superfluous celebration. They claim the Quad for days a time, the university powerless to enforce regulations against seizure of public spaces knowing they would be interfering with the big cheese's wishes. They annex student centers without warning to become headquarters of production for figurines of unborn fetuses (so human, so feeling), thy fall from campus skies in waves of shame. They plaster signs, curated by some half-savvy design student, that scream "ETHICS OF WORK" over any plasterable surface at the university. Their presence grows ever larger, not just in the center of campus but also in neighborhoods in the campus periphery, reflecting perhaps a larger willingness of the student body to succumb to the tides of time. In this manner it comes to the point that Juneau cannot even look out her window in one of the least collegiate of all surrounding neighborhoods without seeing some reminder of encroaching doom. The Christian Crusaders, a name only they are willing to use, call themselves crusaders and comrades with equal gumption and bloodthirsty desire for retribution.

If some part of their state-making manifesto had been co-opted for sinister purposes, others had been totally ignored. Although the people took to using terms like "comrade" and referring to "the cultural hegemony of the Northeast," Delawareans could not stop using idioms related to money. To the contrary, they were much more militant in their usage, and much more aware of their time as a monetary asset; they referred to their newfound consciousness with things like "a dime a dozen" or "that's my two cents," though it wasn't really *their* opinion, but that of Bridge.

They even ended up creating new idioms to refer to this hyper-monetized reality. Since so many workers now had fifty or sixty or seventy-hour work weeks, or at least the most linguistically productive lower classes did, they often stated that "to rest is to go bankrupt" in some delusional self-assurance. And inevitably the more monied classes also took to saying this, in much less of a true sense, of course, since they rested even more than before, and this linguistic colonization was more of a prescription for others than for themselves.

* * *

Juneau and Victor sit down on a Friday night to watch another one of Bridge's speeches. Employers screen these speeches on giant televisions while the workers take escaping glimpses when they can, absorbing more of the audio than the video. Juneau and Victor watch it on a tiny television whose reception depends on the goodwill of the duct tape that binds its corners. Though they often finish such broadcasts feeling despondent and lachrymose, they cannot help but watch again to stay informed, if only as a vocabulary exercise in finding new ways to describe their predicament.

And so today, Bridge refers to the success of his "ethics of work" campaign. He has to stop several times after announcing this or the other fantastical and illusionary statistic of his success to allow the digital audience to howl and scream in nationalistic fervor. Bridge has no qualms in giving them all the time they need to calm down and allow the spirit to flow from their hearts out of their orifices, which often causes his speeches to last for hours.

When he has read through all of the statistical non-information he wishes to highlight, he projects his wishes for a new campaign: as he calls it, ever so delicately, "ethics of thought." The audience roars like never before. People sing in newly invented foreign tongues, chastise themselves in mysterious languages of the Lord for not being worthy, in a fury that can only mean "Oh great master would you please instruct me how to think for I have lost the ability to reason," and Bridge looks to the sky, his eyes closed, and shouts "Hallelujah." He pronounces that he has a new plan for Delaware, a new idea for reform.

He explains that, in Delaware, the Devil threatens to bring down his reign, to level out the classes and give the poor health care, to make fetuses emerge from their mothers only to kill them once they exit. The crowd jeers deliriously, heated anger backing their enthusiasm. "And they want to destroy the kingdom of Delaware, this kingdom that was ordained from up in the Heavens." So Bridge announces, finally, his policy goal: that all Delaware citizens, effective immediately, will be "voluntarily obligated" to attend church services on Sunday.

"Workers will be permitted to take an hour of absence each Sunday to attend these services, and for those citizens who choose not to partake in these services, they will have that option, but they will be punished for it mercilessly." He then specifies that each county would have a designated church to report to, and tithes would be the way for each citizen to record their "well-pondered" decision to attend the service. "These will be grand services, to build the glory of our People. Because Delaware, in the original French, means 'those workers who work for Jesus,' and so we shall exalt His name and the Kingdom he has ordained for us." And so the crowd erupts, with firecrackers and guns and all sorts of devices that gobble up time and space, and the speech is declared finished.

Delaware's Francophone population, comprised of linguistically incompetent teachers as well as harrowed Haitian immigrants, are too busy to raise issue.

the protestant work ethic

Juneau had previously thought her and Victor and all of her fellow college students mostly safe from the madness of Bridge's administration. She had imagined that they couldn't ever expect the students, many of whom without a Delawarean allegiance in the first place, to attend church services and pay tithes like the other citizens. Oh how she had hoped that their youth would allow them to sin without interruption, as long as it was quiet and could be assumed to be the fault of tuition-paying OSSs.

She hoped for some strand of normality to remain. She prayed that Sundays could continue to be large displays of blasphemy, topsy-turvy young women discarding their hangover brunch in church parking lots, their male companions shouting "Jesus Christ!" seeing the proximity of the bile to their new sneakers. Even traditions she was not a part of, Juneau felt a sort of kinship for, at least in this mess that made such nuisances seem homey. But on one certain Friday, Bridge announced his plans to "let Jesus inform us of the wickedness of unions and public health insurance" by providing church services to all, willing and not; the university had followed up with an email that suggested their very collegiate status would make their indoctrination especially painful.

Juneau cries out: "What other ghastly horrors lie waiting in my inbox?"

Victor does not read his email. He had forgotten the password, sometime long ago when his account saw light for the first time. He always tells his professors to send him snail mail, highlighting its crisp physicality. His explanations are always met with quizzical frowns, but rarely with much correspondence.

Juneau, in the voice she uses to explain things that Victor had missed, tells him about the email and its implications.

"We're not exempt, like we thought we were. They're making it mandatory for us to attend church services each Sunday at the stadium."

"We thought we were exempt?"

"I certainly did. Did you not?"

"No."

"Well, you didn't know about it."

"Correct."

"So, you couldn't think you were exempt, because you couldn't think anything about it. You didn't think you were *not* exempt."

"True. I didn't think I was not exempt, and I did think that this was not an issue."

"So, it did cross your mind?"

"No."

"But if you thought, 'this is not an issue,' that had to have been conscious, right? You would've at least been aware of the threat."

"But I wasn't."

"Victor! This is ludicrous. Did you see the thing about 'students with remarkable offshore investments or assets' making 'separate arrangements?' The horror!"

Victor laughs, and Juneau makes her contempt known.

"What's so funny?"

"I mean, isn't this all so absurd?"

"Be serious. 'We are cooperating with the Revered Reverend Bridge to inculcate in our students the Judeo-Christian values that have guided the Delawarean consciousness for centuries, as Delawareans united under the Delaware Church of the Protestant Work Ethic. For those who claim non-Delawarean citizenship, we wish to be hospitable and make your economic life here as comfortable as possible.' And then he goes on with the whole bribe bit. He's totally contradicting himself."

"Life is full of contradictions."

Juneau rolls her eyes. "Is that so?"

"Contradictions don't just *happen* though, at least not most of the time. Contradictions are created. In order to explain behavior that we already have grown accustomed to, we separate our brains into separate categories, each one believing things that radically contradict ideas in other quadrants. And by constantly reimagining our categories and applying strange new laws to each, we can convince ourselves that we are making sense. We know we're not, we just keep that information in a folder that we don't open. Some of the most important truths are hidden deep in the shafts of our gray matter."

"Oh god, no more gray matter, I'm gonna ralph up my lunch." Juneau feels that Victor does not understand the gravity of the situation, nor does he even acknowledge the mundanity of these weekend inconveniences, which is somehow worse.

"On Sunday mornings, I don't move until dinner. Now I have to pay to be wrenched out of my slumber?"

"Wait, wait: *pay?*" Somehow, Victor did not catch this piece of information.

"Because we can't give huge sums to avoid it, we're obligated to cough up ten bucks a week."

Victor wonders how he will manage such a monetary commitment, having been fired from his job on grounds he found completely unfair. "The manager didn't take so kindly to my reading pulp romance at the drive-thru window," Victor had explained so well at the time. He mentions, on the side, that asking his father for a weekly allowance of ten dollars, even in these strange circumstances of indoctrination, is not an option.

"You like romance novels?"

"Only the really smutty ones."

Juneau tries to think of a way out. She wonders if her mother has a secret bank account for her under Caribbean auspices, but something tells her this is unlikely.

"You think I could get a loan? Maybe a few thousand?"

"You'd probably have high interest."

"Good, good, that means I can choose from different lenders."

"No Juneau, I mean that you'll probably have to pay it back at a really high rate."

"Oh." Juneau had forgotten temporarily the second aspect of acquiring a loan, that which involved the return of funds to the rightful owner, along with fees for the inconvenience. Victor vocalizes a phrase he often repeats to himself at night: "There's no way out." Except this time, in the light of day, it is much easier for him to scoff and laugh and appreciate the chaos as spectacle, to pretend that what is in front of him is just entertainment.

* * *

On Sunday morning, Juneau wakes Victor up at 7:34 am. She says they have to leave soon if they want to make it to the stadium. Victor takes his time in raising himself from the fetal position, extending his arms above his head to rid himself of the night's stressors. He chomps on a cigarette while shoving himself into pants a size too snug, the only pair he thinks suitable in a stadium-turned-place-of-worship. Juneau, waiting for him to be ready, asks him if he thinks any Delawareans will be able to avoid the services.

"I'm intuiting, somehow, that we're the main target group. But probably the capitalists, yeah. Business majors."

"You think the offspring of our nation's capitalists are all business majors?" Victor notes how Juneau speaks of "the nation," and shimmers with pride.

"Probably. But there's probably some others who see their duties differently. There may be a few art majors who have the resources. Those that want to reject the trimmings of wealth by trotting around Brooklyn selling graffitied urinals to hipsters and tax-haven foundations."

"I bet there's quite a few capitalists who study economics. Finance, too."

"That's just business." Juneau concurs. The distinction is unimportant.

They resolve to walk to the stadium, not merely by force of will against the vans provided to transport them, but also out of habit. They would lose their lives without the vibrance of the morning air.

Juneau wears a black dress that her mother had lent her, remarkably unsuitable for her body's constitution. She thinks of her fashion decisions as an expression of her disdain, realizing that it would not strike others to notice that her slight deviation from the norms would constitute rebellion. The dress is of a black too garish for a funeral, but too macabre for a party, and so in the narrow confines of Wynona's social life it has little use. Juneau thinks it a perfect number for brainwashing in a sweaty gymnasium. Victor shifts in the tight pants he had aroused from the tomb of his closet.

"Are we dressed appropriately to be indoctrinated?"

"We look ravishing." Juneau includes Victor in her "we" to make him feel better, though they both know she speaks only of herself and her appreciation of her new trapezoidal form.

"It's like showing up to a wedding in a white dress."

Victor sees no room for comparison.

"I would just prefer not to stick out, you know? Like, look at this fool, his testicles scrunched into the pants his mother bought for him."

Juneau looks over, as to ascertain if Victor speaks hyperbolically, or if his pants really are so transparent.

"You can't actually see them. And my mom didn't actually buy them. It's just a turn of phrase."

The walk to the stadium takes half an hour with determination, forty minutes with mopey delay. Today, they are both content to romp around without haste, Juneau seeing it as another small rebellion, noticeable only by her own eyes.

Victor wants to stop to observe every bush, every dilapidated house torn to shreds by co-eds, every wasp languishing in the concrete heat. Even so, they eventually reach the stadium, the slowing of their paces at various critical points along the journey notwithstanding.

They stand in line to enter, as if to present a ticket for a concert. Victor is mortified to see that no one else had bothered to dress in polite church clothing. They wait behind a sea of leggings and oversized t-shirts plastered with non sequiturs, and the two of them together look like a dusty old couple haunting an antique parlor room. Victor refers to himself as a toddler ring bearer uncomfortable in his first suit. Juneau, in spite of the solemnity of their absurd situation, laughs, and ignores the people stomping on the train of her dress.

"At least we're fashionably late," she says with a friendly poke. Victor's face turns a docile red.

A man in thick cowboy boots collects crumpled ten-dollar bills at the entrance. As Victor tries to make acquaintance with the ground, Juneau watches the man. He has a natural rhythm: he takes the dollar bill, switches between several routine comments on the weather or the newest online currency, always with a hearty chili chuckle, and closes his procedure with a firm but friendly finger pointing. He shines in this work, mechanical functions with a touch of brief human interaction. Even far back in the line, Juneau can hear his every word in his husky baritone. As she gets closer to the front, her fascination with him starts to dissipate, and she wishes she could turn down his voice.

She and Victor are just a few people deep in the line when there occurs a breach in protocol. Two dazed men reach the front. The cowboy lays his eyes on them, then attempts to lower his voice to say:

"This here ain't for y'all!"

Though he achieves a modest reduction in sound, it's clear that he is far from mastering the ability to hide his words. He then takes them by the shoulder and directs them back toward the main campus. Juneau watches them closely to figure out why exactly they were left behind. Standing behind them, all she noticed was the overwhelming stench of skunky cologne and expensive hair gel. But as they turn away, kissing their dubiously maintained but massive all the same biceps in self-congratulation, she catches an unwanted glimpse of their chests through the generous slits in their tank tops, and notices the unmistakable shape of the Grand Oppressor, New Jersey, tattooed on the taller one's side.

"Did you see that?"

"I just see asphalt and trampled garbage."

"I just saw a couple of guidos get out of the service." Victor just smirks contemptuously.

"One of them had a New Jersey tattoo bigger than my head."

"The top or the bottom?"

"Uh...the taller one?"

"Figures." It appears that Victor had been paying enough attention, at least, to notice their relationship dynamics, even without raising his head.

They pay their dues and enter the building. The halls are wide, the walls revealing no indication of where to go, and neither of them are well-acquainted enough with the sports buildings to guess. They walk aimlessly, feeling like sea creatures suddenly on land.

So they cannot find their way, despite hearing a faint sound of chanting emanating from some unknown direction. They wander this way and that, approaching the sound briefly just to veer away from it, never locating it. It seems impossible. Then, as they turn a corner, Victor jumps to see a man standing in their path. He wears a virginal white robe with antique slippers. He smiles at them for a few moments, not breaking eye contact.

"I like your Jerusalem shoes," Victor says.

The man's grin does not fade: it expands, recoiling across his entire face.

"You'd better be careful," he warns in brusque falsetto. He turns around abruptly and begins to walk in the other direction. When he looks back, he sees that they do not follow.

"Come," he says simply, no longer excessively cheery, just a simple command to be obeyed. They know nothing but to follow his lead. He guides them for only a few brief moments, turning down one hallway to lead them to the large auditorium they had passed several times. Juneau and Victor hear nothing, see nothing from the room. The windows had been covered up with red paint, and there is no indication that the light noises of worship they had heard around the building had their origins here. But as the man opens the door, they realize they had found their way. The sound is magnified:

"Delaware is blue, money is green, the Devil is red, unions are obscene!"

The rows are packed with people. Most of them students just like Victor and Juneau, disinterested, tired, succumbing to the nonsense. For the most part, they slump over in their seats, drooping their jaws floorwards to provide the appearance of participation. Stationed in each row is a person in a white robe, just like the one who surreptitiously apprehended Victor and Juneau in the hallway, to oversee the masses.

As soon as the man in white led them in, he abandoned them to some other pursuit in some other place. They stand without direction for a moment, unsure of where to turn. Eventually Juneau takes the lead, moving her feet to the left just to have something to do. They climb the rows to find their seats, located at the very top of the stadium seating. The speakers that surround transmit the sound clearly even in their annals, how lucky they will be to not miss a word. They sit down, the chanting becomes more intense. Juneau sees one of the white robes pinch a girl who had fallen completely asleep, and she tries to tell Victor, but then she is reprimanded by a white robe for failing to sing. So their conversation ends.

The chant continues, with some variations here and there, but generally the same, besides the increase in intensity and somewhat in speed.

And then all of a sudden, a white robe on the gym floor makes a hand signal, and silence reigns in a matter of seconds.

"Good morning, Delaware!" A strange concert no one wants to attend. The woman in the white robe handles the microphone as if she had allusions of stardom. She receives nothing but a grunt.

"That's no greeting fit for our king. Let me hear you greet our Revered Reverend Bridge. Good Morning!"

They're forced to participate, every single one of them. The white robes stationed at each row emit a hand signal to report down, making sure each student had been made to be vocal. Juneau whispers to Victor:

"I said good mourning, not good morning."

The white robe in their row, who was beaming the instant before, turns their head suspiciously to give Juneau a look. Somehow it says volumes, implies she had committed the worst of the ten commandments. She doesn't know which one it is, clueless as to what any of the commandments are, besides adultery, the most captivating, but she feels like she had been censured by God himself.

The white robes stationed on the court, microphone in hand, communicate with each other secretly. There's a sort of shuffle, one could observe that someone had forgotten to carry out a duty, or had overstepped a hierarchical boundary, or that there had been some sort of mutual misunderstanding that, for this moment, brings the service to a halt. The crowd grows suspicious. Then one of them takes charge, after apparently deciding to cut out a section of the service previously agreed upon:

"Today's service is about thievery." She waits for a crowd reaction, unsure of what that would be. Hearing nothing, she continues.

"Well, maybe it'd be more accurate to say that our service today is about a *lot* of things. Everything, really. But that would be a hard sell." The joke, if it is intended as such, does not land. She frowns slightly, Juneau can see so even from high up in the hinterlands, and then makes a signal.

A sort of noxious red slime bursts out of the ceiling tiles in some sort of mass cleansing ritual, Victor and Juneau in the hinterlands of the are among the first to perceive the sensation, screams break out BATHE IN THE BLOOD OF OUR SAVIOR JESUS CHRIST, HE WHO HATH WROUGHT THIS HOLY DISCIPLE THE REVERED REVEREND BRIDGE, THE DELAWAREAN RACE PREVAILS!

* * *

In time, Bridge is happy to report that his ethics of thought campaign has been a massive success: "We've got everyone thinking more Godlike than ever!" In terms of logistics, it was actually quite a failure: each Sunday, at the designated morning hour when factories and offices would gracefully allow their workers to take a spiritual respite, the traffic issues created by corralling all citizens of each county in one church were considerable.

Bridge didn't have any advisors, but he did have some people that he trusted in at some level, mainly including high-level clergy members in the state most comfortable with his version of evangelical neoliberalism. When these suggested that he allow citizens to choose their church, or if that was too radical, to open up one more per county to alleviate the massive congestion caused by concentrating everyone in one area, Bridge did not relent, and some were greatly suspicious that this had something to do with the fact that the selected churches happened to be owned by either one of his brothers or one of his cousins, and that the requirement to record attendance was to contribute a tithe.

Seeing that this experiment had been a success, at least for him personally, he was ready to embark on a new mission. He had exploratory ambitions, desires to spread his views further around the world, and so he asked a few low-level interns to research any historical ties Delaware had with any foreign nations. They found that Delaware had a sister state in Japan, the prefecture of Miyagi, and Bridge thought it could be a perfect way for him to promote his faith and his bank account across the world.

With dizzying velocity, Japanese became a priority language in the school system. Bridge introduced the language at all levels of instruction: even pre-schools were required to hire Japanese-speaking staff to educate Delaware's next work force in the language. Elementary schools and higher were required to split their time evenly between English and Japanese. This would have been simple enough, "simple" without taking into account the great logistical struggle that was recruiting and hiring a boatload of Japanese natives to work in the school system, as well as dealing with this sudden influx of educators unfamiliar with the Delawarean school system.

It was however made even more difficult by the fact that certain subjects were required to be taught in one language while yet others were forbidden to be taught in the other, and there came strange inexplicable decrees as to what times of day each language could be spoken, resulting in the fact that schools were forced to teach English class using "the language of our oriental subjects"and Japanese class while avoiding uttering a single word of Japanese. And then there was the question of teaching religion, now obligatory for all students in all grades – many taught that it would be best to teach it in Japanese, if the goal was for students to cross the Pacific Ocean to proselytize, for then they could learn the Christian terminology they would need. While there were some who were opposed to their childrens' religious education taking place through a "communist language," being unaware (just like their leader) of Japan's capitalist exceptionalism, such critics were quickly removed from public and private life.

And it was not just in the school system that these effects were felt. In the ever-growing national bureaucracy, an increasing number of positions were reserved only for fluent Japanese speakers. Besides Bridge's goal to convert the Japanese to his own particular brand of Christianity, he also wanted to become more integrated economically and politically. He claimed to have read many a book in his college years about the rise of Japan and its potential as a labor market, and he thought tight integration with Japan could represent a raw market for Delaware to exploit. Unfortunately, no one explained to him that in the twenty years since he had graduated university and neglected to read a single book, China had largely overtaken Japan's spot as the new breeding ground for Western capitalist exploitation and was due to be overtaken in the future by some new cheap labor force, upon which time the cycle would start over again. The notion of this being a cyclical process escaped him, and he only continued to ramp us his efforts to create stronger diplomatic ties with Delaware's "great neighbors" (neighbor being a very, very loose term attributed to someone with a poor knowledge of geography and the general location and makeup of continents.)

He himself, however, could not be bothered to learn Japanese. He would often recite phrases, or even entire paragraphs in the language during his speeches, to a growing intelligentsia class that could understand him, or would have understood him if his words had made any sense, this great leader struggling to pronounce intelligibly this phonologically limited language. He seemed to wear it as a badge of pride; despite his inability to communicate, he insisted on using the language on as many occasions as he could manage, perhaps believing his exceptionalism rode somewhat on his unwillingness to conform to these sounds.

* * *

Juneau was having a bad day.

She left her French book at home, so she had to share with the boy who smelled like hot peanuts and rotten grapefruit, which meant a level of physical closeness that made her uncomfortable. Then, on the way to her identity politics course, she realized that her shirt had been on inside-out all day. And when the government professor told them their essay grades were uploaded, hers was not so favorable. Her professor remarked that her reflection on the subjugation of Delaware's markets to New Jersey's colonial empire was "based upon a flagrant misunderstanding of basic terminology" and "an affront to the discipline of postcolonial studies."

So when Juneau walks down the street and sees flames brewing, she imagines that yes, this is part of her day, this is something that she deserves. But she cannot see *what* building is burning, precisely, and does not think to wonder why it would be in flames.

She walks ahead, neither avoiding the flames nor directing herself towards them, simply walking listlessly along her usual path. As she gets closer, she sees that, beside the flames, there are groups of people with fists raised in protest, their hearts ablaze like the bricks that tower so perilously before them. Still a bit too far to make out what exactly they shout, she is aroused by the exclamations indiscriminately tinged with passion and fervor. In this moment, she decides that she will enter the chaos.

With horror, she realizes what the burning building is, and what it means for this new nation, the nation *she* created. The Planned Parenthood… that small, non-assuming eggshell white building, built off of the corner, a cornerstone of compassion in the bleakness that is the American health care system. Or, rather, the Delawarean health care system, which is admittedly quite similar to the American one at this point in time, given that Bridge had not yet had time to enact a policy change regarding this issue.

She approaches the sidewalk, where two ideologically separate but physically quite close groups confront each other. She sees students on the one side, raising their vocal tones in defense of bodily autonomy for women and the poor and the queer and others who desperately need these services. Whereas on the other side, Bridge's most adamant supporters, those who had supported him before his rise to power and had accepted his most vitriolic ideas, demanded that "clamshuckers and cocksuckers" be forcibly sent away, without reference to where, that sexually active women outside of marriage be burned upon the stake to preview their experiences in hell in an earthly manner, that refugees be forced to convert to Christianity or else be sent back to where they came.

They are like hounds, their words attacking like jagged jaws, she can see that their animal instincts are coming in quickly; the fear is that the force of words will rise and rise to make physical altercations inevitable. In any case, however, while tensions rise and the numbers in the groups swell, it appears that Bridge's supporters, shipped in from all the desolate post-industrial corners, are winning, as the building is already approaching a state of ignition to which its shape and form is starting to leave it.

The rioters grow to such proportions that the streets around are blocked, inconveniencing motorists who are angry enough to slam down on their horn, but not quite angry enough to drive into the crowd to make a point. Not yet.

In fact, when the fire trucks arrive from just around the corner, the drivers cannot even reach close enough to see the building and can only make out the flames that rise and travel in the air. Juneau notices a perfect cacophony, a disquieting array of splintering vocal cords, horns and emergency sirens, *oh there are ashes, but where are the wings?*

communal delusions

OUR REVERED REVEREND GENERALISSIMO BRIDGE ELIMINATES
SIN, QUADRUPLES WORKER PRODUCTIVITY, HAPPINESS

(The writer of this article would like to report to the general public that
"Our Revered Reverend Generalissmo Bridge" is now the preferred name
for Our Great Leader, not only in print but also in speech. Comrades should
take notice and adjust their speech patterns accordingly.)

In these last few weeks, Our Revered Reverend Generalissmo Bridge has
made great strides in improving our new nation. His efforts have extended
far and wide along our coastal strip, all of which have increased our
communal well-being. We are honored by the privilege to report Our
Revered Reverend Generalissimo Bridge's successes, so that we as a people
may worship Him and give thanks to our Creator. (Amen.)

Our Revered Reverend Generalissimo Bridge's Ethics of Work campaign
was the first of His many noble campaigns to improve the quality of life for
all. He freed us from the tyranny of the "40-hour work week," which many
have rightfully condemned as the "4 hour work week" for its characteristic
sloth and lack of industry, gracefully opening up the door for us to perform
our Passion Projects with more Godliness than ever before.

We are grateful to Him for freeing us from the yoke of idle "free time",
time that as servants of the public knowledge we feel obligated to remind
produces NOTHING and is free for NO ONE. The Department of Passion
Projects has reported a striking 456% increase in productivity across all

Passion Area Fields for the fifth week in a row, most notably banking, proselytizing, husbandry, queerchasing, and governance. This stands in stark contrast to previous years in which zero productivity increases were reported. Experts have attributed this to the negative influence of the *Secular United Satanists of Queerfolk*, professional terminology for the imperialist empire that surrounds our peninsula.

We interviewed a Factory Passion Project Participant to hear the Yeoman's thoughts on these increases on productivity. David Savin, 49 years of age, is a model comrade: a Southern native from Georgetown, he has been able to increase his time at his Passion Placement from 40 hours a week to an astounding 120 hours a week. Due to time constraints, he gracefully granted us an interview from our moving Accuracy News Van as he returned home for his daily Quickie Respite Allowance.

"David, what's your secret? How can we all increase our hours at our Passion Placements?"

"My secret is to keep on working. No matter what. Sometimes there's hurricanes, or a tornado, and it looks like the big GD is coming, but I just figure, that's that Big Red One trying to distract me from my Passion Project. You can do lots of things on the belt: eat, rest, speak to your loved ones. They're there in your head. As long as you keep your eyes on your PP, and never look away, you're free to do ANYTHING."

We also asked him, as he dutifully reviewed employee malfeasance regulations at a red light, to relate to us his satisfaction with Our Revered Reverend Generalissimo Bridge's Punitive Assets Plan.

"David, how grateful are you to Our Revered Reverend Generalissimo Bridge that He has kept our Punitive Assets stable, while providing for us Comrades to put in more and more hours at our Passion Projects?"

"Very very very very grateful. I'm not too good with words, but you just go ahead and print 'very' as many times as you'll let in, that's how grateful I am. I wouldn't know what to do with any more of those green things. I would just lose 'em or spend 'em on something I don't need. It's really what's best for this nation. It was a great decision of His, and we should all be grateful."

In addition to the Ethics of Work project, which has rid our grand Passion

Placements of the toxins and impurities of secular sloth, Our Revered Reverend Generalissimo Bridge has recently also implemented the Ethics of Thought project. According to the most recent census data, the amount of Godfearing folk in Delaware has increased from one to 995,764: namely, every single comrade in our great Nation. Since Our Revered Reverend Generalissimo Bridge has been able to get comrades to the church on Sundays, he has made it that everyone can share in his great knowledge, and hopefully, He won't feel so lonely, anymore, being so spiritually healthy and learned. The Bureau of Spiritual Health has also reported that spiritual impurity has decreased by a stunning factor of 237%, which places Delaware in first place as the Most Spiritually Healthy Nation on Earth.

As if these two great initiatives weren't enough, Our Revered Reverend Generalissimo Bridge has also had enormous success with His Oriental Initiative. In his efforts to spread Delawarean piety throughout the world, especially in the Godless nations of the Orient, He has instituted mandatory Japanese language programs at all levels of instruction and has increased the number of government officials fluent in Japanese by an astounding factor of 4*.

Our Revered Reverend Generalissimo Bridge Has commented that this knowledge was greatly useful for him during his recent trip to Japan, in which he travelled to Delaware's sister state, Miyagi prefecture, to spread the Word of God.

Due to his efforts, the Word of God reached every single Miyagi Prefecture resident, who all decided on that very day to rededicate their lives to Jesus and his Passion Projects. The Word of God, from the mouth of Our Great Leader, then spread from Miyagi Prefecture all around the country's remote mountainous terrain, where millions upon millions of people interrupted their daily routines to commit their lives to Jesus and all of the Work he has in mind for them. "We should be inspired by the Japanese' industrious spirit," Our Revered Reverend Generalissimo Bridge stated, acknowledging at the same time that, spiritually, they are "heathens", and could stand to learn some things from the Delaware Church of the Protestant Work Ethic.

It is these efforts, Our Revered Reverend Generalissimo Bridge assures us, that will allow us to deflect the threats from that Lower Red Other Place that surrounds us, and to overcome them with our great strength and wisdom, being a great big nation of spiritual might and Christlike willpower. "War is God's greatest gift," He tells us.

*rounded up from 3.93

* * *

Typically, past five in the evening all is quiet, as breeders attend to their offspring around the bare off-campus home that Victor and Juneau inhabit. That's the tradeoff they made, for cheap rent, being cut off from the collegiate ruckus. If by "tradeoff" one can refer to a choice made not through sheer will, but out of necessity, as they cannot afford the new high-rise condominiums meant to house the children of parents with room in their pockets to burn.

In happy times, they meet in Juneau's room, which is bright, filled with plants. In times of crisis, they prefer Victor's room, whose *batons de mort* and old movie posters make decay seem aesthetically pleasing.

One quiet evening, as Juneau reads a book about gerrymandering and Victor chain-smokes in bed, their sloth is interrupted by a brief change in atmosphere. Although separated by walls, their sensations are shared; of this they become sure. As is their unspoken custom, Juneau walks naturally into Victor's room, not bothering with a knock, and sits down next to him on his bed, where the only movement he makes is the inch his left hand reaches to and fro to transport his cigarette.

As they convene, they decide it would be factually incorrect and perhaps irresponsible to describe it as a sound, because if this event had caused any sound, surely they would be at too great a distance to hear it in their sleepy residential neighborhood. All the same, if they had been forced to describe it in one word, nonsensical as such an exercise would be, both of them would have said that it *was* a sound. And it was surely *like* a sound: a call for help, a sharp whimper in the dark, in the way that it bypasses their brains and goes straight to their panicked hearts.

"Must've been some tizzy to stop you from reading."

Juneau's words do not come. All she can think about is what she would *normally* do. *Normally,* she would propose a hypothesis, think of some rational explanation for their experience. *Normally,* she would find a problem worth solving, soon after which point she would find the solution. The only thing she can sense now, unfortunately, is the absence of normality, this she tells Victor.

"How can you feel the absence of something?" Victor asks.

"It's like how you can feel the past, how something was there, and then it suddenly is intangible. You feel that moment when that thing vanishes. Like a curtain dropping on a play: you don't see the play anymore, but you have the memory of how it made you feel. You're just feeling how the reality of it was ripped apart from you, over and over again."

Victor furrows his eyebrows pensively. He lifts his cigarette, inhales an even third of it, and extinguishes it on the windowsill.

"Who knows what is to come?"

Juneau says she doesn't know, maybe doesn't want to know.

"Well, I don't know either. But I'd like to. Call it morbid curiosity." He's deeply serious, and something about it makes Juneau feel uneasy.

"People in the old world went on pilgrimages. They were wrapped up in the ideas of the past, but they claimed to be mindful of their present, while also assuring the goodness of their future. But what if what lay ahead wasn't a spiritual awakening, or a reconnection with the earth, but rather complete, utter destruction? Is there not some beauty in pure truth?"

At this point, Juneau stands up without a word and goes to her room, against all conventions of their friendship for coping with difficult situations, to put on a vinyl and weep while her body twists in mourning.

* * *

It's the last day of the week, the weekend approaches. And yet what Victor feels walking to class is not a sense of relief, but a premonition of some future change which comes to haunt this present moment. They walk side by side to go to class, as they typically do on Fridays, and yet everything is different. They're physically together, mentally apart, separated by some chasm that grows larger and larger.

As they approach the main campus thoroughfare, they watch as an entirely unremarkable group of three or four students becomes a somewhat noteworthy collection of ten, to then double into a small agglomeration and then rapidly grow towards becoming a full-blown demonstration. They have no signs, no slogans, they are being recruited one by one for newly-created and rapidly evolving roles. Hectic and spontaneous as it is, anger makes up for the impromptu expression of discontent. As Victor and Juneau stand watching, fascinated, someone walks up to them, shouts "LAST NIGHT FORT DELAWARE WAS TAKEN," and runs hurriedly back to rejoin the ever-growing conglomeration and preserve their spot.

Suddenly, it all makes sense to Victor: the noise from the night before, the crowds gathering before him. It was inevitable, really, that another one of Delaware's terrenal possessions would be reclaimed by the sea. It was a fact inherent in the succinctness of what the people had come to say, "to be taken" in the passive, without need to explain that some higher force or other had ordered destruction. And it makes sense, too, for those angry about the regime and its control of information to have only heard about the ecological disaster through word of mouth, coinciding in the haphazard grouping of people.

The crowd has grown into a single being, with new appendages expanding it on its sides. But those joining now, as opposed to the brave founders who stood alone, are incorporated into a being that already has existed indubitably, one that has decided on its own battle words: "DOWN WITH UNIVERSITY CO-CONSPIRATORS, COMPLACENT WITH HELL'S FLAMES." Watching as students rapidly splat spray paint upon newly acquired poster-boards to memorialize the newly coined phrase, Victor is stunned by how poetic the words have been, and how hell means so many different things to so many people. *As if it were meant to be*, Victor thinks, joining the crowd. He's consumed by its power. If they are unsure of exactly what they want, they're at least decisive enough to choose their battle words and display their prowess. *Is this community?*

But Juneau does not share the moment. By the time Victor is swallowed by the mechanism, his mouth already joining in on the chorus of voices trying to dispel destruction with anger, he looks all around and she is nowhere to be found.

** * **

The next day, in a televised public speech, Reverend Bridge praises his own successes and commits to larger goals of "trimming government fat" and "streamlining private insurance opportunities."

As so often happens in political speech, words take on meanings never imagined before, even those that blatantly contradict their common meanings. Bridge, referring to his desire to "streamline health and wellness opportunities," means that he will dispose of public health care in one clean sweep and decrease the number of insurance providers to one, thereby ensuring that any "opportunities" will be quickly diminished and eradicated. "One state, united under one wellness provider." "Insurance" is out of vogue, no one is sure of anything, anymore.

Juneau listens to this news, horrified, and imagines that, although the crowd she had noticed stirring the previous day had lost, since the building in the end did burn down, they would be back to put up a fight and counteract his evil.

Although Bridge's misnomers may seem blatantly heinous for those that read behind his lines, many of his followers do not read at all, for as long as they've lived they have been committed to reducing their attention spans to such a level that will not allow for reading beyond one sentence, and they praise him with the enthusiasm of the ignorant. They take his words at face value, because they are flashy, and exciting, in a way that no one had dared to speak before in this lame stretch of land. Perhaps it is because Bridge's language is shrouded in the new nationalistic terminology that no one quite understands. It seems that, no matter what he says, he receives a broad base of support, because every goal is connected to "the Fatherland" and "the purity of the Delawarean race" and other such divisive concepts. For those who do not support blindly, they resort to special methods of persuasion.

When he talks of eliminating all government public health benefits, he speaks of "our Nation's economic health," and then when he refers to eliminating options for private insurance, he says that it is "God's wish for all of the citizens in the Nation he created to be under one umbrella provider."

* * *

Juneau grows tired of finding every garbage can she passes by empty, so upon her third disappointment, she simply throws her backpack onto the ground and turns the other cheek. Maybe somebody will use it. How can she know, why should she care?

Juneau has no intentions of returning to class; it will be her last Friday.

She has nowhere to go, just an inexplicable need to move. She makes her rounds around the campus, she explores residential corners right on the outskirts, draws circles and squares and triangles around these familiar grounds. And in these strange permutations, she perceives something alien, as if everything had changed, despite looking, smelling, and feeling the same.

You can't swim in the same river twice.

But she's not swimming in a river, she decides. She's not swimming at all. She has become an island, content in its distance from civilization. She stops at no time to think about the strange places the thought of water has taken her, nor does she wonder why water is so deeply on her mind.

Yes, she thinks, *I'm an island, remote, floating in the middle of a sea unnamed by humans. And if this deep sea is threatening the safety of my shores, sending a deep, primal fear into the exotic birds and virgin wildlife that inhabit me, I have a responsibility to maintain my geographical stability as long as I can, to protect this paradise.*

I am an island.

She repeats her mantra several times over the hours she spends wandering in the new sameness. As she walks, she becomes less aware of the legs that propel her human body, feeling only the waters that contain her, the quiet lives that call her shores home. She thinks less and exists more, as a member of the great ocean. Whether she speaks these thoughts aloud or not is of no consequence; through her oscillations, through the motion of her (nominally) human body, she would become eternal.

But eternity does not last, or at least it must from time to time be put on hold, and so she redirects herself towards the house that is no longer her home.

II

Zukunftsbewältigung: coming to terms with the future

islands and cogs

I'm an island, I'm in motion, no one can see me in this great big ocean.

Their yard is scant, hardly inviting. The gray chain-link fence intended to separate them from their neighbors is only partially functional. Some patches of the perimeter appear to have been neglected from the beginning of the installation, leaving only a rudimentary partition. Other stretches of brown grass move freely along the houses, the idea of fences in these spots having been quietly abandoned. And so, as Victor watches Juneau pace back and forth, the neighbors are able and welcome to co-observe the spectacle.

How strange it is for Victor to hear Juneau chanting so. Thinking of pre-history, he remembers that she never was a fan of rhyme, stomached only the rarest of puns. One of her most resolute non-political agendas was, namely, to ban public acts of singing, which was but one of the reasons for which her Sunday obligations were so nauseating. But when Victor catches up with her after having scoured the campus north to south just to find her in their backyard, she is chanting. She whips her neck to the side to acknowledge his entrance into the scene, then continues to move, continues to chant.

Victor tries to plead with her.

"You're not an island. You're Juneau. No man is an island…" She turns toward the entrance to the front yard that opens onto the street, responding:

"I'm not a man." She continues to distance herself from their collegiate shack; Victor follows after her. At first, the only aim is to occupy their limbs and gather distance. They turn left, away from the dreariness of their residence, shifting into a new era. Words spill out of Juneau's mouth.

Sometimes she pronounces them slowly, as if to savor every last syllable. Other times, it appears she cannot stand the silence that lingers in between her enunciations, and her speech becomes an accelerated jumble.

I'm an island, I'm in motion, no one can see me in this great big ocean.

Victor is content to allow her to speak. He listens without pause, though he knows she is just to repeat the same incantation. He hopes his manners can cure this madness. He hears her out as they cross the streets haphazardly, taking the risk of seizing pedestrian control. He listens to her repeat herself even as they pass curious bystanders, who crane their necks and burst into quizzical laughter. He knows there is a reason for her behavior, even if he does not know what it is. It is a reason unknown to him, perhaps unknown to her, but that is the way of many things, to occur for what seems like no good reason at all.

They walk in concentric circles that grow ever larger, expanding beyond the gown to reach the town, the vehicular arteries that surround the campus. The buildings where Juneau once took notes and Victor dreamt of night, they are like mere folktales in their distance. The student center where they first met, on a day that seems far away but is only separated from their present by a statistically insignificant measure of universal time, is part of a different world.

"Juneau, what are we doing?"

"What kind of question…"

"Suppose I asked you a different one?"

"Suppose you did."

"Who are you?"

"We're starting to ask the right questions, but we are far from answers."

Victor's efforts to understand, as he sees it, are part of his loyalty.

"Where should we go?"

Juneau shrugs. "Who knows."

"I'd like to have a direction."

"Where are you aiming?"

Victor connects his own dots, the words jump from his brain into speech:

"I'm aiming for the end."

His time had come, to embark on a pilgrimage. No doubt about it, no time to question the forces of fate. What a movie moment, when your life clicks into place. He looks around to contemplate the beauty around him, sees only half-empty beer cans and fresh condoms with day-old contents gushing into the cracks of the sidewalk.

A voice foreign to Victor uses Victor's body as a vessel to pronounce its wishes: "We must be one with nature." Juneau does not notice the possession. She continues her mantra, gaining speed:

I'm an island I'm in motion no one can see me in tHIS GREAT BIG OCEAN. I'M AN ISLAND I'M IN MOTION NO ONE CAN SEE ME IN THIS GREAT BIG OCEAN. I'M AN ISLAND I'M IN MOTION NO ONE CAN

Victor knows where to go.

* * *

Victor leads Juneau to the state park. Though it has become national and changed names, it retains its status as a place of refuge for those who remember. He tells her honestly: "I want to be swallowed up in canopy." This *want* he uses, it is so vague, he is unsure if *wouldn't mind* or *will* are better alternatives, desire and fate converging only occasionally. Ending up in the digestive system of a tree, or of multiple trees, for who knows how the forest consumes those who dare to enter it, does not necessarily seem *definitive* enough.

Maybe the end is near, but how near is near, I want to live to see what lies ahead, maybe that's brave or just naïve, maybe what they say about curiosity and cats is true, but I'm on my home terrain, if there ever was such a thing, and I want to feel what secrets it has in store for me.

They enter the park with no qualms or comment from either side.

* * *

Victor thinks they are moving towards heaven, Juneau thinks they're on their way to hell, and in the first hour or so this ascent or descent that they perceive, they are accompanied by other users of the trail.

They view them as passing scepters, provoking them, challenging them. It's something that Victor and Juneau share, though they purport to move into different directions, because they both think that the road to enlightenment, whether it shoots down or spikes up, will be plagued by these neitherworldly creatures. Whoever it is that passes by them in these moments, not that either of them is in a state to discern faces, is not alive, not real, and their laughter can be only a taunt from the other side.

Victor and Juneau take no mind of the middle-aged bikers, of the gaggles of sorority members on an Instagram prowl, of unhappy couples letting nature speak for them: they simply walk forward, hoping to be deeper and deeper in the forest. With time, the crowds thin out. Victor is most content around this peace and quiet. Juneau does not notice; she is too busy watching the waves settle around her shores.

They are alone; the trail becomes more rugged. This is not the trail they had walked before: the trail that made itself known, the trail that had been shaped by those who walked upon it. The shoes, the bicycle tires, the paws that dug into its surface. This trail is an alien trail, unknown to most, untouched. For as miserable as it is to be outside, no one has the stamina to venture beyond the path most traveled, and cell phone service can only be denied one for so long before the self breaks down. They walk, and walk, and walk, all alone.

"I remember the last time we walked this trail," Juneau says, suddenly interrupting the flow of her own affirmations.

"Do you?"

"I remember it like it was yesterday."

"When was it?"

"I don't know. But I do remember what happened. We came to jump into the waterfall. We brought Julia and a couple of other people from my French class. I said that the water was quite *froid*, but they didn't understand me, so I had to repeat it. They laughed with embarrassment when I told them it meant 'cold' in French. We jumped in together. You were nervous, I remember that. Why is it that you are so shy? You keep all of your thoughts in your brain. It must feel pressurized up there.

And you were feeling pressure that day, too, I remember because you took me aside and told me you were feeling anxious and wanted to go home. I listened to you, and told you to stay, if you could manage to get the energy to do so. And you did."

"After we jumped into the waterfall, we laid out a really nice red and white striped blanket for a picnic. You know, like the movies. It was kind of surreal. We had a *baguette*, a French bagel, I guess that's hypocritical. We ate our bread with jams and jellies, drank some red wine my friend told me came from Porto. I accosted her for bringing Portuguese wine to a French meetup, and we laughed like socialites, like we had nothing else to concern ourselves with but foreign wine. You were smiling, after you smoked your cigarette, of course, and after you had some wine. You were warming up to these people. You might have thought they were fakers, or phony. Or maybe you thought that about yourself. But in the end I decided I would remember that day forever."

"I see." Victor does not see. He hears but cannot form an image of the scene in his head. He wonders if the past is starting to fade from his memory. It would surprise him, to have abandoned all memory so quickly, but he would be grateful, too. Grateful to start anew, without the burden of things carried, real or fake, imagined or invented. His brain rolls around in circles, looking to see if this story can be found in any crevice. He orders the system to process the story by elements: does he remember a red and white picnic blanket? Does he remember being shy around two of Juneau's Francophile friends? A beautiful waterfall? He finds no evidence within himself that such an event ever occurred.

They continue to walk. Victor's mind begins to focus on water. Juneau's mind, of course, is already wet, thinking of the shores she believes separate her from the rest of the world, from language and civilization and port-a-potties. But she thinks of water as a protection against the world, and Victor's mind thinks of water as a protection against itself.

There's no water in the park, no waterfalls to be seen in their vicinity. The water Victor experiences, it is all in his brain. He thinks of the duality of it all, water's capacity to nourish and destroy. It flows in and out, wanting to stay but having to leave; soon it returns, Victor feels that this motion complements his vision. He begins to think of his past, the past he thought was already gone. He remembers times when he had swum in the ocean, at Rehoboth Beach. He had been there with Juneau many times, when they managed to scrape up the gas money. They would go in the summer sometimes to find that the beach was unbearably crowded, and they would look for refuge at some neighboring beach to try to sunbathe in peace, him reading about Marxist theory, her taking a rare moment to sit and stare.

He thinks of when a hurricane came to visit them in the bay, on the northeastern leg of its Atlantic tour. The storm lingered. It did not attack directly, or with intent to destroy, but its gray face led beachgoers to flee.

Victor loves such gray. It makes him feel that life can be temporarily suspended in time, to resume at a later date, when the skies will open to announce the end of mortality. He thinks more about hurricanes, about the times he had ventured outside against his own best judgement.

It occurs to him that, the last time he and Juneau went to the park, there was another massive hurricane. It was a storm of such grandeur that the state had declared a state of emergency. The university was closed, all residents were ordered to shelter in place, and some on the coast even had to evacuate. In their interior college town, they were safer, but not remarkably so. Juneau and he had felt antsy. They couldn't be in the house all day lighting matches and listening to Wynona's old blues records. It also wouldn't do to sit by the window and hide while the earth unraveled. They wanted to see.

Victor had felt fascinated by the idea that open spaces could not resist the forces of nature. Humanless, devoid of our presence, they could still be so deeply alive, so immortal in their longevity. Anything that could fall in the forest to be gone forever would have been a sign for him. So, as anxious as they were to participate in the action, they went to the park. The streets were deserted, the entrance to the park rumbled before them. The rain pelted their bare skin. They had not bothered with rain jackets. It was a rain so thick and powerful, their jackets would have stuck to them just as easily.

They had walked with calm, watching the trees around them cling desperately to their roots. Some succeeded, some failed. They had watched reverently as a grand oak fell just a few feet in front of them. There was something majestic in its fall. Neither of them with words. They had stood still for a long while, becoming one with the petulant storm. Silently, they had gone home and shoved open the door, uncooperative in the mighty winds. Juneau had knelt to the ground, crying, said she was scared of dying, not of the presence of nothing but of the absence of anything, this time Victor had known what she meant.

This is the story Victor remembers. But Juneau's mind thinks of other things, she's an island now, like she continues to repeat in whispered tones. *Perhaps she believes that death can't swim,* Victor thinks to himself. He imagines the grim reaper on a grand circumnavigational journey, paddling vigorously with his scepter. He screams "Eureka!" as he digs his scepter into the ground, ancient but rebranded, to begin a new nightmare. Victor thinks of tears, laughs instead.

"This is my pilgrimage." Victor's thought turns into words, somehow, and must have reached Juneau's ears, even though she does not respond. "This is a beginning." Victor is struck by a spirit of blind hope.

He is, once again, profoundly inspired by the openness that surrounded him. He takes in the wide green landscapes, not as green as before but greener than they will become one day, heaving with the gentle up and down of the land. He doesn't dare call them hills, though that is the only word he can think of.

The hills that are not hills give him pause. He feels small.

"I will purify my soul, find grace through silence, connect with my future." He beats around the bush.

"I want to see what comes ahead. I am ready to be taken in by it. I'll see it, I'll touch it, I'll smell it. It can have me, if it wants. I just want to…feel the end."

Who knows where the end is? Only the forces that propel humans throughout history to undertake pilgrimages could know. Whether that's a God, a shared consciousness, a shared delusion or some interesting mixture, eludes Victor, and is of little importance, anyways.

* * *

Night falls gently, foreboding in its scarcity. The clouds cannot make up their minds. The rains come softly, leave quietly. Juneau and Victor at times walk through sheets of water, other times through dry night. They listen closely to the sounds of the clouds opening to resume their weeping.

Victor sees the moon is full, and he starts to yawn.

"Let's stop for the night, shall we?" Juneau does not respond. Victor leads them over to some trees, and they lie down.

The trees had toppled over. Whether it was recently or in the distant past, Victor does not feel confident. It would be a different thing to sleep on a tree that's just beginning to decay, a tree still with memory of brighter, vertical days, than to sleep on a tree that had long resigned itself to the afterlife. It's a shame he does not know.

They fall onto two large trunks, perpendicular to one another. Juneau reaches slumber as soon as her back hits the bark. Victor lies awake, eyes wide open, yearning to know if trees can dream.

* * *

When Victor opens his eyes to early morning, Juneau is lying on her tree branch wide awake. Victor thinks to ask her how long she has been awake, but he reconsiders and decides to say simply, Good morning, and she nods her head to him in recognition. He feels that his back has turned to stone, or bark, or something else cold and rigid. He remembers people who had recounted to him, in a time when people had nothing else more urgent to discuss, that sleeping on a hard surface is good for one's body, and it hurts his stomach to think of their deception. So far this morning, he has felt only pain.

He lies looking at the sky, of a muted blue that suggests less rain. The luminescence of that shade of blue, pale yet all-engrossing as it stretches over the sky, makes him feel that it is time to leave. He allows himself the pleasure of resentment: of the fact that, if he languished all day, the skies would make him feel guilty. He stands up and stretches himself out briefly to attend some knots that have grown in the night. Juneau follows him.

"Did you sleep well?" Juneau looks at him with a face that suggests that both "yes" and "no" are conversational possibilities. He was right to think his question redundant.

They head off towards the north, continuing the path they began the previous night. Their first steps are not as certain as they were before, but soon enough they discover a rhythm once again.

The sky is consistently blue. Not like yesterday's sky, which could not decide on the emotions it wanted to express and so was in a constant state of flux. They walk together, close enough to touch but not touching.

Juneau's repetitions stop. By the way her face is twisted with the effort of thought, it seems that she continues the battle in her mind. But Victor has no way to know. He asks her if she is okay, she responds with a noise that says little, if anything. He asks her if she wants to stop, she responds by continuing to walk. Though he can see, from the limited way her inner thoughts reflect on her visage, that she's deep in thought, there's also much that he cannot see, could never see, and so she seems to be floating off to a more distant point in time and space.

When he strains to observe her from the side without her noticing, he sees her floating. Victor begins to think of her more and more frequently as an island, to think of her shores, her flora and fauna. She had been a welcoming piece of terrain, a place of calm and peace for those who come from busy mainland provinces. Lush but unimposing, beautiful but never so beautiful to attract swells of crowds: a hidden gem. A welcoming island, if not a bit shy to reveal its secrets at first, an island that captivates one from the beginning, leaving you with more questions than answers.

But now, she is different. Some islands are almost peninsulas, so close to greater expanses of land that they could be considered extensions of it. Bridges, planes, trains connect them to larger places, and so they do not feel so insulated at all, and their island status feels more like a piece of trivia. Other islands are remote. So exemplary that they become islands in thought, as well, as those who think of them can only scarcely imagine what they are like, being so distant and improbable. They become symbols of self-imposed alienation, the "happy place" of pop psychology that keeps working mothers subdued enough to refrain from beating their children. Victor would realize, bit by bit, that Juneau becomes more the latter every day, as her island drifts into the sea and fades out beyond the horizon.

They walk; they do not talk. They stop only once in the span of hours, for a brief "restroom break," surely a term Victor will use only at the beginning for politeness before succumbing to the crudeness of their new outdoor life. Fortunately, due to a neglect of hunger and thirst, they need to stop only once; for to stop for more than a few minutes could mean disaster, the way Victor feels compelled in his duties as a pilgrim. With the exception of Victor's digestive needs, they walk continually, leisurely but always towards the final horizon.

It is late afternoon when they come upon sights and sounds that pervert the forest. At the end of a small hill, right after Juneau and Victor brace the hump and celebrate their accomplishment, they see a great valley, and in that valley, construction mangles the land. They hear the large orange cranes whose garish coloring contrasts with the sober foliage. The trees fallen, the horizon is occupied only by the large necks of the cranes, the collections of matter that rise to the sky to support the new structure.

Victor thinks to himself, *the air is less sweet*, unsure if he can really perceive the loss of the aroma of the trees, the life-giving force being dismantled bit by bit to make room for modernity.

"Must be a Delawarean flag," Victor remarks, trying to decipher which flag it is. As they near the structure, their steps heavy like lead, he can see the design, the light blue of the Delaware bay interrupted with images of firearms and warfare, the name of the new nation accompanied by a trademark sign he never noticed before. It's the design he recognized as the one supported by the most nationalistic and conservative, those whose desire for empire trumped all other practical considerations; the desire to conquer nature, conquer the masses, conquer the mind. The flag presides over destruction and stands content. Victor reckons it is some sort of Delaware government building, but he does not strain to see what it is. It would hurt his eyes.

* * *

They try hard to escape, their steps become quicker. Their leisurely stroll turns into a type of jog, a motion neither of them enjoy or are used to, a motion nonetheless necessary to keep themselves encased in nature's sweet innocence. It's almost an hour before the sights and sounds of the construction leave their field of sensation. Before the aggressive beeping of cranes, shouts of workers, cries of greenery escape them, and they can pretend to be walking, once more, in peace.

What is peace, if not the ignorance of turmoil.

* * *

Juneau admires the waterfall, insofar as she can pull herself out of her own mind, as Victor sits and observes a praying mantis. Once, in elementary school, he was told it was illegal to kill these creatures, and he wondered what kind of human being would need a formal penalty to not destroy such beauty. Even if it had not been for their name, he always would have known that they were uniquely spiritual, their arms always raised to the sky, their eyes fixed to the ground. Their earthly appreciation informs their greater universal belonging. When he learned it was not a federal offense to smash a praying mantis out of this world, he first felt happy, *we do not need laws to know what is right and wrong*, later he realized its exclusion from legislative consideration was due to reasons much less lofty.

He had already broken a tenet of his pilgrimage, he reflects as he remains on the ground. *Failure to move.* But perhaps it is not an offense; perhaps it is necessary growth. The water cascades down into the air, like the princess releasing her hair. He takes a breath of the salty air, it feels good in his lungs.

His eyes do not leave the image of the praying mantis, though the creature does little more than stay still. Victor does not dare to experiment with the creature, to see if it would move if provoked by his finger. He just watches it. It sits on the tree, silent and still, at peace with everything around it. The more he watches, the more he accesses the mantis' state of being. He orders his joints to relax, he thinks about his breath, nothing else. He creates himself new again, in the image of the mantis. Eventually, Victor wants no more but to breathe; he feels less of a need to observe the creature, and more of a compulsion to follow its nature, to be one with its beauty.

He has wondered, running past the jungle of construction, if he has the spiritual stamina to continue his pilgrimage. Seeing the image of destruction cast doubt in his mind. Though he figures it is but a taste of the ugliness he may see on his journey to discovering the end, he feels disturbed by this new intrusion. Hot tears fall on his cheeks as he walks, an urge that has eluded him for many moons prior. It's cleansing through despair, purification through an ugly vessel. He posits that the journey will be a series of contradictions just like this. Beauty that leads to destruction, words that lead to silence, nothingness that leads to deep fulfillment. He's learning lessons, knowing growth is pain; he lets himself feel what comes and take from it what he may.

He had not planned to stop, if not to relieve himself, and yet here he is in rest so early on. Looking at the praying mantis, seeing the simple satisfaction in its eyes, leads him to realize that the journey would require much more calm from him than he expected. As much as he goes forward, he will have to stay still, to process all that changes within him, all that changes around him.

Victor thinks about his breath: in, one, two, three, hold, one, two, three, out, one, two, three, repeat. His body moves in time with the praying mantis, in time with the swaying of the trees that tower above him, in time with the wind. He is one with this system, a cog but happy to be inconsequential, happy to be discovering secrets so simple in their wisdom.

Victor thinks to himself: "I am the breath I control." His thoughts are narrow. He ceases to think of the journey, losing sight of the panorama, settles on the here and now. He knows that journeys are comprised of hundreds and thousands of moments, but for this moment, he pushes the thought away to a deeper portion of his brain, so that he can inhale, exhale, share his life with other beings.

I am but a cog.

catsup

The waterfall's lull awakens them in the morning. This time, Victor's eyes are the first to open. He is unaware of the timeline, of when light turned into dark, when he chose to sleep, what hour it can be. He sees only faint light, reckons it must be sometime early in the morning, and that is accurate enough for his purposes.

He sees no need to rush. He takes in the waterfall, not knowing if on their journey there will be other waterfalls to soak up and admire. He thinks of the bodies of water they may see, all different from one another, and thinks still that this one waterfall is special, having shielded them from the ruckus of destruction and served them in a time of need.

He sees no praying mantises, just some ants and roly polies. They are busy with the industry of their day, their communal gathering of food. He admires how strong the ants are, how flexible the roly polies. He looks all around him: at the trees, at the birds, at the waterfall once more; he thinks, *each one so unique*, serving their role in this great ecosystem, and he asks himself what his role is. Maybe that's the human curse, to have to think and consider, there is no calming that internal storm.

"Maybe it's time for us to be on our way," Victor suggests.

As Juneau rises from the branch, her body says "maybe."

* * *

Beyond the park, their world is different. The sun shines on the roads, on the hunks of metal they avoid as they cross raucous expressways. But Victor doesn't trust the gloss. *What is it that is hidden when the world is illuminated,* he wonders, but he does not speak this aloud. His thoughts are lonely and his body not less so. Ostensibly, Juneau is his company, but in many ways, he is just alone on a journey, just what he wanted and also everything he feared. Their paths do not respect the vagaries of civilization. They make their own, trespassing but never loitering, forging their own frontiers through dead-end roads, abandoned backyards in the stillness of the workday, pockets of forest between the developments where the cars look like the houses and the streets look like the sky and everything is so eerily the same.

Their journey would be smoother if they chose a strategy. If they chose to follow roads, to play the role of an automobile, or if they chose to forage through forestland. But all they can do to stay afoot is to head in one direction, undiscerning. Victor knows he's following what he's been summoned to do.

And so, Victor does not feel that this path is of his own creation, but has been predestined by some force greater than himself, how much larger and how much more ancient he has not the faintest idea, not that he believes in God but he also does not reject, alas it simply can't be that this pilgrimage came about of his own free will. It could never be, no, the logic of it just does not stand, and where logic fails, faith prevails. Where the path is nonsensical, filled with twists and turns, designed for monsters of gasoline and not for humans to count their steps, Victor is sure that there is divine creation in such absurdity. He comes to the realization as he dodges offended motorists, ignores the pleas of entitled cyclists, ignores WRONG WAY signs painted hellfire red: he repeats to himself that this journey is for him to awaken, to see the beauty in destruction, and he keeps his heart open to whatever may come.

Whether ordained or not, they continue on northeast and enter a reserve of forest. Victor does not know it, as it has no markers or signs; he assumes Juneau is also equally clueless but does not ask. He feels grateful to have happened upon a more amenable section of their journey, but feels guilty as well, like he has interfered with destiny in some way, and resolves to free himself from the vices of likes and dislikes. *It's fine, it's simply okay, whatever is here is the only beauty and the only evil I'm meant to confront, even nature has its own terrors.*

They walk, they walk.

It is quiet, but there is no calm in the novel forest. Victor, attempting to accept the silence, feels disquiet he cannot ignore. He tries to think of other things, hoping to pile on layers of consciousness to avoid what seems like impossible silence, but these layers intermix so loudly that he winds up again in the present, where he is suspicious of the trees with no names and the oppressive May heat, feeling things he thinks are inappropriate to feel.

They walk, the trees continue to mock them, as if they had sprung up in just this moment for just that purpose. There is no trail, they make it themselves, they see no footprints and feel lost as if in a world just created.

Suddenly it all changes.

Guns fire.

Screams erupt, these are no animals they are people who scream, Juneau's eyes so large they look back and forth but there is nothing to see.

"Cover your ears and let's continue north" but Victor cannot believe his own words.

Screams but also panting, someone needs to flee and it's not only them, how did this forest grow so crowded, steps run closer, Victor's mind is blank, maybe he's become a true pilgrim.

The weapons, they cry, but the humans wail!

It seems like war, not that they know for sure what war seems like, for this war is so close and the feet trod so quickly on the ground, no longer just noise but a figure from the distance who takes them by the hand-

"Follow me!"

In one moment to the next Victor and Juneau pass from inertia to frenzy.

The man holds them as tightly as he can, Victor pulls away, his feet can move by themselves, but the stranger cries *faster!* He grabs Juneau, Victor cannot see her eyes but he imagines they are empty, oh if he could just tell her it would be okay even if it would be a lie.

They are running, sounds of weapons erupt, who knows what they are, perhaps the man, the soldier dressed in green, he is running but he does not tire, Victor feels like he's choking on tears and he wonders if Juneau will be okay but she

"HELP"

The man stops, he's panting still, Victor barely registers any sight because he's transferred his energy to his ears and to his vocal cords to scream, but he is stopped, too, Juneau is on the ground, her eyes are closed. They look to her, check she has not stopped inhaling air, her mouth opens in a wail but the soldier places his hand over her mouth to prevent her recoil.

The soldier swings his head left to right, he wants to know if they are still targets, it seems everything is still but they cannot be sure, he places Juneau on his back, is she conscious?

"We've got to get farther away," Victor looks into his eyes and sees less fear than he expected, they both begin to run and run to distance themselves from the explosions that continue just along the horizon.

* * *

The soldier tells Victor, when they reach the highway, that they are safe.

"Are you sure?"

The response is affirmative. He holds out his arm to greet Victor.

"I'm Raphael," he says. Victor holds still, his hand motionless. Raphael's hand continues.

"Do you have a name?"

"I'm Victor."

"And your girlfriend?"

"Her name's Juneau, but she's just my friend."

Victor looks to her: though she continues to breathe, her eyes are still shut. Victor wonders if it won't be better this way.

"Where shall we go?" Raphael asks.

"We'll go where no one can find us," Victor responds. The roads call to Victor, they continue to walk along the side.

* * *

Victor frowns at the commotion, wonders if Raphael's addition to the journey will impact his spiritual goals. Raphael walks dutifully, careful to support Juneau. Between the two boys stand many questions, and yet they stay silent for a long while, carrying along.

The hours pass, morning turns into afternoon, soon the worst heat of the day comes and they are attacked by rays of sun.

"Should we take a break?"

How unorthodox, Victor pouts, but he nods yes. So many things are better hidden.

There is no refuge for pedestrians on the highway, it is drive or consent to likely manslaughter, their best choice is to roam the shoulder and hope against collision.

Victor feels himself wondering, and his curiosity will not leave him alone. It is strange that a man in a soldier's green uniform should lead him away from some threat, he admits it for the first time. He looks at Raphael, feels that he must be of another place, perhaps some place far away. His skin is bronzed, his body sinewy from the rigors of military service. Why he is here, in this country, on this highway, in Victor's life, Victor does not know.

"Do you like war?"

"No, I wouldn't say that."

"What brings you here? Are you a tourist?"

Raphael's mouth creaks up at the side. His smiles do not hide. "I wouldn't say that, no. I'm with the Israeli Defense Forces, doing my mandatory military service. Or I guess I'm not doing it any longer, now that I've ran away."

Victor nods with sober understanding.

Raphael turns the question on its face. "Are you running away?"

"Well, I think of it like that sometimes, yes. But you could also say I'm running *towards*. Towards what? That's my question."

"What a duality." The cars speed by, angry to be moving shy of the speed of light. Victor tries to look away. Raphael maintains his vision straight towards him.

"I guess you already understand what's going on."

It is a layer Victor has managed to ignore. The bigger context: beyond this soldier, beyond this strange trio.

"Not really, I could use a refresher."

Raphael smiles again. Victor thinks to himself that the devil himself must have a smile just like his.

"Our Great Leader has chosen the side of the Delawareans," Raphael states.

"Why us?"

"Business interests," Raphael says. "Business, national glory, personal glory…

"Just like the Spaniards…"

"He is a great fan of your Revered Reverend's…leadership tactics."

Victor is so astounded to hear of such global reach, he does not believe his ears. He puts it eloquently: "Really?"

"Yes. Delawarean pop culture is actually quite popular in Israel. Everyone wants to be a

Delawarean. We are now the greatest importer of pumpkins in the world. We eat them, we display them, we bathe in their juices. The Delawarean media is the most highly trusted news source in our country. Words like 'canal divide' are ubiquitous, we don't even bother to translate them to Hebrew, they can mean anything one likes."

"Sounds like quite an industry," Victor says, remembering the times when Delaware did

not even have its own news station.

"We love industries in Israel."

"Here too, we do."

"International brotherhood." Raphael smiles again, as Victor hides himself away. He feels the pressure of a great decision, two paths stretching out before him. He sees himself embarking on his own, *goodbye to you both, I wish you a safe journey but I must confront the tides unaccompanied*, or he would stay, his pilgrimage perhaps foiled, stay for his friend. He never thought his pilgrimage would involve so much agency and active choice. He frets, wishes things would resolve themselves.

Just in this moment, his threads of thought are interrupted once more:

Juneau's eyes open, she looks out to the rush of metal on the highway but fears nothing, stretches out and yawns as if any reality would have been plausible.

"Hi Juneau," Victor says, less in the expectation of a response than to offer Raphael a piece of information. She greets him with a somber expression.

"I'm Raphael." Juneau waves, her body separated from her mind through multiple dimensions.

"Are you okay?" Raphael means the question to be superficial, and yet the tone of his voice conveys a more general concern for the girl who does not speak.

"I speak very little," Juneau responds, sitting still, unaware of the silence Raphael elongates to invite her to elaborate.

"You know, I've got some food with me." Victor remembers humans like to eat. He notices the green bag that hangs from Raphael's chest, military grade like his robes and his body. It occurs to him that neither he nor Juneau have eaten since the beginning, nor have they discussed the urge. But Victor is hungry, staring in this boy's satchel he knows he cannot deny it; greedy energy propels his arms to reach for the apple Raphael extends to him.

"Some fruit, some water, some dehydrated nuts…"

The apple is crisp, as Victor prefers them to be, it feels good to focus on a mechanical life process. They sit together, chewing calmly, as the rest of the world rushes past them. The highway is not a quiet place, but in their bubble they do not feel the rush.

The apple separates Victor from a previous moment in time, Victor knows it, he knows that he has propelled himself along one path and can no longer go back.

"I used to love to eat horseshoe crabs," Juneau says.

"We love them in Haifa. They must be a lot fresher here, though."

Victor stares at the silent vegetarian in front of him, wonders when it could have been that she ate horseshoe crab. He does not expect the truth, but he listens more, in hopes that her claims will not contradict reality any further.

"We ate them a lot. I always made my mother save the eyeballs for me.

Under their bellies, too, they hide a lot of juicy, delectable meat. We would eat them as we celebrated our humanity, our capacity for reason and logic, our ability to bring other creatures out of the living world to suck their guts."

"I prefer their tails, myself," Raphael states. "With catsup."

"We say ketchup here, in Delaware," Victor states.

"In Israel we say catsup. It makes us feel special." With this, Victor cannot argue, as what one feels is what one believes is true.

* * *

Where others believe in God, Wynona believes in routine. Every Sunday, she leaves the house at 5:13PM to allow for the thirteen minutes the route usually takes, as well as four minutes for possible delays. When all goes to plan, she's unencumbered by any delays, and she treasures the four minutes she saves to use them on perusing products she is unable to buy. But such days are rare. Most days, she has a two to three-minute delay, with which allotment she sees the same people, listens to the same AM talk radio show, and weaves through the same traffic patterns.

Today is altogether different, exceptional. Some days have their own rhythm. As Wynona would think, they exist to remind you to stay humble, forget about controlling your own destiny. Driving along roads she knows so well to be able to ignore, she notices a palpable tension around her. But in the metal hut of her automobile, protected from the world by glass and stereo, she does not take much note. She thinks only, *how nice to be alive,* continues the route she takes to the grocery store.

But when she exits her car, it strikes her what comes into relief as she feels the sun on her face, *and on Sunday, the day supposed to be holy* she thinks as she sees the green men that surround the buildings. She looks back to the intersection, sees two young soldiers stationed on the sidewalk. She takes note of the men that operate the tank in the parking lot, attempting clumsily to direct it toward the drive-thru burger joint on the corner. She walks towards the entrance, still calm but struggling to understand, notices a green boy posted at the entrance, he greets her but does not say a word.

Wynona imagines, *war has broken out,* but she cannot remember hearing about it. She reads the news every day with her coffee and her cigarette, and yet nothing comes to mind. There had been gentle intimations, *tensions increase at the US border,* or editorials on the importance of safeguarding the nation's pumpkin supply, but the Reverend had assured the public that there would be no war. Wynona reminds herself to think again, there must be some reason for the logical fallacy, she would do a double think and things wouldn't seem so strange.

And once she ignores her eyes, everything seems normal.

The Friday before, her work had been a circus, even though they had pitched no tent to attract onlookers the circus had come to them of its own volition. Some woman ran into the doors, Wynona hardly processed what had occurred before the woman was at the desk, her expression fixed with delirium:

"HAVE YOU SEEN ELLIOT??"

She stormed in so quickly, Wynona wanted to throw up her arms in resignation but instead her lips went to form "No, I apologize, is there some way I can assist you?", the woman had no time to waste:

"HELP ME FIND HIM PLEASE! QUICK!"

Wynona tried to interject to explain that she did not know any employee named Elliot, though she could take a look at the records, but the woman's face glowed in relief:

"OH MERCY"

The woman was sweating, the beads drained onto the counter and Wynona felt pity, but at that moment the woman also pointed frantically to the back room, Wynona went to investigate. In the break room, she saw a brown ferret writhing on the floor, wrapped up in the cracker crumbs it had rolled into itself. The ferret stopped when she looked in, looked up with bright eyes as if to say: "Have you found my owner?" Though the ferret was incapable of speech, Wynona knew it was meant to communicate this very message, on its own terms and in ways only it could understand. She placed a hand under each of its two ends, it was her best guess for how to properly handle the creature, then she presented it to the woman, who proceeded to grab Elliot, say "thanks" half politely, and walk peacefully out of the reception room as if her outbursts had never occurred.

And so, as Wynona enters the grocery store, she does not object to the green man who avoids her gaze, she thinks only *why not*, what could she do as a meager human to confront the logic of power-hungry leaders. The soldier, meaning to perhaps be intimidating or soothing, she doesn't know which, can barely hide his youthful fear.

* * *

His youth flows through her veins, she feels herself take on a new form as if the calamities of the hour had reduced her years, she does something new: she rambles through the aisles wantonly, with no regard for order or determination. She ignores her shopping list, gathers items on whim. She is gleeful to let loose, let her individuality shine.

She arrives in the cereal aisle, *the colors in spring bloom*, what she grabs and throws into her possession she does not notice, it matters only that it is new and different. Three cereal boxes later, she runs to the liquor aisle, a delicacy she usually only allows for weddings or funerals, recently more of the latter and less of the former, she inspects the wine with new greed, *to imbibe without a reason is to be a free Delawarean.*

As she sizes up the wine, wonders which will look best at her side on her nightstand, *oh yes I'll really show the system if I drink in bed-*

RAM

A man bumps into her cart and appears into view. She abandons the Californian wine, no longer tantalized by the allure of the Pacific Secessionist Vineyards, ignores the pumpkin and horseshoe crab-flavored concoction that brands a Delawarean flag: a man blocks her from her activity, she is startled, she shouts.

"Have you been here the whole time?" Her words come so fast, she doesn't know if, upon exiting her mouth, they shall be interpreted as anger towards him or embarrassment for herself. His guess is as good as hers.

160

He panics but then responds with a simple "No, I just came by and noticed you." Wynona could never know how long he had waited for her. She would wonder all her life.

"It's very possible you don't remember me…"

"No, I do!" She affirms an untruth to ease the encounter.

"I'm Russell Brandt, I sat next to you in high school math class."

"Oh…" She thinks back, *boy the years have passed so quickly*, but she can picture his face. Though it has clearly taken on rings, his face has the same juvenile innocence that she places with his earlier image. She does not remember anything substantial from their time together. She remembers only the image of his face, the way his face crumpled with clear bemusement when the teacher spoke of parabolas, how helpless he would look when she would offer him an explanation.

"Oh, yes, of course. How have you been?" She doesn't particularly care to know, really, but this is the piece of language she finds to smooth over the encounter.

"I've been great…". She notices the ring on his finger, it shines incessantly as he searches around for more tales to tell.

"How about you, Wynona?"

"I'm okay. Divorced, one beautiful daughter. She goes to CSD."

"That's great to hear." He refrains from using her name again.

They stare into separate blankness, avoiding eyes. Wynona's cart remains stationary, however, and Brandt holds his hand basket still.

"She asked me to pick up some bread, but she didn't tell me what kind."

"So that's what brings you to the wine aisle?"

He smiles, she does not notice because she is busy ignoring his gaze, he wonders if he ought to make himself scarce.

"Well, it was nice seeing you, Wynona, I wish you the best."

"Thank you, Brandt, you too."

Their eyes intersect in diagonals, *how did I remember he prefers to be called by his last name,* each avoids the other like animals being hunted, Wynona stumbles over herself to leave the aisle. He goes the opposite way, she thinks of articles she neglected to buy, her mind fixates on the words she said and she finds herself imagining ways she could have been more articulate.

162

the Jersey devil

Oh Wynona,

Tonight, I write.

It's been such a long time, years pass, maybe you don't remember me. I only know that I remember you. My mind wanders: when I'm at work, when I'm lying in bed, at morning and at night; it drifts to your memory. I hope I am not too forward.

It could've been sophomore year, or perhaps when we were juniors. We had math class together, have you any shred of an impression? You were exceptional, I was mediocre. Wasn't my thing. But it came so natural to you, easily enough that you went through the motions with time to spare. If I never thanked you, I want you to know I'm grateful for that time you gave to me, helping me grasp what eluded me then and now.

Most days, though your seat was to my left, we did not speak. Who knows what kind of different worlds we lived in. It all seemed very important. Our teacher was resistant to change, she had few years left and did not want to be bothered with new pedagogy, but I always looked forward to the days when she had us work in pairs.

It seems so ridiculous, it *is* so ridiculous, for me to be stuck with this past version of you, the Wynona that was. It is as ridiculous in my head as on paper, I see that now. But when present reality makes no sense, why must the past? I think of the times you helped me find an equilibrium, back then logic could bring you peace if you just tried hard enough, I found you very charming. I didn't follow what you said, perhaps I wasn't dedicated, I would tell you "can you explain that once more?" just to continue with your conversation, but you can only explain a parabola so many times...

It's so silly, I'm ridiculous, I created a version of a person that very well may not exist. I don't know who you are now, I know I think of the past, I interact only with an outdated version of you that I keep in my head.

And one day you asked me, "Do you believe in God?" My mind had little capacity for anything, much less the theological, so my answer was silly, "Well, yeah, I guess," and you looked at me with wolflike contempt. You repeated: "I *guess?*" And I who had nothing to say, I saw you smile, so genuine but also filled with pity, you told me that if that was my reason, *well*, I had better find a new one.

Now, I know. I don't believe in God, anymore, and there are many reasons why. Sometimes, small moments in our lives leave indelible impressions on our souls. I continue to be fascinated by the memory of your admonishment, how it informed my worldview. If my faith in the Lord is gone, I am happy to report that I still have some faith in humanity.

I don't know how you'll react when you see my letter. Maybe you'll think of me as a creep. I would understand and leave you alone. There may be other reactions, many of which do not result in us resuming contact. It's a shot in the dark. If it's your wish, continue with your life, unimpeded by silly keepers of the come and gone. But, if you find it in your soul, I would love to hear from you, to talk about how you helped me find meaning in nothingness.

Warmly,

Russell

* * *

Raphael steers them away from the highway.

"We'll be safer in the countryside," he says. Victor wants to go to the border.

"It'd be nice to see what all the fuss is about." Raphael advises him against it. The border is dangerous, he says, he just came from there, he can tell him anything he needs to know.

"Is there fighting?"

"Yes."

"Is there open combat?"

"Yes."

"Fatalities?"

"Sure."

"I still can't picture it."

"Try harder. We should lay low."

"Who's we?"

"This group we have become." Victor neither denies nor confirms this logic. The three of them, Juneau without opinion, descend from the highway. Raphael calls for Victor to be more careful.

"If I am meant to be hit by an automobile, let it happen. If my pilgrimage is meant to continue, I will obey."

"That would be a lame way to end a pilgrimage."

"What do you know about pilgrimages?"

"My people have a long history of forced movement." Victor gives him silence, follows his lead. They manage to find themselves in the "countryside," industrial and meager compared to what one may wish to think of as rugged, virgin terrain. Their countryside is on a façade: when they lurk between the trees left behind in the race for residential development, they can feel as if they have retreated from civilization, only for the sound of angry motors to bring them to reality. And when their bucolic pursuits are truncated by ruckus, they pass through suburban developments ever so quickly, Victor reminding Raphael to take great care not to disturb the solemn quiet of suburban desperation.

* * *

They've established their rhythm. Between moments of rapid transposition, they find themselves under the peace of the forest, if it is not insulated from all of the terrors of the world at least they can ignore a great deal of them, and as they pass the time between these two states of being, the days begin

165

to fade.

Victor looks to the heavens. The harrowing azure skies drift into pale shades of baby blue, and the movement leaves an impact on the group. As they drift under a new blanket of canopy, Raphael takes a deep breath, Victor begins a conversation.

"Do you believe in the Sapir-Whorf hypothesis?"

"What would you define as the Sapir-Whorf hypothesis?"

"The idea that people's destinies are controlled by the language in which their mothers sing their lullabies."

Raphael's smile brightens the newborn twilight. "I wouldn't define it so fancifully, but I do believe in a version of it, yes."

"Which version do you believe in?"

"I believe that language can serve to unite a people. That, within our language, we contain the multitudes of suffering and joy that come from the past. That, I do believe, with or without evidence."

"Your language rose from ashes."

"We are quite proud of that, you know. Our language carries our sorrows, our desperation, our wild attempts to survive amidst the challenges we have faced."

"Words are beautiful."

"Well, tell me, Victor, do you believe?"

His own name sounds so different parting from Raphael's lips. "Somewhat, I guess. Not really for myself. I don't particularly feel shaped by my language, this idiom of global beige."

"The woes of a colonizer."

Victor is silent, afraid to offend, but Raphael laughs.

"So you're saying that Delawarean identity is not built around your language."

"No, not at all. It's just the default. We have no special linguistic features to speak of, if we tried to claim one, some other state still in the union would claim to have it, too." Victor knows he is answering a question Raphael already understands, having grown up in the sphere of Delaware's influence. Yet his words do not seem pointless.

Victor's mind does not part from this image of Hebrew the linguistic phoenix, *what a brave creature to defy orders of the aggressively intolerant.* He thinks about words, those that live long lives but change unrecognizably, those that emerge and go once again into obscurity, those who live longer than anyone ever could.

"Could I ask you to translate something for me into Hebrew?"

Before Raphael can ask, Victor specifies *modern Hebrew, please,* and Raphael nods an emphatic affirmative.

"How do you say 'I'm tired'?"

"*Ani ayev.*"

Day turns to night, Juneau shivers from the coldness that penetrates their bodies, *one forgets what it is like to feel the cold,* Raphael yawns, *Ani ayev,* and the trees take guard as they fall into sleep.

* * *

Victor's eyes open suddenly, he looks and sees only the moon, its green rays like daggers. It menaces the earth, in the ranking of celestial objects the earth is clearly under the moon's domain, but maybe it is mankind itself it admonishes with its gaze. Victor feels small like never before.

Somewhere in the distance, there's life playing Coltrane on a saxophone older than time. The sounds are plaintive, sorrow jettisoned through a rounded hunk of brass. The music envelops him and yet is nowhere to be found, invisible. Victor sees nothing, no one. He imagines a man whose lips make love to the instrument's erogenous zones, perhaps it is not a man playing after all, but it is what Victor imagines and the saxophone man is real enough to him. *The beauty of the music is that it makes a grave sound sweet.*

Victor inspects his circumference, drenched in sweat and heaving with fear. He is alone. Over the undulating sound waves of forgotten promises, Victor hears only his breath. He tries to calm down, *take a deep breath* but air will only enter in short bursts.

The forlorn aspirations of shattered dreams come to manifest themselves from the mouth into the air. The sounds of melancholy are gentle but do not soothe him. Victor envisions the man, abandoned under an overpass from which the wealthy and accommodated have long escaped, he's left behind and all he's to do is pass empty time. He marvels at such beauty, even here in the forest where it is alien and does not belong.

The beauty pales in comparison to the oppressive heat. Though the night is dark like scorched earth, Victor feels the crushing weight of suffocation, like his body were to be imposed upon by a basilisk of horrid light, sinking deeper, ever deeper, deep enough to-

Nothing, nothing at all. Victor chides himself for making fantasy. He knows that in darkness, there is only darkness; what is not illuminated by the moon's arresting glow will not, cannot hurt him. He lends a moment of attention to the smooth incantations of jazz, attempting to be calmed, but all he feels is a jealous heat, unwilling to permit any other sensation.

Heat, heat, *ani ayev*, Victor is so tired and yet he knows sleep will evade him. There is a path before him, he can make out marks of feet or hooves, he looks to see all the desperate, harrowed beings who've searched for redemption and found only more pain. The cruel moon imprints a swamp upon the wretched earth.

Suddenly, chills rise up Victor's spine as he hears a moan rise from below civilization. Human, subhuman, creature – Victor does not know, this black hole sun makes him feel as if his own humanity evades him. His body has gone taut. He cannot move, to move will certainly be to attract some evil force, the moon shines so bright, he feels hotter once more and-

The earth, shaking. The music accelerates, Victor listens to jazz played at robotic, unnatural speed. Victor hears, faintly at first, voices struggling to turn moans into words. They bellow, their voices mangled with anger. But the sound rises and becomes more distinct, Victor can almost make something out-

The saxophone's cries become wails and screams under a rotting moon, suddenly Victor makes out the words *ani ayev ani ayev ani A-*

Out of the earth burst hands, Victor's body disobeys his impulse to flee, the music turns sinister, it is louder and louder as Victor watches arms sprout from the hands, they try to grasp at the ground to emerge wholly.

Victor cannot move, he can only observe as the horror becomes more acute, the words are so clear *ani ayev ani ayev ani ayev* but accompanying words are other moans, more primal, Victor tries with all his might to bring himself to his feet but his body doesn't listen. Flesh extends from under the ground, Victor wonders what is risen, the squalid heat prevents him from thinking, the fleshy corpses rise, Victor can see their mouths open and close with perilous effort *ani ayev ani ayev* but they're coming towards him *ani ayev ani ayev* he can't get away *ani ayev ani ayev ani AYE-*

* * *

"Victor!"

Victor emerges into the day, the sun is yellow like before. Victor feels no fear once he realizes he has come back into the realm of the living, but Raphael's face is that of one who has seen death. Raphael peers into Victor's eyes, as if to confirm for evidence of love or hate, then quickly moves away to look towards Juneau. Victor only receives a brief glimpse of the hazel grandeur imprinted on Raphael's pupils. Just as he catches speckles of gold, flashes of green, Raphael moves himself away, like a child caught in its mischief.

"You're alive," Raphael says. Juneau chews a peach, peers over briefly to confirm the presence of life.

"I think so."

"You must be tired." Victor ponders for a moment.

"Perhaps."

"It's what caused us such alarm, hearing you shout like that in your sleep. You kept repeating that phrase I taught you yesterday. *Ani ayev ani ayev ani ayev.* Your pronunciation was meticulous, though."

Victor smiles. "Spaced repetition is an effective language learning technique."

"Productive in your sleep."

"It's the modern way."

"Try as you may to force people to change their speech, to reject their capitalist ethos…"

Though their words are light, Victor feels that something may burst within him. It is not the first time on the pilgrimage that he has felt like there was something hidden within him, desperately seeking to climb its way out. Perhaps it will be Victor's true form. A vampire, a mummy, a dragon. Victor hopes he will turn into a dragon incapable of spaced repetition.

Victor points to the sky. He calls to the object he sees as a UFO. The three cock their heads, hear the cartoonish sound of the missile descending. Downwards, towards earth, it takes its time, they watch it as if observing paint dry.

It erupts on the ground, just as expected. Raphael estimates that it's approximately twenty kilometers north of them.

"Likely just over the border," he says.

"Can you give me that measurement in miles?" Victor asks.

"But Delaware prides itself on the metric system, does it not?"

"Oh, that's just for show. No one thinks of the distance from Rehoboth Beach to Wilmington in kilometers."

Delaware's cosmopolitan status ticked away one Americanism at a time. Victor once again feels the pressure in his chest, he thinks it away as his lude reference to the beach that is no more. Raphael suggests they redirect themselves slightly to the south to put some distance between them and the border.

"Why, are you scared?"

"Yeah."

* * *

They cross over into a small section of forest somewhere past Centreville. Raphael recounts to Victor, *how can you be so disoriented on your own land,* Victor is embarrassed but acts indignant. If the forest had consciousness, it would cry, but it is past that point in its life cycle: the wheel has been turned too many times, too many organisms have abandoned it, it has already sunken into a grave. The husks of trees cover only small pieces of sky, the sun can access them so easily out here. Raphael is used to it, but Juneau is not: she signals for them to slow their pace.

"Never again shall I take for granted a yellow sun," Victor states, inviting his company into the realm of his dreams.

"It looks orange to me. Maybe blood red. In my language, I would call it כדם אדום."

"Well, if I see a yellow sun again, I'll remember not to take it for granted. I wouldn't call it blood red, necessarily; maybe just burgundy. In the meantime, I suppose I'll have to admit that, in this instance, the Sapir-Whorf hypothesis got it just right: even our colors are different." Victor notes the heat of a smile on his face. He does not advertise it, but he also does not hide it, and at some point in his ruminations he knows that Raphael has seen. He wonders if Raphael senses the beast lurking underneath the surface of his skin.

They expend effort moving their bodies and trying to ignore the expired life around them. Suddenly, they hear the faint twill of a bird. As the three of them search confusedly in the sky above, they think to themselves *it isn't possible, not anymore*, and yet the sound defies any doubt.

The bird croons with quotidian vibrato. *Could be joy, could be sorrow, could be the nothingness of aspiration.* Victor wonders what the bird could create with a beat-up saxophone to its lips, what stories it could expel from a body that has known so much free sky. He must content himself to the imperfect interpretation he performs as a member of another species, imperfect even when he tries his best not to impose his will on this lower organism.

The bird sails through the air above them. The patch of grassland stirs, startled to receive another visitor: the felled tree trunks appear to notice the change in wind. They look overhead: the bluebird sings with no reservations. It fades away, its song grows faint.

"Blue like our great nation," Victor says with no small tinge of sarcasm. Juneau twists her hand into an approximate shape of the Delaware land mass, snaps her hand to her forehead in salute. Her body is visibly stiff, and her face's contours display no jest.

Ahead, the bird sounds multiply, it's a mystery where their provenance lies. In the foreground, there appears an image of a golf course. From this vantage point, they can see a clubhouse of several stories, composed of lavish marble with ornate trimming. They can see the verdant greens, extending as far as the horizon allows. But it is not the green of the sad patch of nature, no, nor the green of a hungry moon, but the green of paper bills put on display. They can see the fallen trees around them, they sense the lack of life, the forest once again placed in its tomb by the whims of humanity. It becomes clear that their treasured bird, and the sounds of the ones that follow it, could only have emerged from the golf course itself.

They approach the course. In the reception area, phallic limousines elongated along the driveway squeeze open to allow for portly men in stiff white polo shirts to emerge, orange mistresses in hand. Haggled drivers in the back of the line slam on their horns. Young men in tuxedos swarm around the would-be athletes, become pack mules loaded with golf clubs and bags of libido supplements. The rich smile only when greeted by their own kind.

From where they stand, they can also see several water fountains: one of Our Revered Reverend Generalissimo Bridge sliding into a pool of Delawarean dollars, another of a young woman splayed out on a chaise longue swallowing jewels like grapes. They see, in the distance, large wave pools, and they watch the tuxedo men empty gallon-sized water bottles to keep the water fresh and of the highest caliber.

On the course, the men drive their carts into the water and laugh at the fancily dressed servants who dive in to rescue them, all with an industrious smile. The men grab the decorative birds from their cages, stuff them onto their shoulder for an exotic photo op, and throw them into the air when they are satisfied. But due to the reclamation efforts of the staff, only one bird manages to escape.

Above the main entrance hangs a sign, ETHICS OF WORK, but the men do not see.

* * *

Caught between fatal blows and varicose men in shorts, the three agree to move back north closer to the border.

"I'd rather be blasted," says Raphael. Victor laughs.

"If you're so keen to be blasted, why did you abandon the fight?"

Victor suddenly wonders if he has overstepped a boundary. The days are few but they are also long, and he has come to regard Raphael with a certain layer of familiarity. But Raphael could certainly respond negatively, place distance between them. Which would not be the end of the world, of course, not yet; if he does not appreciate the question, they will simply separate and abandon their so-called mutual purpose.

"War's not really my thing, I guess."

"What is your thing?" They have returned to another lowly forest. Amidst cracked leaves and split sun rays from above the trees, they have returned to the natural state they inherited as human beings. Victor wants to speak words to Raphael, to learn about him and interact like humans do.

"I don't know. I don't only have one. But I can say for sure that war is *not* one."

Juneau nods her head. It makes sense to her.

"How many detached limbs did you see?" Raphael is taken aback to hear Juneau's voice. He strains to think: in his surroundings there are only two others, and by now he knows Victor's voice well, no way it *isn't* Juneau asking him. And yet, he remains incredulous; he answers the question in spite of his doubts.

"I didn't count."

"Could you give an approximation? It's important."

"Why?"

"I don't know, information is always important. Ask our Leader."

Raphael sighs. "First of all, we'd have to define what a limb is. It's easy enough when it comes to an arm, something clean like that. But what about half of an arm? Or even more complicated: what about a groin that is severed off, reattached, and subsequently shredded?"

"You can round up," Victor suggests.

"I don't know. Some things are better not knowing. I try so hard to forget, why do you want me to remember?"

The three walk for a moment in silence. Victor hangs his head in quiet reverence.

"It's just a shame Delawareans hate Pennsylvania so much," Victor states after a pause.

"In Delawarean political discourse, Pennsylvania has always been constructed as the fundamental opposite of Delaware. Canada composes itself in comparison to the United States, or what is left of it now. New Zealand thinks of itself in comparison to Australia, or what of it is not charred. It's a classic situation between two lands with similar histories but different levels of influence and cultural import. Ever since we gained statehood, we've staged a drowning of William Penn in the Delaware Bay each year. There's always a long waitlist to be the person who gets dunked. It's really a great honor. Our schoolchildren play in gym class by throwing eggs at statues of Quakers."

"Really?"

"No, of course not. Did you really believe me? Pennsylvania is so benign, they're practically our sibling. New Jersey, on the other hand, is where Lucifer himself enters this realm."

Juneau adds: "I hear he usually resurfaces near Trenton."

hamburgers, cigarettes, candy corn

Victor slips a cigarette from his pocket as the sun departs.

"When the sunset begins, I know it's time for dinner." As he lights it, Raphael protests.

"You had cigarettes this whole time?"

"I did." Raphael furrows his eyebrows and decides to begin a strike of silence. They stand facing the sunset, receiving its eerie warmth. Though the sun is waning, it still lingers in the sky.

"Any sunset could be your last," Victor informs. Juneau shrugs.

Watching Victor suck on his cigarette, Raphael folds his arms. *Such arrogance.* He tries to harden his resolve: the more resolute his silence, the more likely for Victor to notice. But Raphael, unlike Victor, is not silent by nature, only by conscious effort and repression. Soon enough, the sun is gone, and Raphael must speak.

"I've seen this before," he says.

"They call that déjà vu."

"Who's they?"

"People who pretend to speak French."

The three of them occupy a median that lies upon the long boulevard of a shopping mall. There are few cars to pass by and bother them. Those that do pass, however, act as if on their way to behead a regime, blasting by for their passengers to jump out and run into the mall on a time-sensitive mission to purchase soggy pretzels.

Other than the odd kamikaze driver, the streets are empty. The parking lots extend as far as the eye can see in any direction, there are no cars but the holes of their absence remain, *is this what infinity is like, no maybe just the final frontier.* Raphael speaks:

"I've seen this before. I've known this mall."

He looks distressed, Victor passes him a cigarette. Raphael hesitates, the *baton de mort* in his mouth hangs crooked, Victor wavers before raising the lighter to Raphael's mouth.

"*Toda.*"

Victor repeats: *Toda.*

"Thank you, in my language. Those words came from the heart, not the mind." His words leave an imprint, cause distance to grow inexplicably between them; Raphael redirects the conversation after taking a nice long blow.

"I set foot here. I was looking for some socks. There was a woman bathing in the water fountain, totally nude. I looked at her, astonished, but no one else even batted an eye. It was so strange, stranger to feel like I was the only one to notice. I found the socks pretty quickly, which was nice, then I had some time to kill, so I went for the free samples. Deconstructed pieces of cookies, half-cut French fries, spoons of strange flavors of ice cream. Mustard, gasoline, things like that. I ended up buying a gallon of the rusted copper. It was kind of putrid, but the man was just so proud of his creation."

Juneau nods.

"I remember that. I think I saw you there."

Victor squints dramatically.

"No way. I mean, isn't this your first time in Delaware, Raphael?"

"Yes…"

"So how would that be possible?"

"I don't know. Anything's possible. At least *someone* believes me." He looks for Juneau to nod her head in support, but her attention is on the weeds she upends from the ground.

"Maybe it was a mall you visited somewhere else on this continent. They're basically all the same one."

"This is my first time on this continent."

"So, you had this experience somewhere else, and you're projecting it onto this mall."

Raphael speaks in between puffs.

"You might think that, yes. And rationally, if you look at the facts, it *has* to be like that. But I see these gray slabs of concrete here, and they call to me. They're too familiar. These parking lots, the outcroppings of strip malls, I know them like old friends. It might sound crazy…but I've been here."

Victor pauses to gather his thoughts. "It would be easy for you to confuse this mall with any other. I mean, déjà vu is the mark of our times. We've all been here before, in some way or another. When we go to a place we have never stepped foot in, it's not really new. The novelty is either a performance or an illusion."

"You can't swim in the same river twice," Raphael says, almost smiling.

"I disagree. In fact, we do it often. People may want to believe that changing their geographical coordinates may impact their experiences. It's all fabricated. We live the same lives, consume the same food, drool ourselves to sleep fixated on the same screens: anything to the contrary is just a silly mirage."

"What places do you know?"

Victor searches his memory. "I went to Florida once."

Raphael laughs. "Florida is the poster child for the monocultural swamp. Are you kidding me? If you saw other places, places beyond this ocean, I think your opinion would change."

"But what could I possibly see? Perhaps there are differences between the countries of colonizers and countries of the colonized. But that's just a simple dichotomy. Those of us who have been the pillagers all have agreed to follow the same rules. We're one and the same, nowadays, one axis. We sacrificed faith for power, and sent our sloppy seconds southwards."

Raphael frowns. "That's an oversimplification."

"Is it?"

"I don't know. Sometimes it feels like no place will ever feel like home." As Raphael's voice turns from conflict to sorrow, Victor takes a contemplative suck of his *baton de mort.*

"I feel that too. If you ask me where I'm from, I'll say Delaware, of course.

But where am I *really* from? Where are my ancestors from, before they raped this land and claimed to belong to it? Europe, I guess. But what does that even mean? What's my language, who's my God? I want to love the land my forefathers walked upon."

"You don't need to love your land if you own the rights to it."

Victor releases a smile. "It's a twentieth-century anthem."

"What *do* you love?"

"Cigarettes and hamburgers."

"The vices of the conqueror."

The dark settles in.

"What if there's more to love?"

Victor leaves the question unanswered, fumbling for another cigarette to occupy his thoughts and his wandering fingers. The darkness sets in, everything turns still but the air retains hints of abandoned trains of thought. Under the piercing buzz of the streetlamps, Juneau tortures a worm, Raphael whistles to himself, and Victor takes a step back, resisting the urge to squirm away.

* * *

They awaken in the parking lot. Juneau has rolled into the street. Victor urges her to come to the safety of the median, but she does not listen, he decides they better leave.

They walk eastward, following the highway. Victor and Raphael lead, Juneau stays behind them on the shoulder. Victor feels embarrassed at how good it feels to have someone at his side. The boys keep their expressions fixed, no funny business here, they hide their enjoyment to extend the pleasure indefinitely.

Eventually, after some leisurely hours imitating the flight of automobiles, they emerge near the coast. They smell the signs of industry. They are greeted by a large sign that dominates the shore:

WATER SAFETY COLOR GUIDE

Black – Fumes unsafe for inhalation within 50 kilometers

Dark brown – Safe to drink only when boiled

Blue Hen Brown – Cancer levels sufficiently low!

The sign features a friendly animated trash can. The trash can waves, and from his speech bubble he advises:

"A little gunk never hurt no one, no how!"

The swaying wind lifts the scent of decomposing matter into their nostrils. As they inhale the sweet smells of the industrial yards, they cup their hand to their ears to hear more clearly: the water goes *glug glug*, another tonnage of refuse colors the water. The smokestacks breathe cancer into the air. The scene takes on a sepia tone, like a vintage photograph, and the onlookers think of how lucky they are to be alive.

"Let's have a picnic," Raphael suggests.

"What an idea!" They set themselves down on the ground. Juneau moves her body with grace, like a Victorian woman with a petticoat. The menfolk have smiles glued to their faces, they laugh grandly and make great to-do of the moment. A large ship scuttles through the refuse, shouts an extended cry, Victor comments that nature holds astounding beauty.

Raphael extends his satchel to his company. Victor declines politely, signals for him to eat first.

"You are a guest in our great land!"

"Oh, but I insist!"

"You've gone mad, I could never be so rude!"

They go back and forth. Juneau eventually tires of the charade, places her hand in the satchel and claims an apple with as much grace as possible. She inspects it, crushes its skin in her hands:

"The yellow ones have less worm holes!"

They all reach for the food of their choice, and they dine with merriment. The smokestacks blow ashen-gray bubbles into the sky. Cranes forage for food among the dirty water, find themselves stuck in plastic with no way out.

"Those birds are so clever!"

"How serene! What a treat!"

Across the bay, flames erupt. They barely register the event as New Jersey shoots into fire. Victor comments:

"Oh, if I ever tasted an apple so scrumptious!"

Trees across the other side are ravaged by the hungry flames, the ruckus and commotion of mass migration commences across the bay, and yet the three do not take heed.

"Must be Lucifer causing trouble across the bay!" The laughter that follows is gaudy and sticks in the throat. Ships carry on through the sludge, carrying loads of products for people to store in underground reservoirs and subsequently forget. Juneau inquires:

"How are the raisins?"

"Oh, they're ever so slim!" Raphael agrees:

"Yes, slim and milky. The last time I had raisins this good was when that goat was elected supreme leader of Uzbekistan."

"What an incident!"

"Uzbekistan has the most fruitful candy corn reserves in the world."

"Their supplies are simply ravishing. A great place to spend a summer holiday!"

"Have they ousted their latest authoritarian?"

"I've grown so ill lately thinking of taffeta." Sirens erupt across the bay, emergency vehicles collect with the intent to assist, ultimately unable to protect. A scheduled arrival of goods from Delaware to New Jersey is ignored, the ship turns around in a huff. The carcinogenic mix of smells makes for an appealing picnic background.

"I, for one, am sick of having to debate the existence of gravity."

"Graves make good backgrounds in photos."

"Would anyone like to hear of the time I was pregnant with an armadillo?"

"The sky always turns green before the fields turn blue." Victor guffaws with bourgeois delight.

"Yes, my lord, you are quite correct! The ice always melts before it gets to Tijuana." Juneau butts in:

"Don't take any calls, I'm eating pickles."

"So sorry to hear that, but I wish you a speedy re-entry into our galactic orbit."

Suddenly, the flames rip across the bay with new frenzy, the fires have come to conquer new land. Victor announces with a jovial smile:

"Congress is frying turkeys again…maybe it's time we got to higher ground!"

They abandon their picnic blanket, made from plastic labels they've gathered and compiled along the rocky shore.

* * *

It's three in the afternoon on Friday and Wynona is tipsy. She simulated some sounds of retching on the phone to get the day off from work. Her boss hung up before she could ask not to come in, she took that as permission. The weather outside is pleasant, the sun shines without being overbearing, but here in Wynona's bedroom, the blinds are drawn, and her heart is cold like the old blues records she plays on repeat.

It's been a week since Juneau communicated with her. A week of radio silence, completely unprecedented. Wynona tries not to come on too strong. *Please let me know you're alive.* Wynona thinks the worst of things, she swings into anger that Juneau would worry her so, but her anger just leads ultimately to the same sadness.

"Juneau loved boats as a child." Wynona has taken up the habit of telling herself the stories in her head.

"She would pretend to stand at the helm of a ship, directing it in waters kindred and hostile. She was so valiant. But when she tired of her play, I could grab her in my arms…"

She had hoped, back then, that Juneau would never sail away.

The mail has piled up, first it was a neat stack but then Wynona forgot about the pretense of tidiness, and so the bottom bills could no longer support those at the top. A house of cards fallen to ruin.

She is weary. She can't polish her coins, can't clean the bathroom, can't fold the clothes still stuck in the dryer, but she finds the energy to sort through junk mail and bills.

Then she spots a light green envelope, her address indicated in solid cursive. The sender makes her jaw drop: *Russell Brandt.*

She opens it slowly, gently, as if it could disappear into thin air if handled with too much presumption.

The letter smells like whiskey and aftershave, hoardings of men.

Wynona reads through the contents, her eyes speeding away greedily at first, then she takes another round to savor each letter.

She reads it again, again, again, her eyes turn watery from strong emotion, not necessarily from the possibility of future love but from the weight of loves that never were.

She places the letter down, out of the way of the sobs that could spoil its contents. Her head falls onto the table. She breaks down, touched to be in someone's thoughts, distraught to cause so much disquiet.

She gathers herself, using a water bill to wipe her tears. She then rises from the chair, she's dizzy but soon collects her balance, then she makes way to her coin room to gather up change for a postage stamp.

* * *

They wake to the pungent odor of profit that drifts across the land, reaching them even miles away from the bay. The smell is reminiscent of lifetimes of dread. Victor stands up and yawns generously in an effort to rouse his mates. Raphael opens his eyes quickly.

"*Boker tov,*" Raphael states, gesturing towards the sun.

"Boker tov," Victor repeats with sustained effort.

"Language is the only thing worth knowing poorly."

"And what will you say when I master Hebrew and express myself better than you?"

"I guess you'll become a new person." Victor stands with self-satisfaction. Juneau arises from her position on the roadside.

"No flames today," she remarks, and the boys nod in recognition of the temporary halt of destruction.

Victor makes a big display of grabbing his nostrils and twisting his face in disgust.

"Let's get out of here," he says, and they rise.

the Delawarean folk

When one walks in an uncertain direction, guided by nothing other than instinct and a desire to move, one finds oneself in places one could not imagine. Some might see this as a casualty, others as an advantage, but by and large the majority do not dare to think of such things.

As they take off, vaguely towards south, they speak less and less, feeling dread awaken in their souls. It is like the peace in between the industry of Claymont and their next destination is a fabrication, they see the layers peeled back deeper and deeper.

They walk for some few hours, silent near the end of their trajectory, Victor moves closer to Raphael the closer they are to approaching their terminus.

When they are greeted by the smell of soot and human debris (Raphael confirms the traces of sooty flesh in the air), they know they have reached Wilmington.

Towering above all of the destruction is a national headquarters facility. From the floors that appear to reach as far as the sky, perhaps just shy of heaven and redemption, a banner hangs with colossal size:

"LONG LIVE THE DELAWAREAN FOLK"

And yet the building stands over the charred shreds of previous dwellings, corner grocery stores bombed to a pulp, traces of civilization reduced to unrecognizable remains. Signs of life are slight and faint. Those who have any means have clearly abandoned this damned city, and the ones who remain have little to motivate them to rummage around for scraps of rotten fruit.

Bumbling soldiers install poles from which to hang Delawarean national flags in all of their disputed varieties, adding insult to injury. Victor feels a pang of fear, whispers to Raphael:

"Are you safe here?"

"No one is," all lost souls can do is look forlornly in each other's eyes for signs of human warmth.

Juneau closes her eyes, refusing to look at the resigned husks of edifices and people that populate the lost city. A national headquarters sacrificed – where have the technocrats gone? Delaware City, maybe, but they've left the largest building intact as a last sign of indifference.

Victor watches as a delivery truck pulls up to the sole government building, the only sign of endurance in a city tormented by resistance. The driver deposits the merchandise right inside the doorway, no time to linger, then speeds off with a frenzied rub of his tires, driver door still open.

Standing still for so long, they move around, but the city is all the same. Raphael informs them of a briefing he received on the city.

"We were due to move into the city at any time," he states. "They told us that Wilmington was a site of active resistance, that it had to be 'pacified.' I didn't know what that meant, didn't want to know. The next day, I left."

Victor cannot pretend any longer to be in a new city of which he has no memories. He thinks back to the time he spent in Wilmington in his past, innocent times in which national independence would have been laughable even to him. Times he and Juneau came to peruse a bookstore and feel the energy of a poetry slam, times he came for cheap tacos, all those establishments reduced to smithereens.

What with the forces he and Juneau have unleashed, Victor began to realize it would be too late to stop the flow of the tides, and it pains him now to see their well-intentioned efforts squandered.

They stop roaming and sit in a plaza desolated by forces of destruction. Juneau bows her head as in if prayer, eyes closed. Victor continues to take in the sensations of loss. He sees abandoned brown men hiding under tarnished brown blankets in this flattened city, watches the horizon expand further into the depths of the interior than ever could be seen before. He thinks of the flight of people forced away from resistance, and he begins to weep thinking of what he and Juneau hath wrought.

Raphael looks to him for some time, he does not understand his pain as an outsider but pains to be on the inside, his arm laces around Victor's shoulder shyly and Victor fades gradually into Raphael's chest.

* * *

In the plaza they find only some fleeting hours of sleep, in the morning the city is still the same. Raphael and Victor awaken in the same breath, Juneau takes her time arousing herself from the darkness of sleep. All through the blankness of morning, no one moves; a silent pact has been made to make company with a fallen city. Victor speaks first, after the sun has already begun its downward spiral from a sober high noon.

"I come here to confront reality, and now all I want to do is shut my eyes." Juneau plugs her ears, Raphael strokes Victor's arm lightly.

"What are you running from?" Victor feels defensive, and he shuffles a bit in Raphael's arms.

"I run towards, not away."

"You think I believe that?" Raphael's words fade into the air. "I know that you are searching for something, I feel that from your heart. But the person who searches is also one who runs. That doesn't mean you know what it is. Doesn't mean it's even one thing in particular. But I feel there's something you're hiding."

Victor falls into a hostile silence.

"I don't know, Raphael. Maybe there is. I just wanted to see what would come ahead, you know? I had my hypotheses, of course. I foresaw destruction and decay. But when you see it all closing in on you in real time, it's not the same sensation."

"Did you stop to think that your pilgrimage would not only be insight into the future, but also your past?"

"Never. I was transfixed on forward motion. Ever forward, ever towards the sky. But being on this journey, in the midst of this destruction, it feels like my mind is moving backwards."

"Maybe that's just what you need."

Victor does not respond, but he stays attached to Raphael's touch. A forager passes by, hunched over in a coat several sizes too large. Victor waves. The man sees, stares towards them for some moments, continues on sullenly.

The afternoon drones on in its languid stupor. The dead city moves only faintly, the three of them not at all. Hours pass, unremarked.

In the evening, Raphael suggests that they eat. Juneau refuses any food, but Victor takes an orange and consumes it meticulously. There they lie under the soft light of the night, the moon the only force in this world to shed mercy on the city of ruins.

* * *

It's the first day of school, not preschool but real *real* school, I can learn to write words all by myself and make some friends. I was excited in the car, mom even gave me three dollars for lunch, but when we get to school, my tummy feels weird.

Mom kneels in front of me and tells me everything will be okay, I smell cherry blossoms fresh and fragrant. She's got a sparkle in her eye; I won't cry, I won't cry. Mom slips a tissue into my new backpack, I told mom I *had* to have the big green one but I don't want it anymore.

No crying, you're big now. My nose is all runny but that's because it's springtime and springtime brings sniffles. There's some clouds in the sky: one, two, three.

"Are you excited?" Mom sounds excited but her face is a little sad.

I smile big and happy, even though the Tooth Fairy still has my front tooth.

My new teacher comes outside and tells us it's time to go. I tell mom to kiss me quick so the other kids don't see, then I go in the hallway and see her standing outside, not squatting next to me anymore but waving from far away. I think it's too late to run back outside and tell her I'm sorry, she can kiss me if she wants, I'm not so big.

But soon our teacher takes us into the class and shows us our seats, then she gives me a tissue and I hide it in my back pocket.

***

The coffee grows cold, in their cups and in their bellies, becoming just a warm memory. Yet their conversation does not know the bounds of their letters, written with the intensity of lovers who sense the art of calligraphy will soon disappear; the space between them shrinks, but slowly, and neither dares to mention the heat of their postal exchanges.

Brandt asks Wynona what she does with her time, and abruptly she feels she's on the defensive. She cannot not inform him of her obsession with coins; surely, when the time comes, there will be a more flattering word than "obsession." Or perhaps it's time; perhaps, it is best to release such things into the air to give him the chance to abandon the café.

No: she won't. She looks to the wall behind him, up at the ceiling, searching for answers in places with no words. Finally, she answers him: "I watch video tapes, sometimes." *How exciting*, she thinks. She becomes confused by herself, by the way her mind keeps swimming in a pool of nervous doubt. Who's to know what the next moment will bring?

He looks at her patiently, neither demanding clarification nor shaming her silence. She continues: "I don't have cable anymore, you see. But I have a few tapes, of some things I recorded years ago. I really like documentaries."

"Me, too." They hold a pause.

"So what do you do, Brandt?"

"Russell, please."

"Russell…what do you like to do in your spare time?"

"I'm a pretty normal guy, you know. But I guess I *do* have one hobby that overshadows all the others…in that case, I might even say that I just have one, really, because none of the others attract so much of my attention. I'm a bit of a…radio enthusiast."

Wynona smiles: Brandt doesn't know what lies behind it, but she knows a sweet relief.

"What do you do with your radios?"

"I listen and I communicate. I like to tune the dials. Hear its music, you know…I like it when the host tells me what I'm listening to. It's like someone's there to experience it with me, I guess."

"What kind of music do you like most?"

"I like music that buries itself deep into my head. Music that's nostalgic, but timeless. Is that a kind?"

"Who am I to say?"

His grin is playful: *touché.* Wynona feels a sort of warmth in his eyes that he lacked before, something less restrained. She directs her gaze away, but her smile does not receive the message to pull back.

"But if I were to describe my music tastes in less romantic words, I would say I like jazz. Not that all jazz is equal, of course. Some is really energetic, some is really mournful, some just seems to be floating in time." He wonders if he has said too much.

"Well said," she says calmly. "I guess I'm not one for music."

"How could that be possible?"

"How is anything possible?" Her expression turns into a quizzical, questioning frown.

"I'm not qualified to answer that, nor interested enough to try. But music is so universal, so diverse – how could you say that you weren't one for *music*, just refuse all kinds of music in one clean swoop? There must be some sort of music you like."

"Is silence music?"

"Not in my book." There's the smile, back for some seconds.

"Well then I suppose we'll have to agree to disagree."

Silence comes to visit their table. Neither Wynona nor Brandt find its presence pleasurable, despite Wynona's usual preferences. Their eyes seek opposite directions in which to appear busy and fake being unbothered by this sudden arrival. Lips pursed as if to whistle, no sounds dare to come. Then, finally, Wynona's will compels her to continue the conversation:

"So, what do you do with your other radio?" Brandt looks back to her.

"That one's for communication, with people from over the world. You just put out a signal and let lonely souls contact you."

"Would you say you're lonely?" Brandt regrets his choice of words.

"No, I wouldn't say it, I would keep it hidden so no one could see." *Too much,* he thinks. Wynona just looks at him as if expressing vague, socially obligated sympathy.

"But it's really neat. I've made all sorts of friends. There was a man in Chile I used to talk to quite often. My high school Spanish is pretty rusty, and his English was nonexistent, but we made it work. He told me he'd been in the hospital for a bit, got bored and started fiddling around with his brother's ham radio.

Never thought his condition was that serious, until he told me that he knew his time was limited. Like, *weeks.* He said it was a bit of show, the hospital and everything, for the family…"

"I haven't heard from him in a while…last time, he happened to catch me on my birthday. My, uh, wife, she had, um…failed to remember the date. But he knew, somehow, even though we had made no plans to talk that day. And he sang to me. It was really funny."

"But you didn't hear from him after that?"

"I can only assume…"

"Where birth comes there is death…"

"And he was ready for the end."

Wynona's face grows heavy. She changes the conversation with haste: "Did you ever meet anybody else?"

"Sure, I did. There was a young boy in Russia who I used to end up on the radio with every once in a blue moon. He always recognized my voice. He didn't know much English. Mostly he just repeated random sentences, like from a textbook: 'I like to play sport. I felt sick yesterday.' But that was all we really needed."

renounce the condom

They stare breathless at the empty expanse on the bay. Here a bridge stood, from Delaware over the bay to New Jersey, before Delaware rid itself of this continental yoke.

They left Wilmington the day before, shortly after dawn emerged. Victor took the lead, and they headed south, inexplicably south, until they could breathe in the fumes of regime change.

The silence is what most captivates Juneau. Not only devoid of sound, but devoid of memory. There is no commemorative plaque, no record of Delaware's past condition. Juneau ponders the unfortunate unfolding of her plan.

"I'm caught between reality and my own constructed narratives."

Victor feels it so pleasant to hear her voice.

"We all have our own ways to cope," Raphael states. Victor feels a personal renaissance.

"I just feel...mesmerized. It was a goal of mine, you know, on this pilgrimage, to be face to face with destruction. I've seen it already, but here it's so blatant, and the destruction has given rise to some sort of... animation."

"What do you mean?" Juneau and Raphael both listen intently.

"You can feel newness in the air. Forget the smog, forget the sludgy bay. Here lay a symbol that was blown into oblivion. A tangible sign of destroying the old to ring in the new. And yet here, this newness is not exclusively what the Reverend purports it to be. It feels fresh, like there are other possibilities."

Juneau descends to the shoreline to see if any bridge debris remains.

Victor and Raphael stay where they are, standing in a sort of asynchronous harmony, Victor's hands are in his pockets and Raphael longs for a cigarette.

"Would you call it beautiful?"

"I might call it that. But I think there's a lot of words you could use," Victor responds. "Beautiful, captivating, sobering. All of these words express a different facet of it. Maybe it's too gargantuan to put into words."

"I believe in your dreams." Raphael strokes Victor's arm.

"My pilgrimage dreams?"

"Yes, habibi." Victor stands still, allowing himself to be pet and yet making no further move. Something inside him, not so deep but deep enough to be hidden, struggles to reach out to Raphael, but every time Victor tries to put it on display, he feels the threat of a loss of air, a loss of himself, who he shall be if he falls into temptation.

"Raphael..."

* * *

In this constant night, the woman in the sky keeps her eyes open. Long ago are the days when she needed sleep, all she can do now is pleasure herself with memories of dreams she used to have.

She circles around space, flying in an undetermined pattern in the cosmos. In her bubble she is all alone, in the little space she occupies she must lie permanently flat; her legs do not remember what it is like to extend. She lies morose, glancing at the stars that speed by her, but the light does not make her soul feel less dark.

She lies in silence. Silence all around, in her bubble and beyond its reach, the air is thick and it makes the physical notion of yearning much more intense. She twists her hair into fair ringlets, it descends to the small of her back. Having nowhere to go, it grows.

She has resigned herself to most of the realities of her protective shield, the one that allows her to graze through space and forget the home planet that once existed. Everything becomes so ordinary and everyday when you do it long enough, and she has been floating for much too long not to have

192

already given herself up to the tedium of space time.

There is only one of her human desires that continues to plague her in her waking dreams: that of touch. To touch a body outside of her own, as her own fingers no longer satisfy. The desires come to her in waves. She forgets them often, pushes them back into another space, but they always come to conquer her yet again, the waves feel like the undulations of the sea forcing themselves against her spine.

She calls out to the world, "hello, I've fallen in love," but the sound waves travel only within the small bubble that encapsulates her yearning hips.

"Sweet nothings," she groans, "won't you whisper sweet nothings in my ear."

The manifestations of solitude continue to pierce her body, from her toes to her scalp, it is only through these corporal sensations that she can remember to feel anything at all.

"Come to me," she begs, "I see you close, can't you hear me."

She remembers tears, that friend that comes as a reminder of her futile being. The tears cause her fiery ringlets of hair to grow wet.

* * *

Juneau's in a mad rush to master her new game of silence, from the look of resolution on her face Raphael thinks she'll find great success. Meanwhile, there are no other voices to soothe the wounds of broken conversation. Having decided to embark once again on the open road, their words expire; Victor and Raphael walk through the physical and emotional distance they continue to create, their eyes avoiding each other nervously.

Victor feels the hole he digs himself into, is clueless in bringing himself out. Raphael, on his end, feels that Victor is being intentionally sheepish and recalcitrant, and it makes him feel like less of a man. *How dare he impose himself upon me*, Victor huffs, *how dare he reject the advances he knows he wants* thinks Raphael, and yet in both of their hearts all they feel is the nonsense of an evasive strategy that benefits no one. If they hang their heads to express their sadness upon failing to connect, they scowl, turning their faces purple, not to show any outward weakness. The road ahead offers no solutions, just a heap of open space allowing for any matrix of possibility.

Their walk is slow and deliberate. Victor puts a little bit of anger into each step, his movements inculcated with toxic passion. Raphael mutters to himself every now and then, whether Hebrew or English neither he nor the outer world can tell, all anyone can see is that he feels great frustration yet no capacity to address it. He feeds off of Victor's energy. The more Victor withdraws, the more Raphael punishes the earth with retribution. *For every action there is an equal and opposite reaction.* A bird flies above embracing freedom, highlighting the futility of their intrigues, but only Juneau looks skyward to notice the conundrum.

* * *

They awaken under some overpass, today much the same as the day before. A bird greets them on the beginning of their quest, sings its graces.

"Nice bird," Victor remarks in a rare sign of possible compromise.

"I find it ugly."

Raphael's words are unforgiving, Victor makes an effort to manipulate his faint muscles further into anger and scorn.

Juneau giggles quietly, the silly games of these petulant boys bringing her back into reality momentarily.

Victor looks to Juneau, as if to request her support on his side of this great war he fights, but she is evidently unavailable from the way her face says, "I will not get involved in such ridiculousness."

And so the day passes begrudgingly, waging war is no fun but someone has to do it. Raphael and Victor think deeply about the empires they build, so deeply that they fail to see the bliss they keep out through such monumental fortresses. But in such cases, honor prevails over the yearnings of the soul, or so it has been prescribed along centuries, and Raphael and Victor know not in this moment how to stop the cycle of their masculine solitude.

"Let's take a break," Raphael states, maybe his use of the first-person plural is an olive branch extended more or less gracefully, but Victor informs in a voice louder than anticipated that he is not tired, not weak, not willing to stop. Raphael sighs, Victor harrumphs, Juneau's eyes disappear into the crevices of her brain canals.

Victor thinks only of the construction of the grand fortress, no one shall penetrate his kingdom no matter how lonely and devastated he becomes, no matter how much his heart calls for him to tender a truce. The flames in the sky fly with confidence, flames of ire, flames of desire, flames that continue to multiply, stoking a conflict that never ends.

* * *

In the morning, the boys having passed a sleepless night under a mocking sky, they realize they have arrived at Delaware City. If the munitions have taken respite in slumber, it is clear that the bellicosity of Delaware City, in all of its imperial glory, will bring the boys back to their defensive positions.

Workers roam busily around constructing the new city. Construction of a statue of Our Revered Reverend Generalissimo Bridge takes place just around the shore, it appears the plan is for the Reverend's graceful face to greet allied and malignant boats alike. The city's walls go up in extended motion, soon enough the whole town will be surrounded with great fortresses but for now they can only obtain so much forced labor. A reminder of this Delawarean weakness hangs just inside the city limits:

"RENOUNCE THE CONDOM, FOR GOD WANTS YOU TO HARVEST DELAWAREAN KIN"

In a moment of diplomacy, the three marvel at the new city. In what had previously been a sleepy industrial outpost, a new center of empire has sprung up. The departments of trade, of proselytization, and of information control loom over the city, their entrance signs proclaiming allegiance to Our Revered Reverend Generalissimo Emperor Bridge, the title having been extended once more in their absence.

The buildings, the wares that frantic citizens obtain from the large purchase centers, the coffee technocrats guzzle between meetings are all imprinted with various images of the Delawarean brand. Pumpkins abound on every street corner, the trademarked logo of Delaware's new sleek corporate image pops off of every surface, the husks of horseshoe crabs hang from fishlines above the busy thoroughfares.

Planes hover above, busy like the people that rush around as if constantly in danger of seeing something ghastly, painted blue and gold they are like giant birds. They do circles around the airspace, a question is left open: are they protecting the people from the American outsiders, or protecting the government from the people? No one stops long enough to wonder.

Having been entranced by these new visions, Raphael and Victor briefly forget the waging of war, but soon enough the displays of power make them want to stretch out their chests in egomania. Juneau suggests they walk towards the shore, Raphael and Victor eye each other with deep suspicion before following her lead.

They walk through the streets, though the environment is tense like a corpse full of lead Raphael and Victor do not notice, they are focused on their next move.

They reach the shores. Juneau inhales the rancid smell, though the sea is rotting it is surely better than the smells of unwashed bodies on pilgrimage; she prepares herself for a speech.

"Just across the bay from here, a few kilometers away, Fort Delaware stands."

"I don't see it."

Victor sniggers audibly, *how foolish*, until he looks in the bay and remembers that Fort Delaware cannot be seen any longer, as it was swept under the water by hungry waves.

"A layman would say that, yes. But for those who *believe*, it's right there. That's the difference between a Delawarean and an outsider. Fort Delaware just appears invisible because we've created a sort of invisible blanket to cover it, hide it from our enemies across the bay. It's an important monument to Delaware's military strength. Many an evil New Jersey naval vessel pacified there. We would ask the ne'er-do-well sailors to pronounce *water*, and those that did so with the cacophonous patois of New Jerseyans were decapitated with a gliding stroke of the hand. Today, Fort Delaware is a center of naval operations. Its strategic location allows it to be very useful to the regime."

Victor cannot dispute the information, as doing so would make him look weak. He does not allow his face to avow the seeds of doubt. What he knows, that Fort Delaware was already claimed by the sea, he conceals from the other side. He would never allow such information to leak into foreign hands. He peers over to the commemorative plaque: he sees that Raphael is headed for it, so he races to get there first. It reads:

"Fort Delaware lies in the bay approximately seven kilometers from the shore. Although foreign media sources have reported that it was overtaken by the waters, that is only a Northeastern fabrication. With the aid of advanced cloaking technology, Delaware can conduct important intelligence operatives with its strategic position close to the Enemy. The fortress has a long history of protecting Delaware from the sordid lands across the bay, and it continues that proud history today, conducting bomb tests, fumigation attempts, and other experimental imperatives for the further promulgation of our Delawarean exceptionalism."

Sometimes, reality is stranger than fiction, Victor thinks all to himself.

the Delawarean psyche

On the outskirts of Delaware City, Victor relates a sudden revelation: "We must walk by the canal." Raphael must oppose the motion.

"No, we must go south."

"If we keep going south, nothing will change. We must go west, like our forefathers. By the canal, we can return to the simple, reflective roots of the pilgrimage." But Victor, of course, is not purely concerned about spiritual growth. As much as he blames Raphael for the new directions his pilgrimage has taken, his real qualms lie in the control of power. Victor stomps towards the west, the two souls left behind waver. Juneau thinks it is not fair but does not want to argue, so she follows, and Raphael, muttering under his breath, drags himself in the same direction. He gains speed to catch up with Victor and give him a piece of his mind.

"You fool – what will going west do for you? It's all the same, you'll be the same person here as you will there or any point south. So why the sudden impulse?"

"Must've been a sign I've heeded from above."

Raphael scoffs. "You think the messengers speak with you?"

"Well, they would speak to you, too, if you were a better listener."

"But don't we need to go south first, anyways, to reach the lengths of the canal?"

Victor shrugs.

"Southwest, I guess. What do you know about Delawarean geography?"

"Probably more than you do."

Victor asks Raphael to name all of the incorporated communities in

Delaware in alphabetical order. By the time Raphael reaches Odessa, Victor stops listening.

They continue playing their silly games. Juneau lags behind the two, wanting nothing to do with their strikes of stubborn combat. They are two separate poles, Raphael intends to shift the group's direction to the south while Victor pulls towards the west, it occurs to neither of them that the middle point of these two directions will bring them precisely where Victor wants to land.

On and on, they continue; the canal calls.

The division between the industrial North and the great plains of the South, a marker of separation, will accompany them on their journey; as much as they might challenge labels and notions of difference, their minds will think only of war tactics.

Hours pass. Despite the fury they plant into their limbs, they move with the lethargy of those whose energy sources may soon expire. The sky is dark overhead when they finally set their eyes upon the canal.

The three of them stop for a contemplative gaze. All that flows in and out of Delaware, it seems, rests upon this little canal that stretches into the horizon. There is a small sense of disarmament as they rest their eyes upon the bridges that connect the two worlds, the lights that dot both sides, rising up to the sky. For this brief moment, it appears ineffectual to argue about anything, as all three of them can agree that one day their souls will rise to a dark sky and rest forever, and anything else to be perceived is just a distraction from this essential fact. Stars beckon wildly above, the moon smiles wickedly.

* * *

Victor looks forward, thinking of what will come next. He has been transfixed on the future for some time, now, having lost perception of his present self, or at least having chosen to ignore any present sensations in favor of prophecies to come. In this same way, he has begun to ignore Raphael, move him to the side.

But these prophecies do not come sequentially. They come in bunches, in broad strokes of light and darkness. Once he does envision what is to come, he cannot put words to it, nor can he assign any emotions to the things that he prophesizes, and so these thoughts are not useful but simply mesmerizing, like it would be to watch someone in a universe far, far away cry out for help, to be hearing their wretched moans while powerless to do anything but hear. Victor reaffirms that one *can* feel the absence of something as he tries to perceive the scant recollections left after his prophecies march away.

"Where are we going?"

"I don't know," Juneau replies, stale, her words betraying no sign of irritation or impatience, merely a resignation to the present and the future and the past, and whatever other spatial concepts humans have not named.

"Me either," Victor says with wonder, though he does not know if what would come would be bold and beautiful, or an absolute horror. He's frustrated that he cannot interpret the fierce blue that shoots through him gallantly, as if the sky had fallen from grace and were moving through him to hide and keep its dignity.

They walk in silence for some time, him paying attention to the acrobatics in his mind, her grounding her thoughts by looking at the ground, Raphael taking time to peek into the depths of the canal. Victor looks over from time to time to to try to catch something in Juneau's eyes, see if perhaps the eyes really were the portal to the soul, but she is always hunched over, facing the side, and his attempts are null. She notices him staring, feels the heat of a nonverbal inquiry, but she ignores it until her love for her friend overpowers her desire for secrecy; she turns around so he can see a sort of primal longing betrayed in her eyes.

After this moment, she shakes her eyes apart from the water's gaze and faces forward once more. They walk together and feel together, as if they are one and the same, united only by the spontaneous shared idea that they have become true opposites. It is strange to feel they are two sides of one coin that cannot see the same side of the sun, but it is the position the stars has given to them, and so they walk obediently.

Juneau becomes enshrined in thought. She thinks of what has come and what has gone, but not of what has become of them, only of their past forms that live in her head immortally. And as she thinks, she says, "One day, we went to Port Mahon."

Victor wants to ask, "who is we," but he does not have time, because Juneau begins to tell her story, seemingly to neither of them in particular, and if to anyone, mostly to herself.

"Yes, mother took me there. She said we were going somewhere special. It looked like the end of the world. I remember that we had to pass through several worlds to arrive at where we came. We passed through that small, forgotten town at the head of the road, and then the deserted road that led to the road, left unpaved and without asphalt, a relic of another time.

Everything was sandy, mother drove more slowly. On one side were grasses so high, so wild. And on the other, the bay. I couldn't see very far. I made out some land masses in the distance, but I didn't know what they were, so I made believe it was Timbuktu.

And we kept driving, she asked me what I thought, I said I thought it was the end of the world. The point where misfit sailors come to be dropped off into the abyss, a stop from which one does not come back. The sky was big but made me feel claustrophobic, so frothy and tempestuous, it mixed with the sea and I could barely see where we were on land.

And she parked the car, it was a one-lane road but no one else was there, so we could go stand on the pier and pretend to touch the sky. I was short, I was tiny and young, and so she lifted me herself, told me to reach for the stars, as if I could comprise the extra length necessary to reach the heavens."

"What aroused your memory?"

Juneau frowns, confused by an illogical question. "Port Mahon is an integral part of my Delawarean psyche."

Victor nods, his eyes adrift, head in conciliatory motion. They continue by the canal, not stopping for any motive or reason, Raphael huffs and puffs on the boundary. They keep going as is their destiny, to reach whatever it is they are bound to reach. This makes Victor smile, makes Juneau weak. And as they continue, Victor thinks to himself, what will the end of the world look like, what will it smell like, and Juneau buries herself deeper in silence.

* * *

They have slept, it is a new day and there is a new surface to explore. It is not a discovery, no, clearly this land has been known to waves of explorers, and there have been many discoveries and many destructions that have shaped this land into the one they see before them today, to perceive it as what has always been natural and good.

But regardless, there is a sense of another discovery, if the sun sets and rises each day is that not also a discovery about which to exclaim? The light of the brazen sun makes the canal water ooze with sultry power.

Without words they begin to make their way along the canal, and Raphael replaces any disdain he held previously for a new reverence. All is somewhat new, perhaps refurbished, it is not as if things did not exist in the past but they all seem so faint and elementary now, too much so to pay much attention.

This is no canal for walking, the only paths that guide are designed for humans in bulky metal blankets, but they pursue their interests anyways. They walk without a care, occasionally a car passes but they coo themselves and say that cars are more afraid of them than they are of cars, they throw their impediments to the wind.

Time passes gently as they soak it in. They walk upon a boundary, even Raphael as a foreigner knows these tight notions of separation, their own lives reduced to the slight space between one named thing and another. The north, the south, outsiders that stride the midpoint.

Juneau is taken by the water. Crisp and slimy, just as they are used to on the shores by the bay. She beholds it, if the water were clear she would certainly drown in the likes of Narcissus, but all she sees are tossed diapers and dried-up tissues. Without hesitation, she begins to remove her clothing. Though she is in no rush, she is eager to feel the water on her skin; her body open to the skies, she climbs into the water.

While Raphael and Victor stare at her in amazement, she supports herself in the water with calm strokes of the arms. Victor wants to advise her to avoid the waste, but it would be so worthless a piece of advice, given that the entire river is a breeding ground for homeless refuse.

She takes her time in encouraging them to join her. She waddles through the thick waters, glides to and fro with the fumbling motions of one imitating a ballerina.

She calls to them: "Come in!" Her face is resonant with a broad smile, not that of extreme joy but of extreme contentment, which of course is not the same. Victor and Raphael glance at each other, puzzled. They stand in silence, watching Juneau conduct her own symphony in the canal's dirty waters. She calls again: "Join!"

Victor is too nervous, but Raphael shrugs and begins to disrobe. Victor feels tinges of several emotions plague him all at once. He is suspicious, he is nervous, and Raphael is still mostly clothed: how will he feel when they are all exposed? Raphael jumps in ostentatiously, gives Victor a nod of sportsmanship.

Raphael is not quite as overjoyed as Juneau, but seeing her so peaceful inspires similar feelings in him to sprout. Victor tries to occupy his eyes but they keep orienting themselves towards Raphael, somewhat as an enemy but also a temple of theatrical beauty, *look how golden he is in this foreboding sun* and all of a sudden Victor is preparing himself to enter the water.

As he slips in, he feels eyes on him, his stomach feels heavy and fleeting at the same time, he races in to cover his bottom half.

And so there they are, the three of them. There is some sort of harmony that unites their disparate existences. Perhaps it is the call of the ships, groaning like whales in their market missions.

Maybe it is the remnants of consumer preferences that surround them.

A water bottle passes by, crunched up and abused beyond all recognition, except for the brand name that has survived the mangling of greedy hands under a black sun: *CLEAR SPRINGS.* The stench of the water rises, it's noon.

They keep themselves afloat with little effort, the weight of the black suds supporting them greatly. Juneau continues to flutter out and about. Raphael and Victor look to each other various times. It appears they may begin some sort of communicative thread, but there are so many false starts, and neither of them know where such conversations could lead. They're cleansed and they're dirty, their warlike impetuses feel so ridiculous in the midst of such natural turmoil, perhaps being exposed is what will bring them back from the brink of Armageddon.

"They say you can't swim in the same river twice," Victor says, smiling with intention. This smile is not an accident; it is an outpouring of grace he allows to shine through to show he's made effort to strike down walls.

"Who says that?" Raphael glows.

"Beautiful boys," Victor whispers.

And in all of the contradictions of land and sun, filth and rebirth, north and south, nostalgia and future yearning, they lose themselves in the pools of their deep glances, hoping both that they can change.

new syllables

Awake under a sea of stars, Juneau is the only one who finds rest, Victor and Raphael find themselves possessed by similar forces though their bodies are apart. Victor had wandered off hours ago, presumably he thought he would be more successful in his efforts to sleep if he could find his own space; the vague light of his *baton de mort* appears to signal to Raphael that he has lost sight of solace.

Neither Victor nor Raphael are heavy sleepers. Even with the demands of their journey, they struggle to calm their brains, the thoughts that want to continue their voyages even in inertia.

There's a certain peace in insomnia, in the meditative hours of the night that glow like raucous jazz bars having grown empty and abandoned in a dying town. Tonight, the moon shines so insistently, it is as if this whole expanse is alit for them alone.

Raphael had watched as Victor rose with frustration, wandered for several minutes as if one piece of ground would be more suitable than another, had seen him bring himself back down to the earth in resignation. Somehow, Raphael feels that Victor's spirit is kindred in this moment, perceives that the forces that perturb Victor, whatever they are, perturb him as well. Distant and apart, they are together, awake and alive watching the moon and the water make love.

There passes an hour or two, in the time of the deepest, loneliest twilight; Victor produces cigarette after cigarette. In the midst of ashes and fires, Raphael thinks about Victor, thinks about the face he makes when he's filled with spiritual wonder, thinks about the ways in which his own insecurities mask affection. Upon the fifth, Raphael cannot stand to be away from him any longer; Victor shows no surprise to hear steps approaching his side.

"You are here," he says.

"Here I have been." Gentle waves crash upon the shores of the canal, bringing fleeting foam as if to emphasize the presence of this current moment.

"The moon is mesmerizing," Victor says. He inhales slowly, exhales deeply.

"But I feel myself coming closer to it. *My journey to the moon.* Perhaps that's my final destination. How should I know where we shall go?"

"Is that what you want? To disappear into space?"

"Who knows what I want and what I don't."

"You do."

Victor gazes up to the stars that dot the black sky.

"This is a pilgrimage, but it is no longer just my own. My only hope is that we can all heal and be pure, place periods on these sentences."

"I'll tell you a story."

Victor nods with warmth. Raphael pleads with him not to take alarm.

"So far, I've only let you see my most superficial, my most insecure. You deserve so much more…But for me to take this risk, it means you have to see the light and the darkness in me, for my darkness is what drives me to salvation, so I believe it to be."

And Victor proclaims, *so it shall be.*

So Raphael takes a deep breath, knowing that upon starting something he must finish it; he releases an untold story from the bonds of infinite privacy.

"I was young," he says, "younger still. And yes, I had been with a man before…but it had never worked out. I had yet to accept myself, was so distant from accepting another."

"I was studying in Tel Aviv. Far from Haifa, free to be myself, so long as I could manage that. At university, I studied philosophy mainly, but I also took many courses in Spanish literature."

Victor nods, his eyes latent with newfound care.

"And so, one day, I went to an event at a bar. A language exchange. You know, where you meet strangers in order to speak better with people you *actually* want to talk to."

"I saw a boy. I recognized him from some app. He was so handsome, I knew he came from Spain, yet I did not know his name. I thought it was my chance to bridge that gap between cyberspace and the real world. I was scared, quite nervous really, but he seemed so brilliant, I made my way to him."

Victor faces an involuntarily reaction of disgust, *where is there room for me where others still linger*, he quiets the demons that live in his head.

"And we talked, or we shouted, as it was quite loud, and after a while, I was enjoying myself and asked if he wanted to take a walk.

So we did, we walked all the way down to the shore, where we sat in the sand and talked about how much we loved Lorca. One thing led to another, my lips pressed to his, our hearts beating to a similar rhythm in the passion of such speed…"

"He would tease me for my accent, I never took it to heart because it was affectionate teasing in the way of lovers. Turns out he had his own reasons for coming to Tel Aviv that were not all so different from mine. He wanted to get away, have room to turn into himself, whoever that would be. He told me I was his first."

"So we went on dates, took things slow. We would sit in parks idly, learning about the inconsequential details of each other's lives that makes being a lover so sweet. Neither of us knew where we would go and what we would become, we were much too naïve for that. But it felt good, all the same."

"One day, he invited me over to his flat for dinner. Most of his roommates were gone, but one of them was just leaving as I came in.

She introduced herself with a giggle. I knew I had been spoken of. He led me to the terrace, where he had prepared a meal for us to eat under the stars. We became multitudes under the blanket of night, candles and smiles made us feel so warm, we finished eating and became hungry for deeper connection."

"The tension in the atmosphere had risen to such levels as to make touch irresistible. We were naked, he told me, 'I've never done this before,' I told him, don't worry, I will be gentle. And so I was, we made love. And it was all I hoped it to be, at least in the moment. But after it came to a close, the intimacy left me so suddenly; I felt sick, told him I had to leave. And the next day, or the next week he texted me to ask me if I was still in the realm of the living, I ignored it even while knowing I was doing something terrible." Raphael hangs his head.

Victor inquires: "And it was his first time?"

"Yeah, it was. It just haunts me to think, what could lead me to be so cruel?"

Victor looks into Raphael's eyes, hiding nothing, asks him if history is meant to repeat itself.

"Only on the level of civilizations. In the way that empires fall and rise, in the way that people always think tomorrow will be better."

"So history repeats itself. But what about my story, or your story?"

"Those are personal, unique. Stories are ever-changing, written and rewritten as we stretch across our lives and become wise."

Victor's feelings for Raphael, primal and instinctual as they are, are entangled in sheets of jealousy and self-hatred.

"And so if you rewrote this story, one day, what would you change?"

"I would tell someone that I treasure that I'm not perfect, that I suffer from bouts of insecurity and jealousy, that in spite of this it is beautiful and radical to commit to another man and live the way society does not intend."

"Maybe we can write a chapter together," Victor states; their hands clasp together in defiance of the crossed stars that wish to poison their embrace.

* * *

Day comes once again. Raphael and Juneau find no strength to greet it, but Victor announces with uncharacteristic confidence:

"I have a story to tell." His companions fall silent, even Juneau's eyes are rapt with attention; Raphael sees a chance to be ushered into Victor's private world, intrigued to know more about this boy he struggles to understand.

"My mom was in the army." He pauses.

"They sent her to Afghanistan."

His storytelling is patchy, sometimes too direct and other times not attractive enough to an audience; the art of attracting attention is one Victor never understood. And yet the others show love by letting him tell his story in the way he sees fit.

"She was there for a while, seemed like it at least. And I missed her a lot, I did. It was hard to be with my dad for so long, because we never understood each other so well…"

Raphael hears much more in his next pause than Victor ever could have had the courage to pronounce. Juneau hears less, less capable of filling in the blanks of the wretched gay boy's father experience.

"My dad's greatest show of love for me was telling me, over and over again, the story of my mother. I never thought it could hurt him that I preferred her to him, and he never mentioned it, knowing that telling her story was all he could do for me to want to be by his side."

"I tried to call her every night, back then. We never talked about war. Maybe it was because I didn't ask. I didn't know a lot about war back then. And neither did George Bush, I guess. I would tell her about the book I had read that day, or a friend I made at school, or sometimes I would just ramble on about any old thing. She just listened. And sometimes, she would say, 'I miss you, Victor', and I always told her I did, too. And then her and dad would get on the phone, for a minute or two, and dad always left the room for that, looking grim. I tried to hold onto the happy parts of the call, hearing my mom speak, hearing her laugh, not fully understanding why she may have been in danger, but being scared anyways. In that way that kids are scared of things they don't understand."

Victor is overcome with emotion. His eyes seek Raphael, who grants him the closeness he needs, thinking, *his eyes are so beautiful when they are full with tears.* Raphael embraces him lightly and whispers into his ear for him to go on, when he can, when he's ready, and after a long minute, Victor begins to speak once more.

"She was supposed to come home on the last day of school. I was so excited. Dad helped me gather some of my best artwork for her. I took all my stuffed animals and arranged them in a circle around my bed, so it would look like they were greeting her, too, when she would come back to say good night, in person. I told dad to buy her flowers, he wasn't so sure but I told him he could say they were from me, so he got some and placed them on the table."

"I was so excited, I was on my best behavior, I even laughed when my dad told his jokes. And by the time we were getting ready to leave, me biting my tongue to avoid telling my dad I didn't like the shoes he had put on my feet, dad got a call."

"He listened to the call calmly. I felt no intimations of doom. To me, the person on the phone was simply a distraction from the main task; I did not think to imagine that the call could end all things."

"He got off of the phone, snapped it shut and stared down at the ground. I said, 'let's go,' and he just kept looking down, I started to feel my stomach churn. 'Mommy's not coming home…' I didn't ask any questions, I didn't wait to think that I was scared to be sad in front of dad. I just started crying, somehow knowing even then that no amount of my questions could fix what had happened. I guess that's where I learned about doom."

"And later my dad told me what had really happened. That mom had done fine in Afghanistan, wonderful, actually, was bored with her job and ready to come home. And on the flight home, where many troops were scheduled to be shuffled back, there was an engine failure, and they had to stop and land somewhere else. The fuselage was damaged, you see, and the cabin was rapidly depressurized. For some reason or another, my mom liked the window seat, and that was where she was where she was ejected from the window. Some sort of freak accident. So just like that, second grade was over, mom was gone, and I intuited, in the way that only children can intuit and have a feeling with no words to describe it, that perhaps it was the end for me, too."

* * *

The canal stretches on and on, there is no limit to where they can reach if they find immortality on the blank horizon. Victor summons courage, nestling his mouth right near Raphael's ear:

"You know, I've always been interested in your language," Victor says, ignoring the subtleties he should be entertaining.

"Yes?"

"Yes. And in fact, I'd like to ask you something."

"Anything."

"Would you teach me to speak it?"

Raphael's eyes fill with desire. "Of course." For he knows that in language there are multitudes, namely, the multitudes of one speaker multiplied by all those multitudes of previous selves that uttered those same syllables, or ones very similar, and share despair and yearning. "What would you like to learn first?"

"I was scared, I was weak, I didn't know how to communicate…"

"Say with me: רשקתל דיא יתעדי אל, שלח יתייה, יתדחפ…"

Victor repeats, treating every syllable with care, fragile as they are as symbols of pain.

"רשקתל, that's the infinitive."

"They carry on through time, they are unchanging, they are the elements of language we can cling to even when nothing else will stay the same."

Raphael repeats his own phrase, his intentions both pedagogical and interpersonal:

"רשקתל דיא יתעדי אל, שלח יתייה, יתדחפ…"

* * *

Wynona pulls up to the address specified. She expects his house to make her feel small, but the block of cookie-cutter apartments that greets her just leaves her in confusion. She takes a glance at the number she has written on a spare receipt, starts up a staircase. Though her eyes are careful, her choice is wrong; Brandt appears out of plain sight, who knows from where he has emerged in this maze of dwellings for those stuck in an in-between; he gestures for her to follow him into privacy.

The door behind them shuts, he begins to explain. He says his world has changed overnight. Just the day before, he was removed from his post. A curt letter arrived on his desk, short but not sweet; there was no time to

211

mourn, his office had to be empty by noon. That night, his wife took the SUV and drove straight to California, said she needed a change in scenery.

"Her heart was never here," he says, leaving no time to define "here." And so it was, he explains, that he came to end up in his temporary dwelling, neither here nor there, simply floating in time.

"All in all, I'm lucky it didn't happen sooner."

Wynona asks him how he *feels* about it all. He replies, to Wynona's chagrin, by specifying how he does *not* feel: angry.

"Frankly, I'm relieved." So they sit together, the air clear of yesterday's trifles. He wipes his brow and asks the woman in the room if she has any news on her daughter.

"No, still nothing," she would continue but it would make her speak out of turn.

"Everything changes," he states with no apparent expression. "It's the natural state of being."

"We evolve, we lose interest. I woke up one morning and couldn't fathom spending any more time on old dimes."

"So the daily scrubbing routine is no longer?" Brandt tries to wink, but he only knows how to shut both eyes together.

"Precisely. I don't want to look at them, even. What can one do when passions just vanish? It's not a phase. I wish it were. I knew then that it was over."

Energy moves in frantic waves, in the unfamiliar living room they embrace change in the way of those who know no home; if change is sometimes slow and sometimes rapid, here it takes on the quality of light, racing through their hearts. Wynona continues:

"And since Juneau has left…something keeps nagging me, telling me there's nothing left to mourn. She's gone, our bond is a beautiful artifact, what is there to live for?"

Brandt wants to mention the letter she wrote to him, the words she forced onto paper with impatience, but at the last moment he is shy.

"So, you would not accept my help if I offered to help you find her?"

"I could never deny your helping hand." Somehow, Wynona sees enough light to grin. Brandt blurts out a retort:

"So much talk of hands…" Wynona hears a vague reference to her letter, it makes her shiver but not due to a chill, her body trembles with the heat of a new moment. She speaks inside the world of their written words:

"If these hands could speak…" Brandt shifts closer, eliminating the empty space on the plastic-covered couch that separates them both.

"They would say we embraced until the end of times…"

And suddenly the moon shines bright, dinner on the table grows cold, and their soulful pact becomes engraved in the purity of dusk's caress.

the infinitive form

Something familiar in the air rouses Victor's attention: it's the sign up the road just ahead, Raphael makes it out and announces "St. George's", suddenly Victor is back where he started. Here, where Victor emerged into this world, where he took his first steps, from where he promised he would flee for good only to return some short years later.

Victor takes the lead, Raphael follows him gently with a hand on his back. In this familiar environment turned new and cold, Victor still has his senses; even if he himself is unaware of their destination in this small hamlet, he knows that something ahead will make itself known.

"You are familiar here?"

Victor turns his head, sees Raphael gazing at him with affection.

"Really familiar," Victor says, as he follows his body's strange commandments that sometimes lead him to the right, sometimes to the left, and sometimes in a direct line forward. Juneau follows to their side.

They pass by rows of buildings, dwellings where the parents of grown children long gone for industrial centers allow time to do its will. Victor feels foolish, how could it have slipped his mind that the canal would inevitably lead him to the beginning of it all, what when all he searched for was the end. It hurts his gray matter to think of the various permutations that could have led the beginning and the end to mix together and share intimate secrets.

Victor feels the urge to stop walking; his two henchmen stop with him. Raphael points out the schoolhouse in front of them. Victor is absorbed with a sudden burst of nostalgia:

"Here I was when I first learned to write, when I first felt the disappointment of tedium, when I first felt the sadness of platonic rejection."

The sight of the slight edifice with its monochrome brick resonance brings Victor back to many moments in the past. Though the building certainly suffers from the neglect of a community with less and less young people to educate, it is much the same as he remembers it, even the air that enters his lungs makes him feel like a child once again.

"This is where you went to school?"

"Yes..."

Raphael gives a quick lesson, *here is how you say "this is where I went to school" in Hebrew,* it gives the impression that their lives and their tongues and their childhoods are bound together. Victor repeats the phrase, leading Raphael by the hand to the playground.

Juneau speaks up, tagging along: "Victor?"

"Yes Juneau?"

"When you were a child, what kind of playground creature were you?"

Victor's response does not delay one second:

"I was a reader. Sometimes I would swing while I read, but mostly I would sit on the slide, as long as no teacher was there to accost me for it. I read pulp thrillers, understanding barely half of what funneled into my brain." He laughs with childlike brilliance. Raphael recounts:

"Me, I loved the swings. You could ask anybody in my class: I was their keeper. Others would come to pass some time, but they were just temporary. I kept my guard over them, didn't let anybody come to sully my pass to the sky." Juneau takes up her turn:

"I would ask other girls to lend me their dolls so I could light them on fire." The three of them snicker like naughty children.

Victor runs to climb onto the jungle gym. Raphael follows, running to catch him. Victor takes up a race: he jumps over wonky bridges, acrobats his ways through monkey bars, all while looking back with the pleasure of competition.

Raphael blasts towards him, Victor races to go down the slide, Raphael ends up on top of him as they find their way at the exit of the slide.

"This is where I read." Raphael rubs Victor's hair softly, plants a kiss on his head. Juneau shouts:

"Boys have cooties!"

They run to her, she runs away, all three projected with force back into time.

* * *

Upon awaking the next morning, having crept into sleep haphazardly on the asphalt in a twilight match of hopscotch, Victor announces with a shriek of glee that he will lead them on a tour of his childhood home.

It is with less glee, later on, that he reveals there is not much to see. He leads them down various streets, making comments on past events:

"I once saw a squirrel run into that person's window."

"My dad used to buy whiskey from that store, when it was still open."

"I always liked this tree."

Juneau listens politely and Raphael takes in these strange pieces of information with pleasure, reminding Victor now and then of his attention with a gentle stroke. Though there are few people on the streets, those who witness Raphael and Victor's small delights publicize their distaste.

Victor feels eyes crawl on him mercilessly. Middle-aged women in loose jeans and old sneakers look to him and Raphael with amusement, as if observing an act at the circus. Stern men in trousers that defy the boundaries between cargo shorts and chinos, lined with pockets all up and down for all the important objects they must carry on their outings, stare with red eyes. Victor feels that the town has eyes itself, the apple pie ideals it holds staring at him with scorn. Big trucks, their tires raised to relay the upmost masculinity of their operators, look at them through their engines, the trees steal dirty glances and cover up their giggles with intermittent shedding of leaves, on every ramshackle house of worship he spots innumerous pairs of eyes shouting at his sin.

Yet Victor does not relent, in fact he pursues even further, in this case self-advancement and romantic engagement mean one and the same as he and Raphael twist their lives together with ropes of touch and kiss; the town scoffs.

They walk the same circles. The canal extends in front of them, at least the canal does not stare, it being a fortress of limit-breaking and the denial of dichotomous barriers. Victor seizes upon the energy he felt at the canal, that new urge to love like he's never allowed himself to before, taking it into a place where common society can observe his act is political, but he touches Raphael all the same, eyes of the past notwithstanding.

Suddenly it occurs to Victor that his pilgrimage has morphed, as all pilgrimages surely must do at some point.

"This is a new sort of journey," he points out, speaking to Raphael; Juneau notes this, places herself to the side.

Raphael places his lips to Victor's ear, does his best to get close to Victor's mind:

"What kind of journey is it, *neshama?*"

His reply, in the syllables of the language Raphael holds to his heart, hints to a bliss only recently released.

* * *

They spend the day by the bay, responding to sights and sounds as if seeing them with new eyes. Surely, the fumes of industry and toxic waste are not what they saw on the bay as children, but as Raphael sees everything for the first time, they respond to it with the same wonder, as if all that is bad is good with new eyes. But they grew weary with such grand efforts, and as they drag on, Victor mentions that he knows where they shall go.

Victor leads them away from the bay, his direction further inland. This time, he is fully cognizant of where he directs, but he keeps them in suspense. They walk in silence, Raphael grabbing for Victor's hand, in the dimming sunlight their affection feels like it can last for the rest of days.

Victor stops in front of a house: "This is where I took my first steps, where I drew anatomically blasphemous sketches of penguins…"

"Shall I meet your parents?"

Victor just looks to the ground, Raphael must have forgotten already the story of Victor's life, Raphael looks to the for-sale sign and it all rushes back to his memory.

"If only…"

But the benefit of cold real estate is a place for them to stay, enshrouded as it is in the mysticism of more innocent life; they enter the backyard, sullen like lost objects.

For hours, they hide between overgrown bushes and flood-tortured grasses, Victor and Raphael's hands meeting in some accord yet unspoken, and with time, Juneau falls asleep amidst dark stars.

Raphael is close to panic as Victor revokes his touch, but Victor is only on a temporary search for cigarettes; Victor lazily pulls his pack from the back pocket of his faded jeans.

Cigarette secured, he holds the lighter to Raphael's face, this means *would you like a cigarette* in the language of lovers, Raphael lets Victor light his flame. In this brief flash of light, Victor spots something new in Raphael's appearance. Not that he is beautiful, no, as this is not new; this he has seen from far away in the forest, from close up in the waters of the canal, from a variety of angles from which he had stolen glances. Something about the occupation of a cigarette changes Raphael's demeanor, reveals some dimension of Raphael that must sometimes also look to the sky and wonder what worth he has; Victor feels his stomach lurch to the ground.

"I call them *batons de mort*," Victor says.

"You call them what?"

"*Batons de mort*. Or sticks of death, in French."

"I like that…"

"Sometimes I feel so close to the end, I just want to taste it, I want to know what it's like." Raphael exhales pensively.

"And why do you feel so close to the end?"

"I don't know. Doom is palpable. You can soothe it, put it to the back of your mind. But it is stubborn, it looms. Why must I run, when I can just face it?"

Raphael scratches the back of Victor's neck, Victor melts briefly.

"Cigarettes make me feel alive," Raphael says. "It is like, I can taste the end, but I do not hear it, I do not see it. I can tempt it, play with it, mold it to my desires. It is a silly thing I do, to pretend to have control."

"We all do silly things sometimes."

"Surely..." Raphael continues:

"You like French, no?"

"I guess so."

"You take some phrase, say it in French or in another language from a different world, in some other tongue that your conversational partner doesn't understand. How silly but also how beautiful. It's not just the message, right? It's the *medium*. And in some languages, mortality sounds so arousing." Victor responds in broken Hebrew:

"And what is there to make of speech directed right towards someone's heart?"

"Is that love?" Victor ruminates:

"Perhaps we'll exchange obsessions, I teach you French and you tell me of all the dreams you once had."

"Perhaps," Raphael says, savoring new ground.

Raphael asks in Hebrew: "Are you hungry?"

"I smoke to make me forget the pangs," Victor states. They sit for a moment and relish the warmth of two bodies. Victor thinks of change, wonders if anything is solid and immutable, if one can rely on anything in life to stay the same.

"Have you gotten all you want out of life?" The hair on the back of Victor's neck stands on end, Victor wonders if Raphael's chest notices the sensation. Victor knows it is impossible to say yes, impossible to say no. How can he know what he has missed?

"I think there are things I would have loved to have experienced, sure... why don't you answer your own question?"

"I would say the same."

"What kinds of things are missing from your life?"

"Maybe it could have been more stable..."

"You mean you would have liked to have a similar experience every day."

"Well things change, people change, but it would have been nice to feel one thing I could count on."

Victor nods, falling deeper into Raphael's embrace. "And you've never felt that before?"

"Never. It seems like no one wants what I want. Or maybe they all think that I don't want what they want, and we're all just swimming around so worried that we create a big circus where we're left to mourn our loneliness alone."

"They say if you don't get attached to any person, or any object, you won't be disappointed."

"Isn't that a sad way to live?"

"Sure. But that's how we live."

"Doesn't have to be."

"You think you can change the mold?"

"It's our last chance."

Victor's pilgrimage, a first, is also a last chance to give himself in whole to another. A reframing of this spiritual journey: to receive the bounty of alien touch. Oh this metamorphosis. A chance to cleanse himself spiritually, an opportunity to be in touch with land thought to be his home, a way to forget about the present and focus on the future: these things he had imagined, but he would never have thought of finding someone with whom to pass lonely dawns.

He's quiet but his mind shouts, filling in the blanks where their conversation has turned vague. Even in their increasing frankness, they cannot spell out the words that most frighten them: *faggots incapable of receiving or giving love.*

Victor turns his face up at Raphael, trying to say what words cannot.

"Together we're happy," Raphael says.

"It's our last chance," Victor replies.

"רשקתל דיא יתעדי אל, שלח יתייה, יתדחפ.."

"I'll fight the monster that lives inside…"

Their minds race, a wealth of polyglot thoughts responds to this commitment, finally their lips meet and seal their commitment to life and love in the face of doom.

* * *

Raphael says "Victor, my love, I will teach you the future tense." He says it is important to him, but he says it in his language, and by these words he means that it is important not to control the future or even to predict it, but simply to conquer the fear of the future by getting familiar with its territory.

So Raphael puts on his teacher's cap, and tells Victor to repeat after him: "AMUT, NAMUT, TAMUT, TAMUTI, TAMUTU, TAMOTNA, TEMUTENA, YAMUT, TAMUT, YAMUTU, TAMOTNA, TEMUTENA" and Victor repeats it with seriousness.

And Victor says, oh, I do not recognize this verb, what does it mean in English?

"It means to die."

* * *

The canal looms on into the distance, the new day brings new feelings of sentience. Somehow the views are not the same as they once were. The beauty is more striking, the ugliness easier to put away and accept as an inevitable part of life's grace. Raphael and Victor move away from shy grabs and turn to extended expressions of their affection; the night before looms large in their mind. Every step they take incurs the drama of newfound love, they play roles they never dreamed they would have the time to play, the scene resembles antique cinema.

They continue along the canal, just as they did days prior, but now with a renewed sense of vigor. Their hands do not part as they mock the false boundaries the bridges represent, they cover each other in young kisses, the theatre of it all is constructed into a remarkable piece of art.

Juneau floats along on the side, subjugated to a lesser role by this romance they wrap themselves in.

"Do you believe in eternal return?" Raphael asks in Hebrew, the language in which he ponders philosophy. Victor parses only "do you believe...", asks him to explain "eternal return."

"The idea that this will all recur again, that the world will be reborn along these same lines, that everything will lead to this same moment an infinite number of times."

"It would be good, it would be bad…"

Raphael kisses Victor's forehead.

"But do you believe that, the universe having imploded, we would inevitably be led to this same conclusion, end up in each other's arms again?"

"I do, *neshama*," this small expression of commitment recreates the one that they sealed the night before.

The rest of the walk along the canal they spend in the silence of bliss. Their pace is slow, they are in no rush to leave this place.

Juneau walks along to the side, her ears filtering out words in a language she does not understand. Victor glances to Raphael with a recognition of guilt, *oh dear, beauty can also descend into sadness*, Raphael directs himself to Juneau:

"Juneau, do you believe in eternal return?"

She stares at the bridge that looms ahead, perhaps to find inspiration. She stares, she stares, taking her time, leading them to think her response will shed light on the human dilemma they have proposed. Finally, an answer:

"If the cows come home early, I won't be there to milk them."

Fade to credits, when one thing begins perhaps others must end, who's to say it is not inevitable that it would happen again just like this in another couple of eons, as the curtain fades Victor tries to reconcile this prophecy that brings him immense pleasure and unwieldy sadness.

towards the continent

Victor and Raphael expend great effort trying to bond their separate physical forms as the dawn greets the new day. Juneau remains asleep for some time as they enjoy a post-coital cigarette: "Time for breakfast."

The fumes they exhale combine in the air; their lips share the remnants of ashes. It is the

allegiance of the *baton de mort* that reminds them of their duty to live while they can, life becomes much sweeter when surrounded by death. Raphael teaches Victor the Hebrew word for "soot," Victor repeats it like a good pupil.

As Juneau awakens, she does not greet them; Raphael and Victor calm their nerves and lead on. Victor, being intimately connected with the qualities of the canal, feels in his heart that soon they will be too close to the Maryland border and be forced to turn back. But as they walk, there are no signs of border patrol personnel, and Victor forgets it all to focus on the boy who holds him.

They walk for an hour or two as the sun rises toward the top of the earth. As the heat begins to press down, they all think again of dipping their bodies back into the canal, but none of them mention it, especially not Juneau, who feels much too betrayed to extend out such intimacy. Their pacing is slower and slower, little food in sight, all they can do is sustain themselves on what remains of Victor's freeze-dried peanuts.

They creep further on into the distance, and Victor feels the pangs of unfamiliarity once more: by now, they should certainly have arrived at the border, and something feels off. Victor turns to Juneau:

"Shouldn't we already be in Maryland by now?"

She shrugs.

In a few short minutes later, they spot the presence of humanity on the horizon, a small settlement. As it comes closer into the foreground, they are greeted by a sign, freshly painted:

"メリランドアメリカたいりくをせいふくするためのだいいち！" Though the three of them cannot understand the words, they understand the sentiment, and even as a sense of foreboding closes around them, they move forward to witness the calamity.

Victor no longer doubts that they are in Maryland and have crossed international borders; the new doubt that takes place in his head is that of this canal settlement's new political annexation.

They reach the town's main streets. In the central square, a flag burning event takes place: ravenously patriotic Delawareans with horseshoe crabs fixed upon their heads light fire to Maryland flags. Others argue about which Delaware flag to rise to the main square's flagpole, struggle to replace the old flag with the new. On street corners, large images of Reverend Bridge dominate the views, his face in Mao-style positioning accompanied by text appealing to the purity of the common Delawarean.

Across the canal, pumpkins are catapulted to the west, presumably as a sign of the Delawareans' impending westward movement, large quantities of Old Bay are thrown into the water to add acrimonious flavor to brown waters.

In this place, the town that the three of them remember as Chesapeake City, expressions of imperialist destiny overrule the worried looks of residents who peek out at the spectacle from their windows.

"He's expanding," Raphael explains. Victor clutches him. Juneau does not react; she is immune to the shock.

They pledge to cross the canal to continue south, back into Delaware, or what may now be known as the Mainland.

"Let us not add insult to injury."

Having already observed enough conquest for the day, they turn away the way they came.

* * *

"Who knew he had such ambitions," Raphael states. He speaks in English, hoping that Juneau may feel inclined to respond, but he is greeted only with extended sighs. Having left Chesapeake City, they turn back towards the other direction of the canal, this time on the opposite side of it. Raphael distributes parsimonious quantities of foodstuffs that he has snatched from the town they have fled. Any feelings of abuse they might feel in kicking a city while it is down is subsumed to the hunger that overwhelms their existence and clouds their moral judgement.

With some quantity of satiation rising in their stomachs, they settle into their return journey with more calm. Raphael and Victor continue glued together, attempting to experience all of these moments as one united organism.

"Our first meal," Victor says.

"Or the last supper."

The canal from this direction lacks the glamour of the reverse side. From this southern vantage point, its ugly qualities are reflected double. Though their lessened hunger reduces the tension temporarily, it quickly returns to haunt the trio. Raphael and Victor worry about Juneau in Hebrew.

"I've been a bad friend…"

"Don't blame yourself, we had to take this chance…"

"Yes I know, but I need to be there for her as well."

"It is only fair, to do for her what she, as your friend, has done for you."

Victor goes to Juneau's side, briefly removing himself from the aura of Raphael's warmth.

"Juneau…"

She continues to look ahead.

"I know I've been a bad friend to you…"

She stares.

"I got swept up in the excitement of this moment, so much so that I began to neglect you, my best friend…" He walks alongside her, stopping the flow of words.

In this space, Victor walks in the middle of his two loves, different from each other but not so much, he tries to show Juneau that he regrets his neglect. Finally, she speaks:

"I don't resent you for this opportunity you've seized, I just miss simpler times we spent together."

"Me too..."

* * *

At night, Victor's doubts come to tease.

"When will these thoughts stop?" Victor asks, as Raphael removes his hand from his hair.

"What thoughts?"

"I'm so paranoid..." His thought ends without a term of endearment.

"When will I stop feeling like every one of your actions is the final act before your disappearance, before you become just a ghost?"

Raphael digs into Victor's pockets: he grabs Victor's back-left quadrant with a hearty handful, much more than physically necessary to retrieve the lighter, and then the pack of cigarettes, which he knows to be in Victor's front right.

"When we die, maybe."

"So you're saying that, when we die, you'll leave me?" Victor tenses up. Raphael takes a dismissive puff and laughs good-naturedly.

"Not if I can help it." Victor's face shows scorn.

"It appears to me that it is human destiny to feel alone, trapped in this flesh that separates us. No matter what company surrounds us, no matter how blissful nights of passion, we are all separated by these chasms we call bodies." Raphael resumes the stroking of Victor's hair.

"I smoke my cigarette; I pet your hair. These fumes that I inhale, they end on your head. We're both dying together, little bunny, the *baton de mort* touches us both. I enter you to show we are one. I hold you tight, almost like I can pass through your skin. And so if we are not yet one brain, one body, I hope you do not think it's because I did not try."

Victor, gently coaxing the cigarette out of Raphael's mouth and into his, takes some deep breaths, first of tobacco and then of the forest's emissions, and declares in Hebrew:

"I sense that we're alive."

* * *

Upon the highway, a sign in dazzling light green greets them: "Welcome to Smyrna."

"You know, Smyrna was one of the Greeks' grandest cities. Until it was conquered by the Turks, that is. Now it's called Izmir. Is this city the reincarnation of ancient greatness?"

Juneau raises her nose in disgust:

"If this is the revival of Western grandeur, color me unimpressed." Raphael releases his expectations.

They head for the first time into Delaware's southern portion, a whole new cultural experience for Raphael. They had finished with the modest, laughable hills of the north, and now their faces looked towards the coastal plains of the south. Victor whispers into Raphael's ear, "we have left my country."

As the cars whiz by, they pick up on patterns. More and more cars fly a Delawarean flag, but they cannot agree on which flag it is. They notice how the flags that the cars carry make up a myriad of shapes, colors and designs. Often, drivers stop in the middle of the highway to argue with drivers brandishing an enemy flag.

Other drivers get involved to show their frustration in the jam, erupting in large commotion. Though Victor and Juneau posit that these discrepancies are most likely due to the North/South aesthetic divide, the citizens involved in such brawls often come from the same town, and don't even ask to find out.

In fact, there is much that Juneau and Victor do not know, cannot know, having been cut off from their sources of media. They know not of the great rifts that divided communities at the town hall meetings convened to decide on a course of action for the national flag. That the pragmatists who did not want to be rid of the old flag were condescended to as the "imperialists" by Delawareans who wanted a flag that reflected their radical desires for nationhood.

All sorts of designs were proposed and denied. Artists would call into the question the validity of the work of another on account of their familial ties to Pennsylvania, which would invite the accused artist to dig up some relative of that artist outside of the small nation and cause a never-ending chain of skepticism.

Weeks after these fateful meetings, the national government had finally decided enough was enough of the violence and hatred, and so they came up with a compromise: that, on Mondays, one flag would be used, and on Tuesdays another, and so on for each day of the week. But this decision was also greeted with disdain, as it would reflect poorly on Delaware's new international image.

So the government came up with a renewed compromise, that on the first and third weeks of each month, the flag would stay the same throughout the week, whereas in the second and fourth weeks, the flag would be rotated each day. They declined to provide further detail as to whether the flag displayed in the first and third weeks would be the same one forever, or if it would change, and even if it did not change, which one it would actually *be*.

And so on and so on, until the tension grew so large that the government gave up on mitigation efforts, allowing road fury to become an everyday sight on the North-South highway.

But they are unaware.

Victor notices a woman in her SUV, staring forward with her eyes glazed over, paying no attention to the brawl in front of her. Her expression of alarm frightens him.

"You think that woman is okay?"

Juneau assures him that she is fine, but when the fight dies down and traffic builds back up, she remains in her SUV; Victor goes to check on her.

He darts onto the lanes of the highway, running the risk of turning into roadkill, finally reaching her vehicle in the far lane.

He knocks on her window: "Are you okay?"

She opens the window. Her eyes are large with undefined fright. She looks to him, then to Raphael and Juneau on the shoulder.

"Where are you going?"

"I don't know," Victor admits.

"Me either." So she abandons her vehicle, follows Victor to the right side of the highway, and the four of them head south in the tacit understanding that she would join their spiritual journey.

la mer, le sable, l'amour, la mort

Juneau takes the reins, announces to this new group that their next destination will be Port Mahon. Expecting to be greeted with some sigh of recognition, Raphael and Victor are too enshrined in their own small nothings to pay any mind, and Ines is not familiar. Ines tries to be polite:

"Where?"

"A place of beauty."

"Oh…" The truth is it never would have occurred to the Canalite to search for beauty in Dover. All she can imagine of Dover are chain restaurants and room for improvement. She vocalizes her perceptions, which Juneau receives with a quiet acceptance, feeling so strange to be a Middletonian, neither from here nor from there. For as important as the small coastal byways of the south are to her, they are of no importance to Ines, and so there must be something in her soul that separates Juneau from complete Canalite status. She is not ungrateful to learn that Port Mahon and its like are not an ineffable part of the Delawarean psyche, but it also brings her a sort of disquiet, of imagined unity broken into individual perceptions.

"And so this is a port?"

"A different kind of port," Juneau clarifies, trying to cloak a hint of annoyance. Juneau is aware that Ines is imagining the port of Wilmington, a place where boats come to release their market droppings, but this is not a port that brings industry, rather a pathway leading away from civilization. Juneau's eyes become glassy.

"This is a port that leads to the end of the world."

Juneau watches as the mention of the end rouses Raphael from private amorous ceremonies, wishes she had not been so inviting.

"People have prophesized the end of time ever since time began." Juneau shuts him down.

"Well, these times are different."

"That's what they always say."

Victor chimes in: "But *this* time, our wishes may really come true."

Raphael's steps are even and sober, in time with Victor's, quietly confident. Victor addresses some soft words to him:

"No more hiding away."

He who has always positioned himself as the patron saint of reality, of science as the only religion necessary, having recently pondered truth as love. Victor, the martyr, come to soak in the news of end times and receive enlightenment. But just as his previous words are sure, his next words are doubtful:

"What is the purpose of this life we share?"

"To love is to be alive."

Victor blushes, places a wanting hand on Raphael's chest.

"Is that something they say in your country?"

"It's something that I say, outside of my country."

"*Of course*," Victor confirms in Hebrew, "and perhaps it will become a habit."

* * *

With small bursts of innocent laughter, Victor and Raphael come to realize that Ines and Juneau have walked far ahead of them; they readjust their pace to catch back up.

They walk through a small town, pass by houses that hold secrets and stale dreams left from a better time long ago. A shack of a post office, schoolhouse brick faded into muddy brown, holds an "open" sign hung haphazardly upon the door even though seemingly everywhere there is dust and no trace of life. Behind the post office there is a small playground: two swings marked with yellow paint move achingly in the breeze, chipped away in various places to reveal a dull copper. Juneau points out a long road running perpendicular to the post office and its playground companion.

"Just straight ahead from here," Juneau says, but no one moves in response. They are momentarily haunted by a palpable sense of the past, of buildings who cannot tell their own stories. Ines stares at the swings. The seats sway so gently, so much so to lead one to wonder if they are really moving at all, if it is not just a figment of the imagination.

"My daughters loved to swing."

Having said this, Ines begins to walk down the long road, right in the middle without fear of cars coming to disturb their peace, and the others follow.

Juneau speaks: "There are several worlds here." One, she explains, is the town itself, a town so small one could miss it if one had any good reason to pass by in a car. Victor wonders if "town" is the best way to describe this one-and-a-half block collection of faded homes.

"It sounds weirdly quaint."

"Words don't expire, *neshama*," Raphael attests as living proof of the permanence of language, Victor imagines Raphael deserves museum display.

But by the time they conclude this exchange, the so-called town is already behind them, Juneau has already stopped looking back longingly and now just keeps it in her thoughts. They pass into the second world: the long road, on the sides of which used to grow large stalks of corn, which now harvest only broad, ashen fields bearing no fruit. The landscape envelopes them. They take their time, savoring the quiet before stumbling onto the sandy path.

"This is the final world, the one that leads to the end."

They quickly grow tired of the sand collecting in their shoes filling their socks with dead weight and impeding their movement, so they stop to bare their feet. And as Ines is bending down to strip away the separation of her body with the earth, she looks to the right and for the first time sees the bay.

On her left, the grasses sit waiting, the narrow sandy strip lying in between. It separates the grasses from the broad sea, she exclaims "it's so beautiful," she imagines wayward sailors attempting to distance themselves from the world and falling off vertically into the horizon, reaching their goal in theory but not in spirit; she has no idea that Juneau has envisioned the very same thing.

Juneau repeats, "it is the end of the world."

"So that is what you meant."

Juneau nods. Ines is captivated further.

"It's so peaceful."

Victor takes Raphael by the hand, explains to him that these narrow coastal boundaries are so special to Delawareans as a reminder of their insignificance, of the lightness of their existence on this lowly strip of land. The idea that, at any point in time, a Delawarean could move a couple miles to the east and see open waters, is fundamental.

"Juneau believes it's an integral part of the Delawarean psyche," Victor proclaims with pride.

Ines, being so industrialized and suburban, does not share this view, but wishes she could.

"My Delaware is looped with highways," she says. Juneau, in an odd display of emotion, mumbles something about Canalites. Ines hears her and does not dismiss her own dissatisfaction.

"I know I'm not from here, I'm not like you. This place is not my own, I don't explore it with the wonder of someone who wants to take pride in what is theirs. But give me a chance to see your world."

"Which one?" Juneau remarks.

"Well this one is nice," she says, her eyes reflecting pools of the shiny radiance of the great rumbling bay.

"I guess I should've known that the end of the world would be here."

"Where?"

"In Lower Slower." Victor laughs. Raphael takes a look at the way his eyes crease, the way he shakes his head lightly, almost as if to excuse this intrusion into the lives of others by laughing so gently, and Raphael is captivated.

Their feet being bare, they walk along the side of the bay.

Together, but in their own heads, they think of the world bending and curving just beyond where they can see. Victor wonders if it is anthropocentric to believe that the world would end just beyond where their feeble human eye can see. Raphael wonders if the world would end in pieces, or in one clean swoop. Ines feels beauty and nothing else. Juneau tries to name all the objects she could see in French: *la mer, le sable, l'amour, la mort.*

They come across a pier. Raphael suggests they stop to smoke, pulling out a pack of smokes of a brand Victor does not recognize from his military-issue satchel.

"You had smokes this whole time?"

"Yes, *neshama*," Raphael responds, Victor shoves him playfully.

"No thanks," Ines states, attempting to smooth over her disdain but failing. Her and Juneau keep walking, while Victor and Raphael walk to the edge of the pier. Raphael sits down on the very last plank of wood to dip his toes in the water, his hands leaning back to support himself. He feels Victor's absence, sees him looking hesitantly into the void.

"Won't you join me?"

"The sea might eat me whole."

"No, it won't, not if I get a chance to do so first."

Victor draws himself forward, his smile so bare, driven by magnetic force.

Raphael inhales deeply, sticks a cig in Victor's mouth. In no hurry, they take their turns.

"The water runs in my blood; I can't help but be drawn to it."

"Me, too."

"And what about your apprehension to near the end of the dock?" Raphael strokes Victor's hair.

"I am scared of my own destiny." He is relieved to release some sorrow.

"It is human to feel fear, my love." He lights himself another cigarette, his lips hungry by the open waters, the small flame intimates the fire they share for each other deep in their groins.

"These kill, right?"

"Yes," Raphael responds.

"Am I manipulating my own destiny, then, by bringing myself closer to the end?"

"Our choices are part of our destiny, are they not?"

Victor agrees. They stared into the great big bay, patiently, as if expecting to be dropped into the abyss at any moment. But it would be okay, if only to be able to feel the fire in their bellies and know that the flames could burn without fear of retribution. Raphael pulls Victor closer; engulfed by such flames he feels more alive, not less.

"*Batons de mort*," Victor teaches once again. Raphael laughs heartily.

"Of course, *neshama, batons de mort.*"

Victor stops to put the stick between his lips and feel the smoke rise within him.

Raphael does not command his lips to open and reveal his teeth: they do so of their own accord, but he quiets the monster inside himself that does not want his happiness to shine.

"I like it. *Batons de mort.*"

"Oh yeah?"

"Well, now I do," Raphael jokes.

Victor tastes like tar and salt as Raphael strikes a kiss onto his lips.

* * *

Ines calls, "is anyone hungry?", but it is not a question, it is an invitation, *let us break bread together.* From the grasses Raphael and Juneau come over, where Raphael has admired a turtle and Juneau went about bemoaning the ground. Victor stumbles over from the dock where he had idled with a cigarette, still perched in his hand despite having been extinguished long ago.

They sit in a circle. Ines opens the small knapsack she had brought with her upon desertion and distributes some of her rations among her new companions: some apples, some bananas, some nuts and bottles of water.

"Call it a gesture of friendship from Delaware to Saudi Arabia," she states. Raphael smiles politely, he wishes to say "I'm from Israel" but decides against it.

For a few moments, they need say no words, for their communion ties them together strongly enough. It does their bodies and minds good to eat, as small as their meal is. It is much too easy, when one is high on spiritual growth, to forget this human need.

Juneau looks to her audience and scrutinizes their faces with her mouth slightly ajar, as if to begin a story, and somehow decides against it.

They pass some few moments, united in silence. Victor wonders how *together* a group can be while saying nothing, until what point a bond can last until a lack of communication necessitates dissipation. And as he is thinking this, wondering if words must always be the vehicle of closeness, he does not realize that his thoughts draw him farther and farther away from the here and now, bringing him into the exile of strangerhood.

"I love Paris," Juneau says, her voice somewhat stifled, eyes stuck to the sand.

"What was that?" Ines asks gently, trying not to upset someone who must repeat words they find difficult to say. Victor smokes a cigarette in the spirit of dessert, Raphael listens intently.

"I love Paris."

The second time she says it, Victor is brought out of his isolation by a sense of puzzlement. "You mean as a concept?"

"I mean as a city, as a place on which I stepped foot and breathed air," she responds, with an air of fact that conveys slight annoyance, as if her statement did not contradict the reality of her never having even obtained a passport.

"What is it like?" Ines asks, her tri-state eyes glittering in anticipation.

"It's a perfect city. The streets are all gold. They have cafes that dispense coffee made of jade, and you pay for it with a smile. And everyone there is well-dressed, because the Bureau of Fashion sees to it that everyone is up to date with their clothing. That's the first thing you do when you get off the plane, you know: they give you a new suit and a pair of high-brand shoes. The air always smells like flour and homemade strawberry jam.

People amuse themselves all day by sitting on a terrace drinking petite gold coffees and eating fresh bread. No one works, the setting is much too romantic to occupy oneself with such meager pastimes. People write, perform, make music all the day. Paris is just a consortium for the arts. Everyone gets to live in these beautiful little apartments, each one outfitted with jade toilets and ruby showers. Visitors, too. It's a perfect place. You should visit."

Ines looks at both Victor and Raphael before gauging her own response. Victor pays little attention, exhales with airs of blasé. Ines feels that she could laugh, or cry, or react in some way to show her disbelief, but Juneau's face is serious and matter of fact, that Ines just says "Paris would be lovely."

"The people there are a bit different, I'll admit."

"Oh, I can imagine!"

"If you could, I would be really surprised. I would *never* have guessed what it would have been like. You see, no one really *eats* there. They don't need to. Sure, they'll have a pastry or a dessert for pleasure. But that's for the aesthetic. They get all of their nutrients from the air: the rest is just nostalgia. And they get bored, sometimes, so they go elsewhere. But that's easy for them. They can't fly, in the true sense of that word, but they can get themselves in another place when they want to, just by sheer force of will. Japan was the trend when I was there.

It was all anyone talked about: a land in which fish falls from the skies, and the sun sets in the south in some sort of confusion of natural order, and people have the capacity to live and breathe underwater. They left and came back in a matter of hours, would decide they had not gotten their fill so as to go once more, and be back in the café the next day.

There was always much talk of which cafes one must visit in that enchanted land, which are the most delicious fish to eat, where the most authentic experience could be had. And they would remind each other, of course, *make sure you go in the onsen, that's where you can breathe underwater, for as long as you want.*" Juneau's tone is didactic, as if she believes this information vital not only for her survival, but for the survival of those who surround her.

"And despite it all, the people are filled with wanderlust; no matter where they go they always desire to be elsewhere."

Victor says he wishes fish would rain from the sky then so he might eat one. Raphael asks him why he does not go into the bay to find a fish himself. Victor takes a daring look into Raphael's eyes, *silly beautiful boy*, "as if there are fish who live in the sea."

Hearing this story, Ines feels strange and transient. "I think I should go to bed," she announces, despite it being only five in the evening; she searches for a comfy place in the sand. With her decision, they take it to understand that they will stay the night on these shores. Juneau takes her chance to go off towards the grass without a word. Suddenly, only Victor and Raphael are left.

Victor gives Raphael a cigarette without hesitation. They sit together, Victor's head perched on Raphael's shoulder, enjoying the taste of a fading sun.

The horizon turns a solemn gray as Raphael pulls Victor toward him to kiss his head.

Victor makes empty promises that sound so sweet, speaking of the cafes they shall visit in their times in Paris, *someday*, Raphael says "yes, my dear", in the way of obedient lovers, and the day disappears into technicolor dreams.

* * *

Who are you, in this new place? You're unrecognizable. In between the you of the past and the you of the future, who could recognize you now? With these new companions, you're both more yourself and more of an imposter, somewhere in between who you know yourself to be and who they imagine you are.

If the syllables you enunciate are those of another civilization, have you changed your destiny?

Who are you in this sleepy underground bar, from which depths did you stumble here from the streets? Music plays in sultry sepia tones; faint walls of pink invite you into a new consciousness. Is it treason to betray your nation's faults in this tongue so foreign? If it leads to rebirth, perhaps it is worth the trouble.

He looks to you, don't worry what he will expect from you in the deepest parts of dusk, just smile and show your new teeth. Doomed as ever, in the nooks these streets lead you to ponder you are alien and your fate takes on a new appearance, the glasses of brandy shine under faint candelabras.

You walk up to the bar. What is this song that enchants me so, barman do you know? He tells you what it is and you feel you've caused a spectacle, all to preserve a portion of this night that will end too soon, too soon for you but much too soon for the one you accompany here tonight, don't let him know the plans you do or do not have.

It is a great cinematic moment as you thank the man at the bar for his assistance, and you return to the table with the air of an old starlet, one whose gusto for life shines with the knowledge that it will be cut short.

Who are you if not the expressions you fake, the people you meet, those who see you for an instant and claim they know your story?

You laugh along with these new friends of yours, how polite and hospitable, the reel continues even with so many questions unanswered, you pick up your glass and make a toast to hazy smiles.

* * *

"My hopes are low," Wynona says, echoing what Brandt can already deduce from her dejected form as they approach the university campus. Brandt drives calmly, hoping to reassure her with gentle braking and careful consideration of pedestrians, but Wynona seems not to notice. He holds her hand to his face, kisses her gently:

"Everything will be okay."

They pass into the main avenues of campus activity, and yet all is quiet and stoic. The few students that Brandt sees walk by do so with great haste, all around the university the sense of rebellion that dominated just some short months prior has been lost. To his left Brandt peers over to see a new statue of Bridge, constructed on the main quad, dominating tens of feet high over the rest of the buildings. He squints, it is difficult to see what is written but he focuses as much as he can at the wheel, and makes out the words with great effort:

"THINK AND YOU SHALL PERISH, WORK AND YOU SHALL BREATHE," accompanied by a Japanese translation as was appropriate in the functionally bilingual regime. Brandt wishes he knew Japanese so he could fret about the accuracy of the words shifted into this different language, wonders if his lack of Japanese proficiency had anything to do with his demotion.

"How do you know?"

"What?"

"What is it that gives you this ability to see into the future and know how all things will evolve? What is it that makes you so wise?"

Brandt may have taken this for an insult, had he not spent so much time with his new companion to understand that she speaks with utmost seriousness. A smile appears upon his face worn by years of frowning solitude, he responds:

"If only the words we spoke would become the reality we live."

Juneau's campus house appears on the right, Brandt parks on the quiet street directly adjacent. Wynona shivers.

"Russell...." It makes her skin crawl, knowing she is the only one to call him by this name, she speaks once more:

"There is no life here."

They enter and she is proven right. There is no life, just the traces of life that once was: coffee cups lingering on the kitchen table, books of metaphysics and cultural commentary strewn across the sofa. Wynona turns to Juneau's room with resolute determination. Brandt follows her obediently, places a light hand on her back to remind her she is not alone.

It is as if she had left just five minutes prior, neglecting to bring any of her things: her laptop stands on the desk, its screen still open, her backpack spews its contents onto the bed.

"She liked to do work in bed sometimes," Wynona comments.

Her phone is on the makeshift night table by her bed, some random piece of furniture she had once scrapped from her mother's garage.

Wynona taps the screen; her own messages pop up:

Are you okay?

Where are you?

Where do we go when we die?

Wynona starts to sob with polite restraint. Brandt pulls her into his sphere, Juneau's scent fills the room she no longer occupies, *Russell*, Wynona takes no notice of time as weeks of sorrow culminate in great release.

* * *

"Raphael taught me how to use the future tense in Hebrew."

"How interesting, the future tense was always my favorite," Juneau and Victor share the moment.

Victor asks, how does one form the future tense in French, and Juneau relates that instead of manipulating the infinitive form, you just take it like it is and attach a series of new permutations. Save the exceptions, of course, but that was another matter, any rule can be broken.

"Don't you find infinitives fascinating?" Victor asks, his eyes to the sky. Juneau disagrees.

"Infinitives are boring. You don't get anywhere with them. They are stuck in place and time, fossilized."

"Well, timelessness is also the infiniteness of time, no? The infinitive is the past, the present, and the future all rolled into one. Take this fire, in front of our eyes, for example. *To burn:* the discovery of fire, our eager industrial past, this current moment of blind destruction, a future of rapacious, hungry burning bearing no witnesses."

So Juneau clings to this idea for a bit, masticating and absorbing it. She says "you're right, that is true, but I find that also fearful." Victor respects this decision. Ines comments, her feet dragging with regret, that she wishes she could have learned a language. "It isn't too late," Juneau responds, but Ines turns serious and says "it very well could be."

Victor asks, what language would you learn, and Ines says, probably all of them.

"You know, if you only know one, you don't know what it's like. But when you learn the second one, you must think *wow, this is a power,* how could

241

you ever stop." She thinks of all the selves whose possibilities would have emerged upon the learning of a new tongue: a hairdresser in Hokkaido, a professor of bioethics in Hamburg, a wanderer of no particular place.

So Juneau resolves to teach Ines some French.

"How delightful, I would feel so posh," and so Juneau says that she would be glad to do it. Ines asks what she shall learn, and Juneau declares definitively that she must learn to speak of the future, after baptizing her with a new French name.

"Repeat after me. *Les mers se lèveront.*" Ines repeats, with relatively accurate pronunciation. Juneau praises the positives and then tells her where she can remove the Anglo from these gallic syllables. Ines clears her throat and repeats once more, *Les mers se lèveront,* still unsure of its meaning.

Victor feels himself sinking. He turns to Ines and translates for her:

"It means *the seas will rise.*"

give me seran wrap or give me death

Raphael, upon beginning to understand the essence of America, drifts further from understanding the Delawarean psyche:

"You can tell how affluent an American suburb is by how close the cars are together."

Victor immediately snaps back: "Is this America?"

"It's on the continent."

"But it's not part of the United States."

"That's true. But your New World is so general, anyways, what's the difference? America is the USA is the country is the continent. If you all don't distinguish yourselves, what am I to do?"

"I'm not American."

"What are you then?"

"I'm Victor."

Raphael flashes him a clever smile, rewarding Victor for his wit.

After their experience by Port Mahon, Ines had campaigned for a "return to civilization," Raphael had said, why not, maybe it's time for me to see another side of your country, and Victor was content with anything Raphael had to say.

Raphael makes observations. After they trek through some of the more dilapidated areas of downtown Dover, passing through which Ines insisted on being protected by a human perimeter of their bodies, Raphael is shocked by the inconsistencies.

"How strange that the wealthiest neighborhoods are the ones with no sidewalks," he states with a matter-of-fact delivery that cushions a tinge of sorrow. As much as he would like to gawk and stare at any one of the grandiose displays of pseudo-architecture watered down for a white suburban taste, Victor advises him against it: "If we stop at any one time, we could be arrested for loitering."

Though they do not stop, their pace is protozoic. Their bodies languish in the heat, like soggy bread left too long in a furnace, only barely making enough motion to avoid suspicion. And it is also true that their eyes have much to ponder, especially those of Raphael. To him, all sights are new, shining with the resemblance to the North American television aesthetics he has consumed all his life. But there are other things that arouse common interest, having represented changes even in the short while that they have been on pilgrimage. Victor, uncharacteristically vocal, points out the signs plastered on every lawn:

"ながいきするぼくしきょうとかれのぶんめいにんむ"

Unable to read the signs, he exclaims, "Look at the foreign script!", smiling a smidge upon encountering evidence that the world has changed during their hermit journey. Raphael looks at him with slight suspicion:

"Foreign script?"

"Whatever it is, it's simply novel!"

"I believe it's Japanese."

"I guess we all have to believe in something."

They discuss back and forth as to what meaning this could have, speculating wildly: has Delaware been colonized by a race of aliens who have managed only to master one random human tongue, and not bothered to attempt with any others? Has Delaware been taken over by an imperialist immigrant community? Juneau just stares at the signs, finding some sort of peace in total incomprehension. Ines' eyes remain fixated on the homes, sizing them up with lust, trying to imagine their insides as if gazing at a potential sexual partner.

Raphael, in this most American, or Delawarean, of places, says to Victor in his mother tongue: "It is time for a Hebrew lesson." So, using readily available realia, Raphael points to the most common items and teaches them to Victor with a didactically slow pronunciation. *Obesity. The spittle you get during a nap. Corporate litigation.*

Then it dawns on Victor that he has ignored another universal sign: brandished on the outside of all homes is a banner with the name *Delaware: The Holy Land*, stylized with the D appearing as the shape of the peninsula. On most houses, the banner is fresh, undamaged from the potential harassment of new, finicky weather patterns. He can't figure out why it has taken him so long to notice.

"Am I really so desensitized to trademarks?"

"You *are* a trademark."

Victor just looks down at his feet and pouts. It makes him sad to think that his voyage into the wild has not completely erased the mark of consumerism from his body.

"Raphael, do you think we can unlearn what we were once taught?"

"This you know is true, my dear."

Juneau adds a non-sequitur: "Yesterday, I went to the bank, today I'm on my way to the butcher."

As they trudge forward in their silence, a humanoid figure steps in front of them, blocking their path. He's a young man with a pair of ill-fitting black slacks and a white dress-up shirt with blackened mustard stains, smiling sourly. He stands his ground, they look with apprehension, and no one says a word for one long while.

"Konnichiwa, ladies and gentlemen," the young man finally says. He has a slight lisp, which makes the threat inherent in his voice all the more strange. It is too early to tell if their encounter will be comical.

"Hello," Raphael says.

The man is silent for another while. He seems mechanically aware of his actions, comfortable in the silence he creates: it is as if all has been planned, but by whom and for what motive, Victor and Raphael have not the slightest idea.

"You four look a bit lost. Might I provide some directions?" The man's lips curl.

"No, no, we're fine, just out for a walk."

"Bit warm for a walk, isn't it?"

"I'm used to it," Raphael says coldly. Victor inches toward him.

"I work for the Civilizing Mission Team, ぶんめいミッションチーム as we call ourselves in the language of the Lost Land."

"I see."

He goes on to explain that he would be delighted to provide them with information on how they could get involved, in one of a variety of teams designed to promote Christianity in Japan. His sentences are sprinkled with random Japanese words, mainly loanwords from English but also some words that neither Victor nor Raphael can understand and are just lucky enough to gather from context.

"We seek to spread His message to the underworld."

"Who's he?"

"Why, Reverend Bridge, of course. That's surely something any Godfearing Delawarean should know, isn't it?" His face turns blank.

"I thought you were referring to God."

"I thought you were going to cooperate." The silence is heavy with fear.

The man takes an interest in Juneau, who has avoided his eye contact altogether. "What's your name, young woman? You look supple."

"Sarah."

"Lying is a sin."

"So is objectifying women."

He emits a polite smile, as if to acknowledge a clever chess move. "Very well, then," he states, and then walks off into the distance, looking back at them every few feet with a sickening grin.

As soon as they continue their jaunt, shaken by this strange occurrence, Ines begins to act increasingly more strange. She starts to crawl onto the lawns, stopping to sniff the grass on the outer edges, her upper half subsumed to the height of her waist in a pose that gives her a canine-like form. She juts along the yards with increasing speed and increasing proximity to the estates themselves. She grabs flowers from front yards, fails at various attempts to perform a cartwheel, and barks at backyard animals.

"Ines?" Victor knows his voice won't be powerful enough.

She becomes more daring and louder in her attempts to occupy one of the fortresses. When she presses her face and hands to a closed front window, the house does not greet her warmly: a siren emits a deadening alarm.

While Victor and Raphael grab Juneau and run to avoid any trouble, Ines grows more desperate in her attempts to reintroduce herself into suburban life. She runs frenzied around all corners of the house, heaving herself onto windows to see if they will give, grabbing at gutters in an attempt to scale onto the roof, banging her head into glass doors to split them open.

The police arrive: locked, loaded, ready to pry human away from property. The three remaining pilgrims, having escaped to a safe distance away from the commotion, hear Ines' disturbed incantations: "GIVE ME SERAN WRAP OR GIVE ME DEATH GIVE ME SERAN WRAP OR GIVE ME DEATH GIVE ME SERAN WRAP OR GIVE ME"

Shots and a petite *thump*, followed by a familiar surreal silence.

spirituality of the flesh

Raphael assumes power militaristically, insisting that they move into the countryside to avoid other strange confrontations. Victor follows these orders with pleasure. He looks forward to a more intimate and rigorous form of pilgrimage, as if the wear and tear on their bodies, the physical deterioration of their clothing, and their cigarette-based food pyramid of a diet do not show enough commitment. As is her custom, Juneau follows along silently, allowing herself to be blown into place by the prevailing winds.

They flee west, away from Dover, being careful not to the extend too close to the Maryland border. Not that they can be sure anymore where Delaware begins and where it ends, but they stick to traditional boundaries, what to Victor seems like the "real" Delaware. The land between Dover and the western frontier is barren. A sense of abandonment prevails, of people having abandoned geographical ties in search for work in greater population centers. In this forlorn country, they grow more bold walking around roads and prowling around former dwellings, even as Raphael and Victor display an affection that would be considered unacceptable if seen by anyone at all.

Raphael communicates to Victor in Hebrew that they are somewhere near Hartly, in the spirit of lovers who say things not to convey important information but simply to share an existence.

Their energy is low. Victor reminds them sporadically that pilgrimages demand an outpouring of endurance in order to reap their spiritual rewards, his words marking intervals of time. But after a while, his words of encouragement are abandoned, and they all languish in silence.

It is noon; the sun hegemonizes the ever-smaller sky, their clothes radiate filth. Raphael suggests that they stop to have a meal. He announces this first in Hebrew, to Victor by his side. Victor may not know to talk of political developments or write an academic essay in this new language, but he can communicate those things most important to his role as a lover, and that is all he needs.

He is even confident enough to debate with Raphael, ask him why he would use the word "meal" to describe a desperate bite of mere survival. But Raphael protests, he claims that using a slightly inapt word to describe rotten fruit and murky water is important to raising their spirits, and so Victor replies, "Yes *neshama*, let's have a meal."

They sit in a sprawling field that lies adjacent to the abandoned strip of highway whose twists and turns they follow unscrupulously. It has been quite some time since they have seen or heard a vehicle. Raphael imagines all the cars huddled in Dover somewhere, or perhaps Delaware City, in some isolated garage barricaded from the outside. On this land they are safe, on grasses crisp and brazen from years of drought and swelling heat. Safe from unwanted human interference, at least, as they digest these paltry means under the black sun, all other concerns relegated to the back of their minds.

Mid-chew, it seems, Raphael's head drifts towards his chest, eyes closing in obedience to his body's fatigue; Victor straightens him out on the ground, marveling once again at the ease with which Raphael has begun to pass from one state of consciousness to another without effort. Victor envies Raphael's newfound ability to rest as he pleases, for Victor's mind still will not allow him to escape his terror so readily.

Victor and Juneau are left together, the two of them palpably alone. At first, they speak no words; how easy it would have been for both of them to give into sleep, or at least to pretend to close their eyes and deny the possibility of togetherness. Victor extends an olive branch.

"Raphael has given me Hebrew lessons."

"Language like a phoenix," Juneau points out listlessly. Victor's mouth creases sideways in melancholic recognition.

"If only we all could fly so."

Victor wants to share his newfound linguistic prowess but worries that Juneau is uninterested.

"He teaches me things I need to know. It's like a crash course in disaster Hebrew. *Watch out for fire, I'm famished, do you know where to go.*"

"*I love you.*"

Victor nods, his eyes wide.

"Yes. I tell him that too. I tell him in Hebrew, and he tells me in English. He says that's how it reaches your heart, in the tongue your mother used to coo you to sleep."

Juneau is silent.

"There is such feeling in those ancient words. I feel sadness, resilience, reinvigoration of a people."

"When he teaches me, I feel you there, by my side. Like we used to be. Something inside me tried to convince me that it was just because you study French. That was the only argument I could understand for a while. But I kept trying to dig deeper, to remember something I had hidden. It's so easy to forget the past. But you told me, once, that languages bear the burdens and the joys of a people. It just came to me so clearly one day, and now I identify with your words, so much so as if I had spoken them myself."

Juneau looks toward the ground as she nods, a tear the only sign of dialogue.

"I told him to teach me to say *I miss you.* He said why? I know it sounds strange, since he's always there next to me…But is it not some sort of privilege to say so? Some sort of sweet sorrow: *I cannot bear to live without you in my arms.* That's something we'll never have, you know. This pilgrimage is all it is and ever will be. For him, for me, for you. Maybe you don't know it, or you have repressed it. But something tells me the end of our trek is the end of light."

Juneau's eyes betray no hint of agreement or contention. They are mere glass surfaces, imprinted reflections that lead no deeper than the bulbs themselves, her eyes having ceased all communications with the soul. Victor continues to speak to her.

"I think a lot about the future. The real future. But that gets old, and scary. So I make stuff up, too. Or I try to think about *alternative* futures: what could be, what won't be, but what we haven't seen for sure. It's like hope."

"Maybe in some other world, Raphael would take me to his hometown. I imagine that he would show me the spectacular and the pedestrian too: the monuments to Jewish identity, the local market nearest his parents' home, the marvels of human ingenuity; the calls of the birds that woke him up as a child and crow as they crowed decades, centuries, millennia ago. His family is happy, very close. His parents live two blocks down from his grandparents, both sets, and in between live his cousins, his aunts and uncles, collections of bonds somehow all able to inhabit the same rural space they trace their origins from.

They tell me of Israel's contributions to the Grand Rescue of the Earth itself, that which now provokes relieved complaints of reduced heat, of too much breeze, too much sea-touched air to inhale and hold onto. They introduce me to the Palestinians who inhabit the home to their right, as they laugh over distant tales of ancient tension and quickly move on to more pressing matters of neighborhood concern, as in whose cat has gotten loose, whose hydrangeas have grown the most, whose children have just gotten married in a patois-like Hebrarabic.

We announce our plans to marry and they coax a celebration out of the air on a whim, but we tell them there is no rush, we plan to relish in our engagement for the hell of it, for the security that we can marry whenever we like, wherever we please. And we'll have forgotten the diseases of doubt and self-hatred that once plagued men who love men, and so will his family, and all will be normal and hopeful, and all will have triumphed over life's perils."

Juneau pauses visibly to reflect on this tale. "You were so lonely."

"I was. But now another part of me is missing, Juneau, don't you see? You're here, but you're *not:* I know that you've gone through something that's put you on another side of consciousness, and maybe that's all you can bear, since you've fought for justice all your life and just seen destruction in its wake. I don't resent it, Juneau. But I want you to know that I love you, and I miss you, and I will protect you."

"I lost myself in another space and time."

"I know."

They embrace.

* * *

They spend lazy days walking along the western interior, Victor taking pains to make known to his lover the differences between his native north and the foreign south, Juneau to their side. They sleep wherever their bodies fall, eat whenever it becomes urgent.

On one day of these many, Raphael gives Victor another Hebrew lesson as the flames engulf the trees around them. Raphael informs Victor, teasing lovingly, of the one pronunciation error that prevents him from sounding like one of Raphael's countrymen.

"It's your r, baby," he says, "it's so Anglo." Victor does not take offense.

"Why don't you show me how you say it?"

Raphael makes a clear example, exaggerating the movement of his tongue in the back of his throat. Victor watches with the amusement of a pupil trying to be obedient. Then Victor tries to imitate it.

"You're getting closer, *neshama*," Raphael says, applauding.

Victor shifts his body onto Raphael as Raphael lies onto the ground. They gaze into each other's eyes. Victor repeats the word he has been given as a vehicle with which to practice his Hebrew r's:

"...דחא רשבל דפוה, דחא רשבל דפוה, דחא רשבל דפוה"

Words formed carefully turn into a sacrament of movement down below, their bodies move as one as Victor masters the phrase:

"...דחא רשבל דפוה, דחא רשבל דפוה, דחא רשבל דפוה"

Raphael commends his pupil for his efforts, "look who we're becoming together," their low jives are a song of the flesh.

It becomes an incantation, with every syllable uttered they are reduced to their forms in which they entered this world, at once Victor rests on Raphael's force that wants in, so sweet:

"...דחא רשבל דפוה, דחא רשבל דפוה, דחא רשבל דפוה"

Raphael's hands grab Victor's chest with avarice, he thinks not of the time they wasted but of the times they will have to be one in these members, he knows Victor biblically:

"...דחא רשבל דפוה, דחא רשבל דפוה, דחא רשבל דפוה"

Their bodies glide into the shape of a question mark as Victor descends to meet Raphael's lips, undulating motions make them feel complete, two pieces of soulmates having coalesced after all this time.

Heavy sighs grow more desperate, flames grow but their heat is all they regard with any real importance, everything grows rapidly, expanding into new spaces that bring them to celestial knowledge, *the spirituality of the flesh never ceases to amaze.*

The act explodes and then vanishes, they are left shocked by the forces their bodies have produced, Victor savors the bits and pieces of Raphael that he has shoved into him, hoping he could hold on forever. דחא רשבל דפוה דחא רשבל דפוה, דחא רשבל דפוה, they pass many days melting into each other.

utopia

Fighter jets buzz overhead like angry wasps, their bellicosity on grand display. It is public knowledge that the Delawarean jets are a distinct shade of blue while the American ones possess a dull green, but in wartime the colors are mixed so as to confuse the other side, making it impossible for soldiers and civilians alike to know who is who. They've arrived at Rehoboth Beach, or the remains thereof.

How strange a sight for these Delawareans, the beach in so pitiful a state: its sands revoked, its coastline having moved almost so close as to touch the highway. Even Raphael, suckled on the waters far from this ocean, senses that what was once full of life is now full of war; what a crass reminder of mortality, of the silly and absurd reasons for which humans could gasp their last breaths.

Raphael, having by now seen long stretches of Delaware, gives his opinion. "You all told me Rehoboth would be magnificent," he says, his voice dark with sparks of desolation, "but in fact, Rehoboth as you knew it was gone before I possibly could have laid my eyes upon it." Victor thinks of the tales he had recounted to Raphael of innocent promenades and childhood romps in the sand, the rapture of local pride in his stories, curses upon foreign tourists that used to jam the streets.

"But you saw some other beaches too, *neshama*," Victor points out, to which Raphael laughs good-naturedly: he remembers only having stopped at little alcoves of small coastal interruptions, infant shores, tiny moments of watershed.

"You Delawareans are made up of hundreds of small waterways in your heart, being so small you naturally take joy in these miniature delights."

"How well you understand the Delawarean predicament," Victor gushes, rewarding Raphael's efforts with a kiss.

"If only I could see Haifa…", Victor says in Hebrew, reminding Raphael of the ways they had gone about interweaving their lives. It was just the exchange of hearts that they wanted: for Raphael to understand Victor's soul through the land and waterways that raised him, for Victor to understand Raphael's through the syllables that Raphael uttered as a child trying to make sense of a world without order, in this way they bypassed fears of eternal solitude.

Yet in the midst of such happiness, there is also horror: Juneau falls limply and suddenly, crashing into sand. Victor remembers how dejectedly she refused the food random saints sympathetic to their political causes had showered upon them days ago. He and Raphael gather around her, trying to protect her from the punishing sun, trying to surround her with love. Though her constitution is weak, she lies in peace, her head resting on top of her hands as if in prayer, her eyes still open and receptive to the world.

But her body is losing energy. Victor ponders the scene around him, the jets swarming and threatening attack, the seas in tempestuous arousal, Juneau in this state: he sees some relation. It looks as if her lips will open to speak several times, but then the words escape her, or she reconsiders her final words. She peers into Victor's eyes, looks to Raphael, trying to express the yearnings of a lifetime in the few short words her body will allow her.

Her mouth opens with a final burst of confidence: "We did not fail, we tried our noblest," Victor wishes he could tell her how much she means to him, but her eyes shut closed, Victor's hand wrapped around hers, and in a few short moments they know she has departed this earth.

* * *

Two lovers arrive at the beach, or what of it is left in its wake, Wynona points to the calamity and commotion of the fighter jets ahead. It is not in hope that he and Wynona come to this beach, in fact it is in the defiance of both hope and reason: Wynona felt desperately that she must be at the beach at this moment, asked Brandt so gently to accompany her to this place.

It is not a search mission, no; Wynona has long succumbed to the notion that Juneau is gone for the rest of days. But Wynona knows that Juneau held this place close to her heart, here on the water looking out toward the rest of the world, and somehow this brings her closer.

Brandt holds Wynona's hand to his chest, kisses her fingers lightly every few minutes or so to reassure her and give himself a task to occupy his wandering mind. In the midst of the troubles of the skies and troubles of the heart, there are certainly places to feel grateful, and in this bodily caress they both feel like they are at home.

"Beauty asserts itself in the strangest of places," Brandt notes, and Wynona tears up, falling in love once more with his wisdom.

The clock on the dash strikes four in the afternoon, Brandt comments that it is a strange time to be doing this, Wynona just shrugs and replies that no hour of the day could make it less strange.

All of a sudden, they feel a rumble from underneath. Neither of them feels alarm. The sedan begins to shake, gently at first but then with terrific force. They just hold each other tighter.

What life remains in this deserted place also begins to titillate: the few other cars parked somewhere in the sand, the abandoned buildings that narrowly avoided the previous catastrophe.

From the horizon a wave of blue mounts into the sky, growing into the foreground as it climbs higher and higher.

Brandt mentions the past, *yes it does resemble Rehoboth's downfall quite a lot from what I heard about it,* in the backseat they huddle together to watch as the wave swallows up fighter jets in the sky.

The lovers say what must be said before an extinction: *I love you, I love you too, hold me so we can leave together,* and in the warmth of this moment the wave invades, destroys the small world they built so carelessly.

* * *

Destruction comes in sets of twos, threes, unlimited digits; the sun blazes down on them harshly, the fighter planes whizzing around each other, and they suspect that there can be chaos in any moment.

Raphael's watch reads four, all Victor's prophecies come true: the two lovers see, looming in the deep horizon, a great rumbling of waves that produces an echo so great they experience it with all senses. The wave is a collector, just like Juneau's mother, coercing any water it can find into joining its mass, and they both understand that this wave will swallow them. There is no reason to flee.

"It is over," Victor says, repeating in both Hebrew and English. Raphael confirms, "yes, my dear, this is what you've been waiting to see." Victor holds onto Raphael's chest as he proclaims a poem into his ear:

I hope when this is over
When our breath is free once more
That you think of me
Like I think of you
Of kisses that make me sore
And if this sphere
Fills with gas
Turning our lips purple and cold
I hope you know
 I wanted to grow
 Old in our utopia

Raphael longs for Victor, Victor yearns for Raphael; their bodies cannot merge but they do the best they can. "When did you have the time to write that poem," Raphael wonders with tears in his eyes, but Victor thinks of Juneau's soul: "Is it better to see your destruction, or to vanish before it comes?" Raphael kisses him deeply with dazed passion, his hands traveling around the delicacies of Victor's body. His words ooze into Victor's ear:

"She would have wanted this, to pass on with hope."

"Surely you're right."

They embrace, like a broken record *I love you* sounds on loop: the wave collides with the ground, all good things must come to an end; two lovers molded together like carved marble are carried into oblivion under a blanket of ocean.

About the Author

Matthew Anderson was born and raised in Dover, Delaware, which may explain why he is so drawn to the outside world. Proficient in five languages and working towards his goal of ten languages under his belt, he is passionate about disrupting the fall of language amidst the global hegemony of English. In his reading and writing, he is drawn to the melancholy and the absurd, the deeply profound and the seemingly nonsensical. He feels most at home in unfamiliar surroundings that allow him to expand and see the world through the idioms and inflections of other tongues. He plans to continue pursuing his writing craft long-term wherever he finds himself in the world. He currently lives in Taichung, Taiwan.

www.ingramcontent.com/pod-product-compliance
Lightning Source LLC
Chambersburg PA
CBHW031449160726
47994CB00005B/1945